The Ghosts of Varner Creek

By Michael Weems

Dedicated to my parents, the finest people I know.

A thank you to Robert Guinsler of Sterling Lord, Literistic, who originally believed in this book and helped me try to send it out into the world.

"An idea, like a ghost, must be spoken to a little before it will explain itself"

—Charles Dickens

Chapter 1

Six-twenty a.m., November 3, 1984

That dead woman is standing out in the hall by my door again. I wake up, open my eyes, and as I give the old body a stretch I see her out there, still as a statue and fixated on me. She's been visiting more often of late, eerie damn woman. I wish she'd carry herself somewhere else and quit staring at me like that. I don't know what she finds so fascinating about me, 'cept maybe she's figured out I can see her. I guess that might be something of interest to the likes of her, but it's only a nuisance to me these days. *Go on and get,* say my thoughts, as though she'd hear them and leave. But she doesn't. She just stands there. I don't pay her much mind, though. I've gotten used to this one popping up. She's the one that doesn't have a face, just a kind of blur where it should be, like someone smudged her features out. I've never seen another one quite like her before, no face and all, but it don't matter. I ignore her just the same. *I got nothing to say to you, ghost, so you might as well go somewhere's else.*

I change my view to looking outside the window. There's just a hint of orange on the fringe of the gray dawn. Pretty soon there'll be yellows, reds, and purples, like a child's watercolor set splashed out over the world. There's a nice smell drifting in from across the fields, too. It's the smell of home for those of us who've grown up with it, the smell of a cotton crop freshly picked. You've got to know what you're looking for to catch it as it's almost overpowered by the strong odors of cleansers and medicines in this place, but it's a beautiful smell. I've seen folks who could poke their nose down a glass of wine and come up telling you everything you'd want to know about it. Me, I prefer the smell of the good earth. With it, I can tell you what the cotton crop is looking like this year. The richness and nutrients of the soil outside drift through the air like perfume. The summer heat didn't scorch the crops too bad this season, and we had ourselves an extra three inches of rain above average this year, just what the cotton wanted. My nose says they had themselves a good harvest this year, and my nose always knows.

The cotton will all be ginned and bundled now, and that means they'll be having the Harvest Festival soon, a tradition that takes me back. It used to be the biggest thing in town once upon a time. Oh, but it's been such a long time since I've been to a Harvest Festival. I'm so out of touch with the world I don't rightly know how things are now, except I know the tradition still continues because I hear talk as it gets closer to festival time and we get a new beauty queen who makes a round every year. I just don't know if it's as important to folks as it once was. I like to think so, though. I lie here in bed while memories dance in two-step to the sounds of old country and I recall past festivals, past days. I let myself get a little lost in the memory, it being such a nice one. I wonder if that dead woman is still there? I peek back over at my unwelcome guest to find she's gone. *Good, go haunt somebody who gives a damn, why don't yah.*

I don't have nothing to say to dead people anymore, seeing as how they've never had anything to say to me. I see them now and again standing around like folks who forgot what they were doing and now can't remember why they are where they are. Used to scare the beJesus outta me in my younger years, but we can get used to all sorts of things, I suppose. I've gotten use to living in this nursing home, for one. Besides the living patients we've got a few residents still here whose bodies were wheeled out a long time ago. Nobody else seems to notice them, but I see them from time to time, including that one, walking down the halls at night or popping up here and there during the day.

First time I saw Faceless was one morning when I woke up and there she was at my window as though she were watching the dawn like I so often do. I couldn't see her face but I remember thinking how pretty her hair was, still so shiny and black without a spot of gray, the proverbial black sheep in this place I guess you could say. She was wearing a white cotton nightgown like some I've seen, so I just figured she was just some lady who had wandered out from her room.

"You get lost, ma'am?" I asked her. But she didn't answer.

"What room you suppose to be in, ma'am?" I asked politely, trying not to startle her. She didn't even turn, though. Then I thought she have might be one of them Alzheimer's folks that lost her reasoning so I rang for the nurse.

When she came in I told her in a whisper so as to not offend the lady at the window, "I think this here lady done wandered off from her room."

That nurse looked around and asked, "What lady, Mr. Mayfield?"

I looked back towards the window and she was gone. Well, I knew right away I'd been fooled. Just another dead person, someone who had passed in my room some time back, I figured.

"Never mind," I told the nurse. "Must have been a dream that woke up with me."

Faceless has been popping up now and again ever since, though. Why on earth she'd be inclined to visit here is beyond me. Seems like one would be glad to be rid of a place like this. Ghosts like her, as I guess there's not much else to call them, aren't all the same, either. Some are skittish and are gone in a flash if they realize you can see them, while others seem to seek out company, like Faceless sometimes does. Some look faint, like only shadows of their former selves, while others look so real it seems like they could sit right down and have a conversation with you, though they never do. At least, I've never had one do it. Those ones just look like they still have thoughts, though. And some, though not many as it's been my experience, can affect things around them. How they affect things can vary. Sometimes it's just a chill or an odd feeling you can't quite place, but there are those rare ones than can do a whole lot more.

Years ago I was in a hotel room on a business trip and I woke up because I felt the mattress get pushed down close by my feet like someone having a sit. At first, I was so sleepy I thought it was my wife getting up to use the restroom, but then I remembered I was in a hotel room and my wife was miles away sleeping in our bed at home. As my mind woke up more, I felt the oddest of sensations.

The air seemed to be sucked out of the room and stillness fell over it like no sound would ever be heard in that room again. It was like an invisible sponge was sucking everything up . . . the sounds of the air conditioner and the cars mumbling along the highway outside, the dim light through the windows, even the very air itself. They all seemed to draining away into an unseen hole. I'd never felt anything like it. It was like having a hand put over your mouth and suffocating you, except it was placed over the entire room, suffocating everything within.

I sat up and despite the retreating light, I could just make out the silhouette of someone sitting at the foot of the bed. They weren't moving or doing anything, but I knew what it was. I felt more empty and alone than I'd ever felt, and the feeling seemed to be coming not from within me, but from the one sitting on my bed. Everything was still draining away, and then it was darkness. I panicked a bit. It was like being buried alive in that room. I needed light, something warm and friendly that would break the grip that was beginning to choke me. There were some matches by an ashtray on the night stand, so I grabbed one and slid it along the pack watching the little flame jump to life. Its feeble glow pushed back the darkness a little, and right there in front of me was a pale young man, naked as a jaybird but white as alabaster. He looked like a man, but he didn't feel like one.

He was sitting with his back to me, and he could've been an ivory statue someone just carved except they'd made a mess of his head. It sunk in on itself and the back had a big chunk missing, revealing a mangled mess of spongy white tissue that I guess was brain. There wasn't any blood, though. Not a drop. I figured right away that he must have shot himself in that room or something, because whatever happened in there, he never left. He liked to give me a heart attack because he was so much there like a real person, yet he also seemed to be the source of the hole that had consumed all the life out of the room. When the light from the match hit his face he turned towards me and I could see his hollow eyes, like two pools of swirling black ink.

A deep depression flowed over me. As he stared at me I felt like I didn't want to live anymore. I felt worse than I'd ever felt. Then he opened his mouth like he was going to say something to me, but the only thing that came out was a plume of smoke like the bullet which had killed him had just sped its course to his end. His gaze trailed from me to the smoke, and it seemed as though he realized for a moment what it all meant. The plume disappeared into nothingness and his hand crept to the back of his head and in his eyes I knew he realized the awful truth . . . he knew what he was, and he knew what I was.

He was the ghost, the suicide who had sought and found his death in this room, and I was the living, who saw it now as it had happened then. He looked at me and I saw in his expression true emotions. He was scared, angry, and almost seeming to ask something of me. It was like he wanted help, but wanted to hurt me both at once. The black pools of his eyes seemed to churn a little more furiously and the room swayed a bit. Where he had a moment ago sucked the life out of the room, he now seemed to be filling it back up again with his misery and suffering. Emotions pulsed from him to me like the crashing waves of a storm pounding to shore. I felt his rage, anger, and despair . . . I felt all of it and it hurt something terrible.

"I'm sorry," I told him. The words came on their own. I meant it, though. Looking at him, young, lost, angry and afraid, still living out his own suicide in this small room, I felt terribly sorry for him. And the things pouring out of him into that room were the stuff of nightmares. I was sorry for whatever had brought him to his end, and I was sorry there wasn't anything I could do for him. And I wanted him to stop whatever he was doing that was making me feel the way I was feeling. He didn't, though. It just got worse and worse so fast I couldn't understand what was happening. I even found myself crying, yet didn't know why. I'm not a man to cry much in my life, but the horrible things I felt at that moment were just that overpowering. I felt like I'd forgotten what happiness was, that I'd never love or be loved, that I was nothing but a waste upon the world. I truly wanted to kill myself. "I'm sorry," I told him again. "There's nothing else I can do but tell you I'm sorry, so you just stop now." And to my surprise, he did.

The despair broke like a fever and I immediately felt more like myself. He tilted his head to the side and looked at me with a strange expression, curiosity, maybe even pity, I didn't know. I looked back at him, and for a split second I thought maybe our moment counted for something. Maybe I'd reached him in some meaningful way. In the pools of black that were his eyes, I thought I saw a tear form. But when it fell down his sculpture-like face, it was a tear of blood. Then quickly, more fell behind it and beads of blood droplets formed upon his brow and then they, too, ran. His expression had changed to one of immense anger, like he was suddenly very mad I was in his room and intruding on his loathing. I believe now he'd played his game before, with other people in his room, but they couldn't see him like I did, and he didn't like being seen for what he was. The next thing I knew that ghost covered in blood was lunging at me. I thought he was attacking me and I threw my hands up in defense with a flinch, but all I felt was the mattress bounce a little, and when I opened my eyes again he'd disappeared. The room was as it had been before his visit, and not a drop of blood soiled the comforter. He was gone.

Thirty seconds later, so was I, thankful I hadn't been torn apart, and thankful he had lifted from me whatever curse he held in that place.

Remembering that one used to keep me up nights, and I'm sure he's still sittin' on that bed in the darkness, going over his last moments again and again. And if there's been an unusual number of suicides in that room over the years . . . well, I just try not to think about such things anymore.

I've read about possessions and the like in the Good Book, and while he didn't jump in my body and run me around, I think I know now what possession really is. King Saul himself was haunted by a troubled spirit that made him feel murderous. I've never really spoken of it to other people, but there's no convincing me it wasn't a spirit like what's in that hotel room that the Good Book was talking about when it said "unclean spirits", and that possession is when they fill you up with their own misery.

That was a long time ago, though. I'm old now. Too old to be worrying about ghosts who are trapped in their own despair, and I've seen more of his kind since then, though none as bad. The only thing I've learned from the angry spirits is to steer clear of them, because there are ways they can hurt you even if they don't physically lay hands upon you.

Most of the ones I've come across are less temperamental. I even used to try to talk to them. It became somewhat of an obsession of mine to get a ghost to say at least one word to me. Just once I wanted to hear a voice from one of them. I wanted to find one that talked and sit them down for a nice long conversation about all the things I didn't understand. In fact, at the peak of my obsession, if I did come upon a ghost I'd start chasing them down yelling, "Come talk to me! Come on, say something!" That got a reaction, I can tell yah. The ghosts who seemed to be really there didn't know what to do, what with some crazed living person barreling down on them demanding conversation. Most would be gone in a blink. Others would stick around for a moment and look at me as though I was the oddity and that I wasn't talking a normal language. Then they, too, would fade out like a fart in the wind.

My little obsession went on like that for years before I gave up on trying to talk with the dead. I figured if I didn't give it up, I was going to end up in an institution doing finger paintings all day. I don't reckon they can talk, since I've never heard one. They can affect, though, and sometimes they let that speak for them. He never said a word, but I heard that young man in that hotel room loud and clear.

That's about all I have to say about the dead, I guess. I've lived a long life, seen a lot of things, and that's pretty much the extent of what I've learned about them, which is to say not very much. They're just another nuisance these days, anyway, as it's not the dead that keeps me up but the living. There's a man next door to mine that moans and groans all hours he's awake and the lady across the hall sounds like she's spitting up a lung when her acid reflux kicks into gear. This getting old thing sure is a bothersome business, and I'm no longer getting there. I've arrived, unpacked, and been settled so long you can smell old on me. My grandkids say it's something between mouthwash and mothballs. At least I haven't started making old people noises, like the moaner and the spitter-upper. You get used to it, though. It's just plum amazing what you can get used to after you've been around it a long time.

Now that Faceless is gone I reckon I'd better go on and get outta bed. I gotta take a leak but I was waiting for her to leave me be. I'm a bit bladder shy, whether the one watching is alive or not. It's nearly six thirty and they'll be serving breakfast soon, and I don't want my eggs to be cold. I know they'll be soggy, they're always soggy, but at least they won't be cold. Luckily, I can still move myself around. It's not pretty, but I can still haul my old bag of bones about the place without a wheelchair or one of those IV things on rollers trailing after me. The tile is cold as I shuffle into the bathroom and as I'm relieving myself I catch a glimpse of the man in the mirror. I have to wonder, who's this stranger looking back? Damn, but don't he look old. This mirror must be broken. I give a big smile and stick my tongue out at myself. The teeth are yellowed, the gums receding so much my teeth look like I yanked them from a horse's mouth, but they're mine. How many eighty-seven year olds can say that? Not many in this place, I can say that much.

I look at the person looking back at me and didn't expect his face to ever look so old and worn. It creeps up on you, old age. You look over your shoulder and it's stalking you from about twenty or thirty years out, then the next thing you know it's sinking its teeth in you. Your body starts staging a revolt and hairs start popping out of your ears. They crawl back into your skin on your head leaving you bald and then start crawling back out in the weirdest of places. Then you get more lines on your face than a highway map. I study him now and wonder where the man I once knew has gone. His gray hair is receding far back and the bald spot on top of his head is shiny from the reflection of light. Undoubtedly that spot is where the ear hairs came from. There was a time when the hair was thick and black as midnight. The skin that once was tanned and unblemished with youth now hangs loosely on the body, like a suit that once fit perfectly·until the man lost too much weight and shrunk into himself. It's spotted now, too, as though it needs a good cleaning. But soap won't clean these blotches away. Years ago his skin held tightly, like a fine wrapping to the gift of youth. Now it is thin and frail like silk. The slightest bump and it bruises like an over-ripe plum.

His face is weathered and creased. I make funny faces sometimes, like now, just to watch the wrinkles fold in and out. I can do the most uncanny impression of a Pug, those wrinkly faced dogs, without even moving a muscle. I can't remember first seeing these wrinkles. It's like they were always there and just got more noticeable with age. I know there was a time they weren't there, though, because I can remember a different reflection staring back at me from behind the glass. This body's the same old house that time has redecorated. I heard someone say that once long time ago and damn if it ain't the truth.

Chapter 2

Outside where the morning sun is rising with its colorful introduction is the small town of Varner Creek, a rural town in southeast Texas. It's a typical small town with a Main Street that runs through its center with two stoplights, one on each end. There are little stores lining Main Street that have grand openings and closing sales just like the seasons. The only ones that have stood the test of time are the barbershop, the mechanic's place, the grocery store, and of course the Dairy Mart where the kids can go for a burger. The other stores that use to be here years ago, the hardware store with the locksmith, the clothing stores that used to have hats and Sunday dresses, the old movie house, they all succumbed to the Wal-mart and mall that moved in just down the highway. The town's got an old railroad track the trains come through on, but they never stop anymore like they used to as they trek their way to load and deliver various goods. The railroad reached Varner Creek around 1900, when a branch of the New York, Texas and Mexican Railway was laid down. It used to be that we had a train station where we could commerce with the outside world. Nowadays, though, the cotton, sugar cane, and other agriculture grown around here by the few farmers left gets loaded on trains in towns farther west. Most everyone here works for the various chemical companies down in the Freeport area or they drive up to Houston. It's become a community of commuters, so to speak.

The town was established in 1877, not far from West Columbia, TX, where the first capitol of the Republic of Texas was established in 1836. Varner Creek was named for a Chicago man named Colonel Pritchard Varner who came to the south after the civil war. He claimed to be a former Union officer who, like a true carpetbagger, believed he could resurrect the plantation lifestyle and claim it for his own. Nobody knows if he really was a Colonel or not, or even if he served in the Union. The only thing the town's historical society could muster up was that he had been running a fabric business in Chicago with his brother, but sold his brother his half and moved to Texas. There he found himself some rich bottom land with a creek running through it for a good water supply, and bought two thousand acres for cotton, corn, sugar cane, and cattle raising.

The Colonel's dreams of becoming the rich land owner in a slow southern lifestyle ran awry, though, when he swindled one of his laborer's out of two dollars and twenty cents. An argument ensued one day out in the fields and it ended with a hoe being squarely planted in the Colonel's head. Local lore has it that he suffered a heart attack at the same moment that hoe found its mark, and in the technical sense, he was dead before he hit the ground. The man who had swung the instrument of the Colonel's demise, a former slave named Henry Mullins, took off into the woods never to be seen or heard from again. He was an avid cock-fighter, old Henry was, and when he disappeared into the thicket he took his prized chickens with him. Nobody ever heard from Henry again, but his chickens lived on in those woods, and for generations after their descendants crows occasionally echoed in the trees, to which I can personally attest.

As for the Colonel, his wife put him in the ground, sold the house and all their land at two dollars an acre for wooded land and ten an acre for the crops, and went back to what she described as "civilized society" in Chicago. The folks who bought up the farmland moved in and families expanded eventually creating my hometown of Varner Creek.

I don't know why I think of the town's history as I look out over the cotton fields. A mind unhindered goes where it likes, I guess. And looking at the town I'm from makes me think of where it came from. You get to thinking about beginnings near your ending. It's just the natural way of things.

After breakfast I make for the game room to play some dominoes. It's how I spend most hours during the day. There's a few of us who sit around and talk about the old days and about what our children and grandchildren are doing. My wife, Helen, she passed some twelve years back from the cancer. We were married forty-seven years. She was a beautiful and lovely natured woman. I never saw her after she passed. I didn't really expect to, but if I'm to be honest part of me hoped now and then over the years. She had gotten the cancer and I knew she was ready to go when the time came, even if it meant leaving me. I miss her often, but I'm glad she don't have to hurt anymore. The cancer had cut her down next to a shadow of herself and that's just no way to live. The day she died she had awoken to constant pain. She lay in bed, unable to move or speak, but her eyes told what her words could not. I kissed her on her forehead and told her if she was ready to go, that she should go on, because I knew she was hurtin' and it was making me hurt, too. I told her that even though there were some spirits in the world, there weren't very many, so wherever we go when we die must be pretty nice, 'cause most folks seem to prefer it. She looked at me with tears in her eyes, and I knew she was feeling guilty at the idea of leaving me a widower. That was my Helen. She was the one dying, but still worrying over me. "It's just temporary, Hon," I told her. "I'll see you soon, and miss you every day in between." She couldn't talk by that point, but she gave me a little smile, squeezed my hand, and closed her eyes for a nap she'd never wake from.

After my dominoes and talking with my neighbors here I head back to my room. There's a couple of little girls visiting their great grandmother in room 34B, Miss Fitzgerald's room. She's ninety-three years old and will probably never leave her bed again, but she's happy today and basking in the glow of her own reflection in the faces of her great-grandchildren. One of them is wearing a ballerina outfit and doing a little twirl with her arms curved over her head. I hear her Mama say something about a recital later. A shadow in my memory stirs a little bit but I tell it to stay in its corner.

There's a little television in my room my son set up for me. I have to get the nurse to work it for me, though. All those little buttons give me a headache trying to read 'em. I press my call button and in she comes. It's not the young one I like looking at but Ms. Rita, a large Hispanic woman with a smile so big it like to blind you.

"How you doin' today, Mr. Mayfield?" she asks, molars just a sparklin'. Either her toothbrush must be huge or she must spend half the morning just brushing her teeth.

"Oh, you know. Same ole, same ole, I reckon. Still alive and here, ain't I?"

"Sure enough, Mr. Mayfield, and not looking like you're going anywhere anytime soon. You want your Wheel of Fortune on?" She knows at three o'clock I watch my Wheel of Fortune. Chuck Woolery's gone, but that Pat fella, he's all right. And that new lady what turns the letters, Vanna or whatever, she's definitely all right. She's got better legs than even that young nurse I like so much.

"Sure do, Miss Rita. Gonna see if somebody don't win a car again today. That young girl yesterday got herself a brand new Volvo." It was silver and worth nearly as much as I used to make in a year, all for guessing the word Superintendent.

"Shoot, I wouldn't mind winning me one of those new cars, Mr. Mayfield. Mine, I got, is on its last leg, I tell you what. If that husband of mine don't find himself a job soon to get me a new car it'll be him that gets tradin' in, Ha Ha!" She laughs and for a moment there I'm dazzled by her brilliant smile like a deer caught in headlights, "You play along now and see if you don't best those contestants." She sets the channel and is off to see my neighbor who's moaning a bit louder than usual. I think there's a whiff of his bed pan floating in. I wonder what they're feeding him in that tube of his, cause Lord whatever's going in, it do smell something terrible coming out.

I hear Miss Rita in the other room, "Wheeew, Dios mio!"

Luckily, I still got pretty good control of my bowels. I get the flatulence, but that's not so terrible, 'cept maybe that one time I farted in my sleep and it smelled so bad I woke myself up. I rolled over ready to complain to Helen about eating her dried apricots before coming to bed again, but she wasn't there, and that meant the gas was mine. There's just something uniquely unpleasant about waking up to a smelly fart and then realizing it's your own.

I spend the rest of the day watching television until it's time for supper and then bed. I got this unsettled feeling, though. Something about today has my thoughts churning and won't calm down. The air conditioner is whirring full blast and the moaner next door is now soundly asleep, so I should be down like a baby right now, but I'm not. I think it was the little girl in her ballerina outfit. There was something about her that sent a shiver through me. It's an old memory, but it never stays in its corner like I tell it to. I roll around a bit and listen to the air conditioner's comforting consistency until I start to feel heavy.

I think I'm dreaming. I have this sensation, like I'm holding on to an invisible fishing pole and somewhere out there a fish is nibbling at my line. It's a little tug, then another, and then Yank! It pulled the line so hard I went tumbling in right after it. It feels like I'm drowning in something dark, but before I can panic I feel this *pop*! It was like a bubble bursting except I was the bubble and now my body's in one place and I'm in another. I'm looking down at myself and can see someone standing by my bed. It's that ghost of a woman with no face. She's standing over my body, but she's not looking down at it. She's looking up, like she can see me floating around the ceiling. At least it seems so. Her head is tilted towards me but with no distinct features it's only an assumption on my part. I don't have long to wonder, though, before she's gone, and so is everything else, the room, the building, the town, the world, it's all disappeared. Or should I say I've disappeared, because I have no idea where I am. There's nothing around me but blackness and it's pulling me down and down into its depths like a hidden magnet pulling a paper clip. I can feel myself somehow being propelled, but since there's nothing but pure blackness all around it's hard to tell how fast I'm moving, or really if I'm moving at all. I try to breathe but there's no air. It's calm, though, a peaceful nothingness. I'm in an ocean, black as emptiness, and I know there's nothing but the watery stillness above and below me, everywhere. My eyes are open but I see nothing but the darkness, and then the obvious realization sets in . . . I just died! So this is what dying feels like. Well, it wasn't exactly unpleasant, just a bit odd. You feel that little tugging sensation right before you pop out of your body, get one last look goodbye, and then whoosh, you're here. But where here is I ain't got a clue. And where I'm going if I am really being pulled along in this nothingness is another mystery.

Somewhere above I imagine there are waves licking the air, but I'm miles away down in the deep and it's quiet and calm with no sense of time. I don't know if I've been here seconds or hours. The unusual stillness reminds me of the hotel room so long ago, except it's peaceful here. There's no torrent of terrible emotions pressing in on you, just the quiet solitude.

I've been like this a while, lost in this place where my thoughts alone exist. It's like being on a long train ride at night. You feel yourself moving, but you get so used to the sensation it almost becomes a lullaby. After a while something seems to change. Part of the blackness is becoming illuminated and I'm not alone. I think someone is coming towards me in this black sea. A dim green light that I remember from my childhood grows in front of me, and then I can see a hand. I feel it as it reaches out for me and touches me, closing around my own hand and then pulling me even faster towards this unknown destination. I try to see who is holding on to me but can barely make out a small figure. I can't see exactly who it is, it's still too dark. I think she's looking at me. Is she smiling? As we move I can make out just a bit of her. Something about her looks so familiar to me, but I'm so out of touch with my senses from this strange journey I don't think much about it.

Down the rabbit hole I go. I wonder if I'll end up on a heap of dry leaves like Alice. Mother had just started reading that story, I remember. But why am I thinking of that now? There's a light in the darkness. It's so far away at first that I think I've imagined it, but then it sparkles like a jewel. We're getting closer to it. There's a bright white glimmering as though a giant diamond were ahead of me, dotted with dancing sparkles like glitter tossed up into a clear night sky but seen reflected in a rippling pool, and it's getting brighter. It's coming much closer, I realize. I remember the near-death experiences I'd heard people talk about on the television or in books, and I'm struck with the notion that this might be what they saw. This light ahead of me is beginning to look a lot like a light at the end of a very long tunnel. It's so bright now I can barely look at it and then it's light all around me, like we just emerged from a tunnel into a world full of nothing but light. And there are faces here. Do I know them? I'm still so dazzled from the brilliance of this place I can't make them out. Someone is still holding my hand. I look and through the brilliance I can see next to me a girl in a pink dress kind of like the one Miss Fitzgerald's great granddaughter was wearing. I struggle to see her as the light is still so blinding.

Well, there may be no rabbit and no pile of leaves, but darned if there isn't an Alice. She's a young teenager of about thirteen with black curly hair and she's wearing a cutout crown made of folded paper with sparkles on it. In her other hand is a little paper straw that has a pink star on top of it that spins around. It's covered in sparkles, too. She seems happy, very happy. And her happiness is spilling out and washing over me, filling me with happiness, too.

She tells me, "Sol! Isn't it pretty? I've been waiting for you for so long."

My mind sways. Who is this girl? *I want you to have it because you remind me of Alice.* Those were Miss Thomas' words. Down the rabbit hole. Then what was it? Oh, yes. The Pool of Tears. Mother had just started reading from The Pool of Tears.

"You don't have to feel bad for me anymore," says the girl. "I've been so happy here and never alone. Now I'll be even happier because you're here now."

The light gives way and a perfect blue sky appears above us. Grass tickles my feet as it pokes out between my toes and grows all around us. The world takes shape around her and me as she holds my hand. And in an instant we're standing next to the creek where we both grew up. I'm twelve again, barefoot in my favorite pair of overalls that I used to have. My hair is thick and wild on my head and my body feels so light I could jump a hundred feet straight up. There's a cool breeze and it's the prettiest day I can ever remember. We're standing on the bank of a creek hand in hand and she's looking down into the water as it flows along. I look, too, and I see that I know this place. This is the place that has hidden in the back of my thoughts most all my life. And then I know who the girl next to me is. Of course I do, the obviousness crashing down on me. I'm still happy, but I also feel tears fill my eyes and begin to run down my cheek.

She looks at me with sweetness, "Don't be sad. I only wanted to come here to thank you." She holds me tightly and I'm surprised at how real she feels next to me. "You don't have to cry for me, Sol, not ever again."

I look at the creek, remembering how cold its waters could be. "I kept seeing it in my dreams," I tell her. "This place was always following me."

"I know. But you can let go now. I never wanted you to have to go through all those things, see all the things you have."

"It's been more than memories haunting me," I say.

And in her eyes I can see that she does know what I'm talking about. "I'm sorry I scared you."

I remember the first time I ever saw a ghost. It was my sister, Sarah. "It's all right," I tell her, "I know you didn't mean to."

"I was scared and I just remember wanting to find you, and then somehow I did. I was in the dark, something trying to pull me away, but I wanted to stay because I didn't know what it was or where I was going. I just kept thinking about you, and how much I wanted you there with me. You were the only one who still made sense to me. It was like an onion, though, layers on layers from me to you, and I couldn't get through them all. I could see you, but you couldn't see me."

"But then I did see you," I remind her. She nods. "I saw you, and I saw what he'd done." My tears were gathering, but like I'd done with that memory so many times before, I send them to a corner.

That was when it all began, with the ghost of my little sister finding me in the darkness. Seeing her in the same dress she wore that last day makes me realize how different she's become. This is not the same girl I knew in life. She's not stuttering anymore and her words carry lucid thoughts she was never able to find in life. She even looks like any normal girl. She's still Sarah, but she's the complete Sarah I'd always imagined she could be, always hoped she'd become. "You look so different now. The same but not."

"You see me like you remember me, but also how I am now. People don't have to stay broken here. This place can mend anything if you let it." She takes a step back and looks me over. "You look like I remember, but also different in a way. Have you been sad all this time?"

I don't answer. I thought about it all the time, even in my later years, but I got used to pushing it behind a closed door.

"It's because of what happened, isn't it?" she asks. Still, I say nothing. Sarah spins around in her pink dress. It was handmade by our

Mama. "Do you remember it?"

I look at the dress and say, "Of course. I remembered it and you every single day."

She holds up her pink straw and blows on it with a smile to make it spin around. The sparkles dance just like I remember, and she whispers to me, "It's okay, Sol. I know why you've been sad. It'll be better now, I promise." Somewhere inside of me a door that has been locked for many years slowly creaks open, and Sarah and I both walk through to the place where I'd hidden so many of my childhood memories.

Chapter 3

On August 10, 1909 my sister Sarah turned thirteen years old. There wasn't going to be a lot of presents, no expensive porcelain dolls with exquisitely crafted features, no tortoise shell combs with an ornate hand mirror. There weren't any of those things that a typical girl her age would have loved. She did get a dress, though. It was a pretty pink dress with lace sewn on the sleeves and collar. Mama had saved up for the material for months and made it herself. She had gotten the pattern down at the general store, but of course she had to improvise. The original pattern was for a Sunday dress, but Mama had need of a princess dress. There was a drawing of Cinderella's splendid silver dress in Sarah's book of fairytales and Mama did her best to borrow from the design. It wasn't perfect, but the hours spent on the task were evident. There was a lot of love in that dress, and Mama was proud of the end result and looked forward to surprising Sarah.

As for me on this day I was outside doing what twelve year olds do. Mama walked over to the kitchen window and hollered out, "Solomon James Mayfield! Get inside this house this instant and help me get the table set."

"But Mama! I got a diller by the tail! I'm gonna haul him out." Living out in the country sometimes requires a bit of creativity when you're trying to entertain yourself, and believe you me, playing tug of war with an armadillo down its hole was good sport for a boy my age.

She wasn't in the mood for it today, though. "Boy, don't make me tell you again. And I done told you not to get out there and dirty yourself up. It's a special day and for once I'd like you to look halfway clean."

Mama just didn't understand the importance of winning a tug of war. "Yes ma'am," I whined. And I let the little diller's tail go. It clawed down deep into its hole and let out a final hiss at me to make sure I knew who'd won. "We'll just see who wins tomorrow," I threatened.

I scampered into the house only to be immediately fussed at again. "Good Lord!" Mama said, "You look like a pig that's been rollin' round in the mud." She grabbed me by the arm and hauled me right back outside where she began beating the dust off my overalls and shirt when my feet lit up with the pain of a thousand hot needles being poked into me. I let out a scream and she spun me around to face her, "Well what's wrong now?" she asked with a slight bit of panic in her.

"Ant bed, Mama! Ant bed!" She had walked me right into a pile of red harvester ants that were attacking my bare feet with a vengeance.

She helped me slap them off my feet and legs, "Well, if you'd wear your shoes like a normal somebody them ants wouldn't eat you up like that."

"They not comfortable."

"Oh, and having a bunch of red ants biting on yah is, huh?" When she finished slapping off the ants and beating away most of the dirt on my clothes she proceeded to poke and prod me back indoors where she took the edge of her kitchen apron, licked it with the end of her tongue, and then started wiping my face clean. "Honestly, son, couldn't you just stay clean until after the party?" I hated it when Mama used her saliva to wipe dirt and smudges from my face. I always figured spit was worse than dirt, but there's just no telling a mother that.

"Sorry, Mama."

A giggling squeal of a voice drifted into the kitchen, "O-o-o-oh, Sol's in trouble." Sarah hid behind the entryway from the front room, which is what we called the living room back then. Her black hair and big blue eyes were poking out from behind the corner. Then she laughed and disappeared back into the other room.

"Don't you run off on me, little Miss Sarah. I'm gonna need you in a minute," chimed Mama.

"Sol's-in-trouble! Sol's-in-trouble!" came the sing-song response from the other room.

Apparently her little song and dance was enough to rouse our Pap. He came out of my parents' bedroom with a scowl on his face, "What the hell's all the racket out here?" He walked into the kitchen and bared down on me threateningly. "What'd you do now, boy?"

Mama answered for me. "Nothin', Abram. Sarah's just getting excited is all, this being her big day and everything."

"That damn girl thinks everything's funny. Must be nice." Pap rarely thought things funny, unless they were his own little jokes, which most everyone else rarely found funny. You were always walking on eggshells when you around Pap, particularly if he'd been drinking, which was pretty much all the time.

Mama sucked in her breath and said, "It's not her fault, Abram. She's just excitable is all." Then she lowered her voice next to a whisper, "And she can't help the way God made her."

Pap let out a sarcastic little laugh, "God, hell. It's that Chinaman blood she got in her from your side, Annie," he said to her, "that's why she's one of them Mongol idiots, something in that foreign blood of hers." Mama wasn't part Chinese. Pap never seemed to understand what the doctor from Houston meant when he said Sarah might be suffering from something called Mongolian Idiocy. Our own town doctor, Dr. Wilkins, had sent her up to Houston to visit a specialist when he became concerned Sarah wasn't developing correctly. What the doctor in Houston had diagnosed as a possible case of Mongolian Idiocy was what they called Down's syndrome back then, up until 1961. Pap thought it meant Sarah was part Chinese, though, and since he was positive he was as white as a white man gets and Mama had jet black hair, he of course assumed someone on Mama's side had some tainted Chinaman blood. That kind of reasoning might not make sense to most folks, but like Pap's sense of humor, most things about him seemed a little left of center. I suppose part of it wasn't his fault. He only made it through the third grade when his father died of tuberculosis and his mother sent him to live with his uncle. That probably had more to do with the way Pap turned out than anything else.

Today like every other day, though, Mama bore it well, "I know, Abram. But it's her special day. Let's please try to make it a nice one for her."

Pap muttered to himself, "Like she knows the difference," as he disappeared back to their bedroom.

Mama looked at me and said, "Now I'm going to take Sarah to y'all's room and get her into her dress. Why don't you go and get your surprise you made for her while I do that?" She gave me a wink like she and I were partners in mischief.

Sarah had been playing princess ever since Mama read us Snow White and Cinderella from the Grimm Fairy Tales. Miss Thomas lent Mama the book. She was the town schoolteacher, if you could say we had one since it only went up to the eighth grade. I didn't attend, though, because until most recently we didn't have a horse and town was several miles away. Instead, Mama home-schooled me and Sarah from the books Miss Thomas let her borrow. Sarah, of course, loved the fairy tales from the big book the best. Miss Thomas had told Mama it was a collection of German folklore stories that two brothers, Jakob and Wilhelm Grimm, went all around Germany collecting. It was so popular they translated it into lots of languages and now people everywhere were reading them. Miss Thomas was a charitable and smart woman who liked telling people small and obscure facts she picked up along the way. It seemed that after her husband passed she found a new purpose in life by being the town's benefactor. She looked after everyone like they were family, and made it a point to stay up to date with what people were up to for the same reason. She was the Sunday social and the towns' gossip column all rolled into one. And as the towns' benefactor, she saw to it the children got a proper education. She also thoroughly pitied anyone lacking books to read and saw to it that those who didn't make it into her classroom still had the chance to enjoy the wonder that is literature, as she liked to say. The quickest way to get on Miss Thomas' bad side was to show no interest in learning anything new. Naturally, she and Pap didn't get along from the start.

Like Mama, it was the fairy tale book that gave me my idea for what to make Sarah for her birthday. In fact, since that was the only things Sarah seemed truly interested in, we all were on a fairy tale theme for her birthday. I knelt down beside Mama in the kitchen and opened up the cabinet, "I put them down here last night to dry," I told her. I pulled out a paper crown along with a wand made from a large paper straw that had a pink star on top that spun around. They had sparkles on them that Mama and I had made ourselves. We had taken some rock salt and made three little piles which we dyed each a different color, yellow, red, and green. Mama had bought some glue from the general store and I covered the paper crown and the little wand's tip with sparkles. It worked rather well so long as you didn't let any moisture dissolve the salt. The glue was nice and dry now and I admired my handiwork.

"That's perfect," Mama said encouragingly. "She's going to be princess for a day today." She gave me a little kiss on the cheek, "You did real good, Bubba." I knew it must be true because Bubba was her little pet name she called me when she was happy with me. If Mama called me using my entire name, including the middle name, I was in trouble, but if she called me Bubba, things were good. It was nice knowing where you stood with Mama like that.

After she humored me with a few oohs and ahhhs about my present, she went and disappeared into her and Pap's room for a second and came out again with the dress wrapped in paper. I had already seen it but Sarah didn't have a clue about it. Mama called out to her, "Sarah Jane, I got something for yah." Mama had a genuine bright smile on her face and I could tell how much she'd been looking forward to this moment.

Sarah popped her head out from the room she and I shared. "Mama got a . . . p-present?" Her occasional stutter was part of her condition, but Sarah did remarkably well considering her handicap. She had been getting told for weeks that her birthday was coming up and Sarah knew birthdays were like Christmas. Uncle Colby and Aunt Emma would come over with their kids, and probably Miss Thomas, too. She liked to attend anything that might be considered a social event in the small town, plus she was partial to us. And Sarah also knew that birthdays and Christmas meant presents.

"Look what Mama made for her little princess," Mama said as she took the dress out of the paper and held it up for Sarah to see.

Her eyes lit up like two saucers, "Princess dress!"

"That's right. A pretty pink princess dress made just for Princess Sarah on her birthday." Sarah ran up to it and stroked it with her hands like it was fragile silk instead of the dyed cotton from the store in town. Mama had fussed over Sarah a few weeks ago taking measurements all over. She told her she just wanted to see how she was growing but really she was getting the measurements to make her the dress. "You wanna go put it on?"

She squealed with happiness, "Now! Now!"

"Okay, come on sweetie. Let's get you all prettied up." Mama and Sarah disappeared into the small bedroom Sarah and I shared.

Right about the time they went into the room I could hear the distant sound of a horse and wagon coming up the dirt road to our house. I went out to meet the guests and waved to Uncle Colby and Aunt Emma as they arrived in their new wagon. They had given us their old one and it sat sharing the little pen area Pap had made for tools and our chickens. Attached directly next to that was the pen where our own horse, Lilipeg, stood craning her neck out of the pen trying to reach some Johnson grass. The barbed wire was starting to dig into her but I guess that grass was worth it. She bit off a large clump and smacked on it in enjoyment with ears poked our way as if curious about what we were up to.

Uncle Colby and Aunt Emma had brought Miss Thomas with them along with their three children just liked they had planned at church, Sunday past. The kids were in the back of the wagon and the three adults had crammed themselves on the front bench. Aunt Emma had another child on the way, we'd all recently learned. They had two girls and one boy already. Francine was a little bit older than me and the other girl, Amber, a couple of years younger. My cousin George was about a year younger than I was, but we were pretty close anyway. There weren't a lot of other kids in our parts so we were normally each other's only playmate. It was nice having each other since we both lived with sisters, though I wouldn't have traded him Sarah for Francine and Amber for all the candy at the store in town. They were regular little nightmares compared to Sarah, I thought. They teased poor George about anything and everything. I didn't blame him at all for the pranks he liked to pull on them now and then. It was the only way to keep things balanced.

Uncle Colby called to his horse, "Whoa there, Joe," as they reached the house. He put the brake on the wagon and they all climbed down. The girls were whispering to each other and probably laughing at my feet, which at this point were pockmarked with red bites all over them from the ant bed earlier. George hopped down ready for play.

"Where's your Mama at?" asked Aunt Emma.

"She's inside getting' Sarah dressed up nice."

"And your father? Where is he at, dear?" asked Miss Thomas. She had a head of hair that looked more blue than gray and she was wearing a blue Sunday dress that almost matched. I was trying not to stare, but it was remarkable how similar in color they appeared in the afternoon sun, and I smirked at George who would have laughed except Aunt Emma's eyes caught him too fast.

"He inside," I said, straining to keep my eyes on hers instead of her hair.

"He is inside," corrected Miss Thomas. "You mustn't leave out the essentials of a proper sentence, dear." She had a little wrapped gift in her hands and that I knew right away was a book.

"Yes, ma'am."

The adults and children filed into the house and I supposed Mama and Sarah were still in the bedroom because I heard Aunt Emma holler, "Where's our birthday girl?"

I held George back while the others went into the house, though. "Hey," I told him, "there's a diller down a hole in back. I had him by the tail earlier and we was having ourselves a hell of a tug of war. You want to go and help me haul 'em out? He's a real mean 'un."

George was of course all for it, "Yeah, let's go get 'em. I ain't never pulled one out of it's hole before!"

We didn't get the chance, though. Before we could even disappear around back , Aunt Emma called out. "You boys come in the house. You don't need to be getting into a mess out there before we eat." Mothers always seem to know when you're up to something. And so yet again, that armadillo was blessed by a parental reprieve on its behalf.

Pap had come out of his room to greet everyone and you could tell he'd started the celebrating early. His flush cheeks and sloppy conversation were evidence he'd been drinking. Before long Mama and Sarah came out, too, with applause for Sarah's birthday dress. Miss

Thomas told Sarah how beautiful she looked while Aunt Emma complimented Mama on her sewing. Francine and Amber looked at each other and then looked like laughter was threatening to explode from them at any moment. A quick sharp glance from Aunt Emma cured that, though. The ladies went into the kitchen and started bringing things out and before long the birthday dinner was spread out. Pap had to make a makeshift table in the front room since our regular one couldn't accommodate more than four or five people. It was easily accomplished, though, with two saw horses and some spare wood with a blanket draped over it. The food itself wasn't anything spectacular but better than what we normally ate. There was even a white frosted cake with candles. It was amazing what Mama could do with just a little bit of money. Mama had egg and butter money she made and she also earned a bit making clothes from old feed sacks, which were of strong material and made for good work clothes. She'd somehow managed to scrape enough together from this, despite the fact that Pap would sometimes find and take from her savings, and she managed to buy the material to make the dress, all the things I needed for my gift, and all the things she needed for the dinner and cake. It all came together well, especially since both Aunt Emma and Miss Thomas had also brought dishes. It ended up being a right little feast. Miss Thomas' raisin pudding didn't last long at all. Pap heaved himself out nearly half of it as soon as it was put on the table. Miss Thomas gave him a disapproving look, but he just nodded towards her as though she had just said hello. He had noticed the all too obvious book she had brought as well.

"Maybe that'll be a cook book so Annie can learn herself how to make something' like this here, huh, Miss Thomas?" He smiled as he shoveled in a mouthful. It was meant to be a compliment in Pap's way.

Speaking of Mama, she wasn't herself. We went all through the singing and dinner without her saying much of anything. She kept chewing on her nails and looking around like a nervous squirrel. Mama always chewed on her nails when she was fretting, and her eyes were puffy and red. She was just plain out of sorts. She particularly kept looking in Pap's direction. He didn't seem to notice, though. He ate heartily and drank down his whiskey. He was in a good mood as he drank with Uncle Colby talking about the crops this year and who was up to what. He and Uncle Colby had known each other since way back and worked on the same farm, so there was plenty of conversation for them to find.

Uncle Colby didn't drink too much, though, citing Aunt Emma's watchful eyes, "I reckon she'll be gettin' on to me if I touch too much of the lightning."

"Yeah, they women folk 'll do that," Pap bemoaned, as though Mama ever nagged him about anything.

During all this time Sarah was just as happy as she could be. Everyone was being especially nice to her. Even Francine and Amber, who normally took every opportunity to exclude Sarah from anything, were being kind despite their near giggling episode earlier. It may have been their natural inclination to laugh at Sarah and her dress, but I think they might have also been a little envious. Any little girl is going to like to play dress-up, after-all, and Sarah's dress was beautiful and different than anything either of them had seen before with its fairytale touches. I caught them both staring at Sarah's dress with what I took to be a bit of admiration, though I'm sure they'd never have admitted as much.

Miss Thomas' book turned out to be Alice's Adventures in Wonder Land. She handed it over as though passing on a family heirloom, "This book was published in 1890, dear," she told Sarah, who was busy admiring the picture on the cover with all its interesting characters, "And it has a letter from Mr. Lewis Carroll, the author, wishing everyone who reads this book a happy Easter, because that's when it was published." She opened up the book and showed Sarah the author's note inside. "This is one of my favorite books, child, but I want you to have it because you remind me of Alice."

"What do you tell Miss Thomas, Sarah?" asked Mama.

Sarah picked up the book and hugged it, "Thank You." She couldn't read herself, of course, but Mama would certainly read it to her and she would certainly enjoy the whimsical pictures inside.

Miss Thomas told Mama about what a wonderful book it was. She told her about the rabbit hole and how there was a queen, knowing how Sarah liked stories about queens, but it was a mean queen who chopped people's heads off, but it wasn't written in such a way that a child would be scared. Rather, it was a perfect story for someone like Sarah. Yada, yada, very imaginative, yada, yada, and something about a grinning cat, but Miss Thomas didn't have much of an audience. Mama nodded like it was all very interesting but most of it was flying in one ear and out the other. Her nails were suffering a terrible punishment from whatever had Mama so preoccupied.

As for me I was nearly bursting with impatience. I still had my gift to give. "And look what I made for you, Sarah, just look!" I popped in the kitchen and was out again with the paper crown and wand. "Now you can really play princess! You got a crown and everything." I put the crown on her head and gave her the decorated straw with the spinning top. I was never really sure whether it was a royal scepter or magic wand, but I figured it could be whichever Sarah wanted it to be. That is, assuming it made it past the birthday party. When Sarah got a hold of it she started waving it so hard it the star on top nearly fell off.

"Wait! Wait, Sarah!" I yelled, "Don't shake it. Look, it spins when you blow on it, see?" and I blew on the star and around it went just like a miniature windmill covered in gems. "And it has sparkles, too, just like jewels and things on it. You can't see it so good in here but under the sun they really shine."

She bounced out of her chair and ran over to where the front room window was letting in a few rays of afternoon sun. She put it in the light and blew on the star. It lit up with reflections and Sarah's eyes danced with the light. I felt good seeing her so happy with my gift. She held her new princess wand with reverence. You would have thought that paper was gold and those colored rock salt sparklers real precious gems the way she looked at it. She stammered a little bit, "P-pretty, Sol. Pretty." It's all she said as she admired the sparkling star spinning under the sun's rays, but it was more than enough. I knew that after Mama had explained what a prince was in Snow White and all about princes and princesses, kings and queens, and Sarah just in awe of it all, that this would make the perfect gift.

Watching Sarah at that moment filled me with happiness for her, and hope, but it also kind of made my heart hurt, too, though, because Sarah knew she didn't look like her two cousins who had come to visit her today. She knew she was different. Some of the other kids in church wouldn't play with her and made fun of her saying that she was so stupid you could see it on her face and about how she couldn't talk quite right. Amber and Francine weren't mean like that, but they were a bit embarrassed that they were related to Sarah, so they pretended like they weren't whenever she was around them. It was hard on Sarah being excluded and cut off like that. But today was different. Today she felt like the most beautiful girl in the world. Sarah took a step back to make sure I got a good look at her new dress. "I pretty, t-too, right? Right, Sol?"

I stood there looking at her in her faux princess dress and paper royal jewels and admired who she was. She might have been made different but she had a heart of solid gold. She loved everyone without a thought to it. She was as sweet and giving as a person could be and I always thought it was a bad choice from above that she should be made like she was, so nice but so slow. "Yeah, you look really pretty, Sarah. As pretty as I ever seen."

"You is a pretty little princess, girl," said Pap from the table.

"You sure are," agreed Aunt Emma "Isn't she girls?" she asked her daughters.

"Yes, ma'am," they said automatically.

"I wonder if Pap got anything for his little princess?" asked Pap. He had a drunken smile that almost made him look affable. He put down his glass and disappeared to his room for a moment, re-emerging with something small and lumpy wrapped in plain brown paper in his hands. He sat back down and motioned for Sarah to come over to him. He lifted her up on his lap and handed her the gift. We all watched as she unwrapped it, particularly Mama who seemed to be studying this gift intently.

Sarah, of course, was thrilled to have one more thing to unwrap. She tore away the paper to reveal a remarkably well carved castle done out of cedar root. The bottom of it was still a gnarled piece of root, but it quickly faded into a beautiful castle. Not only did it look just like a miniature castle, but the cedar smelled wonderful as well. We were all impressed with it. Miss Thomas, who didn't know Pap had a way with whittling, raised her eyebrows in sheer astonishment that Pap could make such a thing.

"I saw it in that picture book your Mama used for your new dress," said Pap. "What's a princess without a castle?"

Sarah ran her hand over the tiny towers complete with little windows and a big archway that looked like the closed drawbridge of the small kingdom. It was a tiny thing that Pap could have held in the palm of his hand, but he'd paid attention to its details. Sarah just smiled and petted her new gift. It looked just like the one from her story book and it was obvious this had completed her princess day. Despite my own knowledge of Pap's skill with a pocketknife, I had to admit this gift took me back a bit. Hours had gone into that castle. I'd never known Pap to put so much effort into a gift.

Miss Thomas leaned in towards Sarah and asked "May I?"

Sarah was a little confused when Miss Thomas held out her hands.

"Miss Thomas wants to see your castle, honey," said Aunt Emma.

Sarah handed it over and Miss Thomas held it up, turning it around and squinting to see all the details. "Well my word, Abram. Did you carve this yourself?"

"Why?" asked Pap defensively, "Don't think I can make somethin' nice for my own girl?"

Miss Thomas handed Sarah back her little castle and said to Pap, "I just didn't know you were a wood carver, I'm afraid. You did quite a job, Abram, I must confess. I think anybody would have to admire such workmanship."

Pap should have been happy to have such a compliment from Miss Thomas. It quite likely was the first and only time she'd ever pay him one. But instead of just saying thanks, Pap said, "Maybe I'm not so worthless after all, eh?"

There was a bit of a tense moment after Pap said that. I looked to Mama to say something, but she just stared blankly at Pap. It was Aunt Emma who managed to change the subject. "Nobody ever said you were, Abram. You just surprised us is all. How long did that take you?"

"Oh, not too long." His thin lips stretched back into his drunken grin again. "Well, it probably would have taken most folks a good while, but it seemed to go pretty fast for me, I reckon." Pap went on to explain about finding the cedar root from a debris pile near the thicket of trees at work and how he got the idea to go through and look at the pictures from the books Mama read to Sarah to find something to make it into. "Weren't really all that hard," he explained with pride. "Just a few square blocks for towers and then some touches here and there."

We all visited for a little while longer before Uncle Colby and Aunt Emma called it a night. "We best be on our way before poor Joe has to find his way in the dark," Uncle Colby told us.

Mama walked them and Miss Thomas out to the wagon, and Miss Thomas couldn't help but to admit to Mama her surprise at Pap's gift. Everyone knew she wasn't big on Pap, but she and Mama had formed a strong relationship over the years so she tried to overlook Pap's shortcomings. Aunt Emma and Mama used to be closer, but I think with the three kids and everything Aunt Emma kind of drifted away from Mama. In turn, though, Miss Thomas had taken a shine to Sarah from early on and that caused her and Mama to become very close. They sat together at church—Pap didn't go of course, and Miss Thomas would have both Mama and Pap over for dinner now and then when they had reason to go into town. Normally Miss Thomas had strong feelings about having folks she didn't care too much for over for dinner. She'd lecture them about morals, try to help them find God, and even help them find work if they needed it, but having them under her roof was another matter. She was very particular about who she invited under her roof, but she made an exception for Pap for Mama's sake. And it was because of this closeness she couldn't help but notice that Mama just hadn't been herself today. "Are you feeling all right, Annie?" she asked. "You're looking a little peakish, dear."

"Huh?" asked Mama. "Oh, no, Miss Thomas, I'm just fine. Happy as a clam after seeing Sarah have such a perfect birthday. I can't thank you enough for coming and for the book. I'm sure she's just going to love it."

"Well, I know it's difficult sometimes, Annie. But God made your child just as loving and pure as she can be." Mama didn't respond but Miss Thomas knew something was eating at her. She was thinking that maybe Sarah's condition was weighing on Mama lately, and in times of need Miss Thomas relied on the scriptures. "'Blessed are the pure of heart, for they will see God'. —Matthew five:eight'," she told Mama. Miss Thomas had an arsenal of her favorite verses memorized and she was quick to whip one out for appropriate occasions, "And she's blessed to have a mother like you, Annie. You're doing very well by her."

Mama paused a bit and looked in Miss Thomas' sturdy eyes with her own frail hazel ones. She had her left pinky between her teeth working on it a bit. She still didn't say anything, though.

"What is it, Annie?"

"Nothing. I'm just wondering if I have done right."

Miss Thomas gave her a little hug, "Well of course you have, child. You've done as well as anybody could ask of you. The Lord has given you burdens, to be sure, but He wouldn't give you more than He thought you could bear, Annie."

She had hoped her words would have a cheering effect on Mama, but instead Mama said something that took the cheery wind right out of Miss Thomas' sails, "And what happens when the devil throws his lot in on top of what the good Lord done give me?" There weren't any tears in her eyes but there was something deep and painful in them that really struck a chord with Miss Thomas. "What do you do then?"

Miss Thomas paused and thought a moment. Uncle Colby and Aunt Emma were waiting for her and this wasn't the chance she'd have to try to get my Mama to open up some more. "Then that person must ask Him to help them bear it, Annie. Isaiah forty-one:ten, 'Fear thou not; for I am with thee. Be not dismayed; for I am thy God. I will strengthen thee. Yea, I will help thee. Yea, I will uphold thee with the right hand of my righteousness.'" That was just the right one, I'm sure

Miss Thomas was thinking to herself, “Whatever shadows or storms come, Annie, they pass. Just be strong like you have been and you'll weather them."

Mama kind of nodded in feigned agreement. "I know. Thank you again, Miss Thomas. I'll see you Sunday at church."

"We'll talk some more then if you feel like it, okay?"

"Of course, Miss Thomas. I'll see you later." She gave Miss Thomas a hug as the lady in blue climbed in the wagon and they headed down the road.

I helped Mama clear the dishes and Pap dismantled the makeshift table. Sarah followed Mama and me around modeling her princess dress and casting spells with, what she had chosen for the moment to be, her magic wand. She wanted Mama to read to her from her new book and was trying to enchant the dishes clean so Mama would hurry up and finish them. Mama seemed to be moving at a snail's pace, though. Her expression was distant and she moved as though somebody else was directing her around on hidden strings.

Eventually, the house was put straight again and Sarah and I climbed in our beds while Mama read us a bit from Alice's Adventures in Wonderland. Mama was on *Chapter two, The Pool of Tears*, and she read: "Dear, dear! How queer everything is today! And yesterday things went on just as usual. I wonder if I've been changed in the night? Let me think: was I the same when I got up this morning? I almost think I can remember feeling differently . . ." but Mama's words trailed off. It seemed that for some reason she had been struck suddenly dumb. Her hands were trembling as she held the book. I couldn't see her features very well in the lamplight since her head was lowered towards the pages, but she almost looked like she was crying. I was going to say something, but before I had the chance she closed the book and said hastily, "We'll read more tomorrow. It's late and Mama's tired, now." Then she stood up, still keeping her head lowered a bit, and left the room with the lamp.

Had it not been for the all the food I had eaten that afternoon, I might have been alert enough to ponder if something was terribly wrong with Mama and follow after her. I might have had the sense to ask her before she left the room if everything was okay. I might have done something other than just fall asleep. But as it was, I was exhausted and barely awake when she left our room that night, so such things were only a passing thought that quickly faded in my tiredness. I rolled over, comfy under my quilt. Sarah, too, seemed tired from the day. She hadn't let

Mama take the dress off of her earlier so she went to sleep wearing her princess outfit. She held her cedar castle close in her hands, its sweet smell permeating the room as she dozed off. Before I knew it, I was asleep, too. I always remembered what a great day she'd had before we went to bed that night. It was one of the few things that gave me comfort. At least she'd had a perfect birthday.

The next morning I awoke to the sound of a strange silence in the house. I was used to either hearing Sarah's heavy breathing in her bed near mine or else her high pitched voice bouncing off the walls of the kitchen, but this morning there was neither. I went into the kitchen and Pap was there with a glass of whiskey in his hand. Normally he didn't drink before going to work, just a lot when he got home, and there was a very unusual expression on his face. I didn't know what kind of emotion it was that put that expression on his face, but I knew it was something I hadn't seen before. He hadn't even looked at me when I walked in the kitchen and looked around. There was no breakfast on the small table, no fire in the oven, no Mama telling me to sit down and eat, and no Sarah. There was just Pap with that new expression and glass of whiskey. Seconds passed and he still didn't say anything or make any facial change, so I did the obvious and asked, "Where's Mama and Sarah?"

He put the glass to his lips, swished around a mouthful of lightning like it was mouthwash before swallowing it down and then said, "Your Mama done left us, boy. She done took your sister and they're gone."

Chapter 4

There was a lot of back history about my parents I never could have known in those days. When I got older, my uncle Marcus told me quite a bit, as did Aunt Emma and others, and eventually I was able to put together much of the past that ended up having such an impact on my future.

Annie Stotley was one of four children born to Tom and Mary Stotley on April 4, 1881. They lived in a three-room house Mr. Stotley had built in the new town of Varner Creek. Like so many others in town, Tom Stotley was primarily a cotton farmer, or to be more accurate he worked as a farm hand for Mr. Wilkins, the actual land owner who had purchased hundreds of acres from Pritchard Varner's estate. There were some sharecroppers, too, who simply leased land from Mr. Wilkins for their own crop and then paid him from their individual profits, but others like Tom felt that wage earning was a more stable income. Mr. Wilkins had cattle and other crops that could offset the loss if the cotton harvest had a bad year, so Tom was content to stay in the service of his employer. Besides, Mr. Wilkins was a fair man. When he did well, so did his employees. And when things were tough he and his workers could rally around one another. Everyone pulled their belts a notch tighter, and in that way nobody was ever left to starve. It was the same with other land owners in the area and it made for a very close-knit community back in those days. It was Mr. Wilkins' son, in fact, who at the time was at the state medical school in Galveston, who later become the town's first doctor.

Mrs. Stotley was a woman between two worlds. She had grown up a fire and brimstone Protestant, raised by Bible-thumper parents, named for the preachers who would pound upon their Bible as they rained down sermons of punishment and vengeance. She'd been taught that God is not a forgiving deity, but rather should be feared always and obeyed without question lest He punish those who stray. But when she married Tom and they moved away she found most everyone around her didn't follow the fire and brimstone way of thinking, and she never seemed to quite know what to think of people who thought God was so forgiving.

The Stotley's small home sat just a mile or so outside of town on land they made payments on to Mr. Wilkins. They had four children, their oldest being a boy and then three girls, my Mama being the second youngest child. When their son Marcus was old enough Tom and Mary had him join his father working in the fields. Like his father he was quiet and reserved, but a hard worker. And when harvest time came around the entire family would put on their work clothes, which was everything except their Sunday clothes, and labor out in the fickle Fall weather picking the tufts of cotton out of the dry and prickly plants. It was mostly during the harvest time that Mr. Wilkins would pick up extra farm hands to help bring in the cotton. It was in this way that Annie Stotley ended up meeting Abram Mayfield.

He wasn't from Varner Creek. He was in his early twenties and walked into town one day with a couple of other buddies, Uncle Colby included, looking for work. It was the harvesting season of 1895 and there was work to be had so the boys were in luck. His boots were old and worn from walking and his clothes dirty and full of holes. His walking companions were just the same and they were a rowdy bunch from the start. Mr. Wilkins hired them none the less and offered them thirty-five cents a day with three meals regular and a work house that they could rent by having some of their pay withheld. It was basically a one room shack that had a wood burning stove next to a few other shacks that shared an outhouse. It was set up just like the old slave rows, but since there weren't any slaves anymore, everyone just called it worker's row. As soon as they got their first pay the boys bought the cheap liquor called white lightning that was sold in town and stayed up late drinking, playing cards, and trying to find a tune with a harmonica and a fiddle that only had two strings left, not to mention a big chunk missing out of the back.

Abram noticed Annie Stotley his first week working. She was a pretty, petite girl of only fourteen with bright hazel eyes and long black hair that was as dark as midnight. Everyone was picking the cotton and she was hauling the water bucket around one day offering people a drink. When she got to him he gave her a charming smile and tried to strike up a conversation. "Hey, how're you?"

"I'm all right. Hot out here today, though," she responded. The weather had gone from a cool morning to a cooking afternoon again, as Texas weather has a nasty tendency to do.

"Damn sure is." He dipped the communal ladle, took a deep drink, and wiped his mouth with his sleeve. He was a tall young man, about six foot, with brown hair and brown eyes. He had a somewhat nice smile but his lips were thin and his teeth were yellowed from too much chaw. Annie hadn't had a grown man smile at her like he was just now. She wasn't sure what was different about it but it made her feel a bit awkward and she felt flush on top of the heat. "Don't go too far, now," he told her, "I might want yah to come back pretty soon." He gave her a flirty wink, "Might want some more water, too."

She smiled back at him, more out of habit than anything else, "Um, okay. Bye."

As she went off to the others working in the field Abram whispered to one of his housemates standing next to him, "She's a bit of a stick, but I bet she'd be a good roll in the hay, don't yah think?" His friend Colby glanced up briefly at the girl Abram pointed at and went back to work without saying anything.

And so it went on like that during the rest of the harvest. He'd find her in the fields and manage his way close by while they both walked down the rows stuffing their bags full, or sometimes her father would ask her to go fetch the bucket and get everyone some water, and Abram would always make her wait those few extra seconds so he could flirt a little and look her over. Finally he worked up the nerve to let her know what was on his mind. "You sure are pretty. What's your name?"

She pushed her hair back over her ear and looked around like he had just said something that might cause an uproar. "Annie." She looked around a bit more and seemed content nobody was paying them much mind. "Annie Stotley. What's yours?"

"I'm Abram." He watched her gaze dart around. "How come you look so scared all of a sudden? I just ask your name."

She kept her voice low, "I don't think my Mama would approve of us talkin'. She awfully strict about things like that," she said nervously.

"And how're we talking that's so bad?" he asked. "Nothing but telling our names and me just making a polite compliment. That's nothin' to get worked up over, now is it?"

She watched her shoe and kicked around a dirt clod. "I reckon not, but like I said, she's awfully strict."

While they had been talking, Mrs. Stotley noticed her daughter taking far too long with one of the workmen some ways off. She didn't much like the looks of their conversation, either. She yelled out to her, "Annie! Go on and finish up and then come help me with this row."

Abram was still giving her his most charming of smiles. "I gotta go," she said. "That's my Mama."

"All right, then." She turned to go and he said quickly, "Maybe we could meet up some time and talk some more."

She paused. "I don't think I'd be allowed." She walked off but turned around again before she was too far away to be heard, and in a hushed voice called out, "Harvest festival's coming up, though. We could talk then." She wasn't sure quite why she said it. He was obviously too old for her parents to approve of, but maybe that in itself had something to do with it. She didn't wait for a response because she could feel her mother's glare, so she walked away with a brisk skip in her step.

Abram in the meantime had sex on his brain. He gave himself a little rub in his nether regions as he watched her trot away. His eyes followed the way her dress moved over her tiny frame and the way her pretty dark hair curled a bit at the ends despite the sweat. Mama was always pretty and it's a fact that wasn't lost on Abram Mayfield that day as he watched her. His heart beat fast at the idea of lying down with Annie Stotley. He had heard of other men who'd get so wound up they'd sneak out and do their business with animals, sheep, calves, and what not. There was an old story on Worker's row about a man who had been found moaning and bleeding in bed with a rear-end full of buckshot. The story goes he had been trying to put his pecker where God never intended it to go at a farm down the road during the night. The farmer had woken up thinking someone was trying to steal his animals and let go a volley of shotgun fire on the culprit when he saw him running bare assed from a pen by the barn where some calves were being kept for branding. The unfortunate recipient had managed to run off into the night and limp home to worker's row, but it didn't take long for everyone to figure out the bleeding miserable in the bed was the same animal fornicator from the barn. Or so the story went. Mr. Wilkins seemed to think it funny and never would confirm or deny its validity. No doubt Abram Mayfield was thinking that he'd never stoop to sneaking around barns with a swollen pecker. He made up his mind then and there he was going to lay with Annie Stotley.

When all the cotton from all the area farms had been gathered, ginned, weighed, and sold, the small town prepared for the Harvest festival. It was three nights of dancing, eating, and general merry-making. At the end of harvest, the big tin building where the cotton had been weighed and stored before it was shipped, was cleaned out and converted into a big dance hall. A small stage was erected and long tables were brought in and put on one side. The festivities began on Friday night with barbecue and dancing. It flowed over into Saturday night with much the same, and it wrapped up Sunday with morning church and an auction that sold everything from arts and crafts to tools and livestock. Harvest Festival was the biggest social event in Varner Creek.

During the day Friday, Annie and her sisters were busy fixing each other's hair and arguing over who got to wear the pretty floral pattern dress. Annie had one younger sister named Candace who was ten, and one older sister named Emma who was sixteen. All the Stotley women shared the same black hair and hazel colored eyes, but Annie was certainly prettier than her older sister, Emma. Annie had inherited her mother's petite figure and had very pretty, girlish features. Emma, on the other hand, was a large girl with a big chin and a somewhat masculine look about her. And seeing how the floral dress was a hand-me-down from their mother, Mrs. Stotley knew it wouldn't fit Emma.

"Why don't you wear that yellow dress, Emma?" encouraged Mrs. Stotley, "It looks so pretty on you."

"Mama, I wore that dress to last year's festival, not to mention last Sunday at Church," she complained., "I can't wear it again tonight. People will think I got nothing else to wear."

"I'll tell you what, Emma," her mother said. "You wear the maroon dress you got for tonight and tomorrow you and I will take one of my other flower dresses and we'll see what we can do with it. Now how'd that be?"

Emma was a little embarrassed that she couldn't fit in her mother's dress, but she knew she couldn't fight the truth of things. She quit arguing with Annie with an air of resignation, "Okay, Mama."

Even though Annie's younger sister had also played at arguing for the dress she knew just as well as everybody else that nobody was going to let her wear it. Besides being too small for it she'd be running and playing outside with the other children as soon as they reached the dance hall and getting dirt all over herself. She was put into one of Annie's old feed-sack made dresses, just like she'd worn out in the fields.

Mr. Stotley threw on a plain button-up blue shirt and didn't look much different than any other day, except that he was cleaner. It didn't take him more than two seconds to decide what to wear and he couldn't understand all the fuss the girls were making about who wears what and who had this on last week and that mess. He stepped outside away from the chaos, lit his pipe, and thought to himself, *what I wouldn't give for some peace and quiet around here.*

Marcus, on the other, had been pestering his mother all day for his best shirt to be ironed for the second time. "I can't understand what your worry is about this shirt, Marcus," she told him, "it looks fine."

"He wants to look nice because he likes a girl," teased Emma.

"Really?" Mrs. Stotley couldn't hide her pleasure. She had secretly worried about Marcus and his finding a good girl to settle down with.

He was already eighteen and hadn't shown much interest in anyone. He just kept to himself and wouldn't hardly talk to nobody. "Who do you have your eyes on?" she asked him with a curious smile.

Marcus' cheeks went red and he tensed his eyes, "Nobody."

"That ain't true," offered Emma, "He likes Mary Jo Greenley. They been talking for weeks now. I seen them holdin' hands the other day."

"Why don't you mind your own business!?" fumed Marcus.

Candace started up a song, "Marcus and Mary Jo, sittin' in a tree. *K-I-S-S-I-N-G . . .*"

"Shut up, Candace," Marcus said. He didn't yell it, though. Marcus never yelled. He just tensed up his eyebrows and shot her a warning look.

Candace giggled but stopped singing. Marcus could produce a most intimidating look when provoked. He had intense blue eyes unlike his sisters, and they could be both beautiful when he was in a soft mood, or downright menacing if he wasn't.

Eventually, everyone was dressed, ready, and they started walking down towards the dance hall. They had a mule but didn't own a wagon of their own, so the family walked together. They hadn't gone more than a quarter of the mile to town, though, before Mr. Wilkins came by. "Y'all want to climb in back and hitch a ride?"

Mr. Wilkins favored all the Stotleys. He knew them to be hard working and trustworthy people. He had already talked to Marcus about learning the blacksmithing trade from the man in town so that Mr. Wilkins could hire him later on to do all his metal working.

"That's mighty nice of you, sir," responded Mr. Stotley. "You don't think it would burden your horses too much pulling all of us?"

"Oh, not a bit Tom. They're young and strong, just like your kids there. And a little bit of exercise is good for 'em. Y'all climb on up."

Mrs. Wilkins gave them a nod in her bonnet with her gray hair poking out, "How do?" she asked.

"Fine, Mrs. Wilkins. Just fine. Sure is a lovely dress you have on this evening," answered Mrs. Stotley. And they all made their way into town.

They pulled up to the dance hall and Candace leaped out of the wagon before it even stopped. She saw some of her friends playing tag outside and went to join in. "Don't get dirt all over yourself, girl!" yelled her mother.

"I won't!" she hollered back, running straight in to the cloud of kicked up dirt with the other children.

"I swear, that girl sometimes," mumbled Mrs. Stotley.

Annie and Emma got out and started walking around saying hello to everyone they knew. Emma looked downright scathingly at all the pretty dresses the other girls were wearing. Neither hers nor Annie's were much different than the other dresses, but somehow Emma felt Annie fit right in and she didn't. As they rounded the corner to one side of the building a big burly fellow poked his head from behind the building to see who was coming. He seemed oddly happy to see them and called out, "Hey, Emma!"

Her eyes lit up, "Colby! What are you doing back here?" Emma immediately went around back to talk to him and Annie was obliged to follow. Apparently, Emma and Colby had sown the seeds of a secret romance.

Behind the building, a number of men, mostly the out-of-towners but also some of the bachelor locals, were drinking, smoking, and swapping tall tales. Abram was among them, of course. He was puffing on a rolled cigarette and, noticing Annie, he walked over smiling, "Hey, girl, what're you doing back here with us no goods?"

Annie just looked towards Emma and said, "My sister."

Abram glanced over to where her and Colby were chatting things up, "Oh, yeah. She's got a thing for my friend, I think."

Annie looked over and it seemed to be true. Both Emma and Colby were wearing grins. Emma was talking away and Colby just seemed to be contently listening. Annie just shrugged her shoulders and said, "Guess so."

There was an awkward pause as neither could think of something to carry the conversation forward. Abram held out the little cigarette for her, "You want to try this?"

She made a facial look like he was offering her a booger from right out of his nose. "Naw, I don't want none," she said.

"Go on," he said. "This here's good tobacco, come all the way from New Orleans. We done planted some seeds around our place and as soon as we get some land of our own we're going to get rich with it. It's a might better than anything they got around here."

She stared at the smoking paper in his fingers, "I don't like the smoke. My daddy's got a pipe, and it smells okay, but that stuff don't smell too nice."

He laughed a little bit, "No, I reckon you're too young nohow." And he started smoking on it himself.

She frowned a bit, "Am not, just don't like to is all. Besides, if my

Mama smelled that on me she'd tan me."

Abram put his head back and let out a little circle wisp of smoke that floated above his head, "Ain't seem to bother your sister none."

And sure enough Annie looked over and Emma was now taking puffs from the same little kind of cigarette with Colby that Abram had. "Emma! Mama's gonna whoop you and me both if she catches you."

"Well how's she gonna know less you run and tell her?" Emma asked accusingly. "Just hush up!" And she went back to her conversation with Colby.

Annie wasn't liking being behind the building anymore. It was bad enough Abram telling her she was too young and her sister treating her like a little child in front of him, but the men smelled bad and Abram's smoke kept drifting in her face. "I think I bes' be going inside now," she told him.

Abram quit leaning against the tin siding and scolded her, "Why? What's wrong with being out here and visitin' a little?"

He kind of scared her the way he got so offended like that, "I promised my Mama I'd help her with some of the settin' up," she lied.

"Fine," he said disappointedly, "go on, then." And as quick as he had gotten mad he was smiling at her again, "I hope to get to dance with you tonight, though."

Annie went back around into the building and decided she would help the women set the tables, after all.

As the night's festivities progressed Annie forgot all about being upset with Emma for talking down to her or being bothered by Abram's moodiness. She was having a great time. The fiddlers were fiddling and everyone was on their feet. She had danced with her father, danced with Candace, and was currently dancing with Gerald, a cute boy her age. He swung her around and spun her so fast she got dizzy and fell right over on her butt and laughed herself silly. Gerald went off to find someone else who could handle his fine dancing abilities without falling over and going into hysterics. Annie was still sitting and laughing at herself when she felt two hands come up under her arms, the fingers of which were unnecessarily close to her breasts. She heard Abram's voice and smelled whiskey on it, "Here, let me help you up, girl." He had already started picking her up so it wasn't so much as an offer as a statement.

She felt herself being placed back on her feet and turned around. Abram then took her by the waist and started dancing. Well, it was a dancing of sorts. She might have been the one falling over a minute ago but it was him that was lacking the proper balance now. He tried to give her a little dip and nearly stumbled right over on top of her. "H-h-had a bit too much to drink, maybe," he breathed in explanation. His breath was so rank she could practically see the words coming out of his mouth.

She turned her head to the side trying to deflect some of the foulness. She tried to walk off or at least take a couple of steps back so he wouldn't be hanging all over her like he was, but his arm was holding around her waist too tight. Just when she felt she couldn't stand being next to him anymore she felt another hand grab and yank her away from him. Marcus pushed her aside and stood glaring at Abram.

"What'd you go and do that for?" asked Abram, wearing a look of true confusion.

"Cause I don't like you hanging on my sister like that," warned Marcus. He was a few years younger than Abram but Marcus had a temper not to be trifled with.

"We was just dancin'. She fell down and I helped her up." He looked over in Annie's direction, "Ain't that right?"

Annie figured even if he had been dragging her around like that on the dance floor, the part about him picking her up was true enough. "Yes. He did help me up, Marcus."

"Don't care," Marcus said flatly. "You stay away from her."

It probably would've ended there, but Abram made a poor decision in his intoxicated state. He took a couple of steps towards Marcus with his own glare in his eyes and said, "Well fuck you, you little . . . " but whatever else he was going to say never came out. Marcus hit him so fast and so hard that Abram didn't know he'd been hit until after he was on the ground. Then a dull ache, which quickly became a throbbing pain, pounded in his jaw. Blood dripped on the dirt floor and the music stopped as people began to stare and whisper. He tried to get up but his entire head was pounding, and every little movement seemed to make it worse. He could feel his lip busted and swelling and the whole right side of his face felt like a sledgehammer had just made his acquaintance.

Mr. Stotley came running over when he saw it was Marcus in the scuffle, "What's going on over here?"

Marcus pointed down at Abram. "He was hanging all over Annie."

Mr. Stotley looked at Annie. "That true?"

She felt a little torn. She appreciated her brother looking out for her and didn't much care for the way Abram was acting with her, but he was drunk and Marcus didn't really need to hit him so hard like that. "He's just drunk, Daddy. He didn't mean no harm and Marcus was just being over-protective is all."

Mr. Stotley looked at Abram moaning on the floor and at Marcus, who stood with his fists clenched and the same look on his face that he had given Candace earlier that day, except now it was intensified. His father knew that look and that more trouble might follow if they stayed, so he said, "Well, I think we better call this a night. Marcus, you go wait with your Mama while I round up your sisters," and he strolled away to go find his remaining two daughters.

Marcus sternly, but without anger, grabbed Annie by the arm and marched her towards the other end of the dance hall where their mother was standing aghast in embarrassment. But after just a couple of steps Abram called out to him, "Hey, boy!" He tried to get up but found it difficult being both intoxicated and knocked stupid. "Dis here ain't done. I'm gonna get you, boy. You hear me? We ain't done!"

There was no reply from Marcus but Annie looked back with worry.

As if Mary Stotley hadn't been mortified enough by the night's events she got a double dose when her husband informed her during the long walk home that he had found Emma outside with some fella's tongue down her throat. He didn't know Colby's name to immediately identify the offending tongue's owner to his wife, but after briefly describing a corn-fed looking fellow with big bushy sideburns and broad shoulders, she knew exactly who he was talking about.

Mrs. Stotley decided she'd give it a night's rest before discussing the various things that occurred on that Friday night, but over Saturday breakfast she addressed her scandalous children, "I'm thinking we might just let your father and Candace go to the dance tonight and maybe you three stay here with me," she told Annie, Emma, and Marcus.

Annie and Emma broke into an immediate uproar, "What? But, Mama . . ."

Marcus might have been disappointed, or maybe just overly concentrating on his bacon, it was hard to tell.

"Well, after the way you three behaved last night, I just think it's best if . . ."

"What'd I do?" interrupted Annie. "Weren't none of that my fault, Mama. Some drunk man come up and grab me and Marcus flies off the handle. How's that my fault?"

Mrs. Stotley huffed a little, "Maybe if you hadn't of spent such a time out there in the fields with that man he wouldn't think it's all right to go grabbin' you like that. I saw y'all out there jibber-jabbering all day long.

It's no wonder he's taken an interest. You might as well have wrapped yourself up in a bow for that scoundrel the way you stood out there eatin' up his advances." She looked over at Emma and said "And you, Emma. Sneaking off and offending your upbringing by making out with some brute none of us knows anything about. Ain't no tellin' where he's from or what kind of upbringing he's had. What were you thinking?"

"He's not a brute, Mama," Emma said defensively. "He's nice. And he's the only boy that ever liked me so much." There was a sad truth in Emma's words and it broke her mother's sternness a little, but she was still severely disappointed in such behavior.

"Well, that's still no reason to be acting like you were raised up to act like a harlot, Emma Stotley."

Dramatic as ever Emma burst into tears, "We was only kissing! Oh, please, Mama. I just have to go tonight. Everyone's going to be there and it only comes once a year."

Annie threw her misery in as well. "Please, Mama. We won't do anything to cause no trouble." Marcus looked over at her as well with a slight plea in his eyes. After all, until the trouble last night with Abram he had been having a grand time with Mary Jo Greenley.

With so many pitiful eyes on her Mrs. Stotley felt outnumbered. Mr. Stotley had been doing his level best to stay out of the conversation up to this point. He knew Emma was a powder-keg of emotions and the less he had to deal with womanly outbursts the better, so far as he was concerned. He sat quietly mopping up the last bit of the gravy on his plate with half a biscuit.

"Well, what do you think, Papa?" asked Mrs. Stotley. "You think these three should be allowed to go to the festival after their antics last night?"

The table was quiet and when Mr. Stotley looked up he saw all eyes were on him.

"Oh, please, Papa, please," Emma said.

He chunked the last of his biscuit in his mouth and chewed slowly to buy himself a few extra seconds of peace. Truth was he didn't really care. He was proud of Marcus for standing up for his sister and even though he loved his daughters he didn't worry himself much about them. He figured the two oldest girls along with Marcus would be married and moved on soon enough and he'd finally have a little bit of quiet around the house. And if Emma fell in love with that big oaf she was kissing on, then the quicker she'd be out from under his roof. "Well, I reckon it does come only once a year. And besides, weren't such a big deal, I don't think. Not less we make it out to be."

And so Mrs. Stotley accepted her defeat. She was outnumbered and her marital alliance had broken down with Mr. Stotley's indifference. They worked around the house for the early part of the day. Mr. Stotley hid himself in the garden out back enjoying the peace and quiet of the squash, zucchini, peas, tomatoes, beets, cabbage, and carrots. There was a secret Tom Stotley walked around with. One of the reasons he was such a hard worker in the fields, always early to arrive and late to leave, was because he couldn't stand being cooped up with his family. Among Candace's girlish squeals, Annie and Emma's squabbling and emotional outbursts, Marcus' eternal solidarity, and his wife's being so opinionated about every little thing under the sun, he felt completely without his own individuality. Four kids and a wife in a three-room home had consumed his personal freedom years ago and the only place he found solace was at work under that infinite sky that let him breathe. Going home each evening to the confining walls of his life depressed him. He could feel the walls closing around him at night as he slept, crowding in on him and taking more and more of his personal space. It was only the thought of the waiting freedom outside in the fields and the fact that some day soon his children would be grown and out of the house that gave him any sense of optimism. He never told his family, of course, but Marcus always suspected a little. In a not so different sense, he felt the same way. Mr. Stotley loved his family, he just wished they'd leave him alone for a good long spell, let him breathe a little in his own home.

Since the children had won their cause Mrs. Stotley and Emma spent the day sewing on another floral patterned dress so that Emma could wear it that night. Annie played with Candace and Marcus walked on down to the Wilkins' house to help Mr. Wilkins make repairs to his porch for a bit of spending money.

While he cut and nailed the boards Marcus was being watched. Out in the distance on worker's row Abram Mayfield sat telling himself all the horrible things he'd like to do to Marcus. His bottom lip was swelled up like a balloon and he could hardly talk without an aching pain shooting through his jaw. He had been smoking hemp all morning to dull the pain and his eyes were glazed over. One of the friends he had made by sharing some his stockpile with was with him, too, and said, "Hey, Abe, ain't that the fellow what punched you last night?"

Abram just kept right on staring out towards Marcus, "He sucker-punched me and I was drunk as a skunk. That's the only reason he got the better of me. But I aim to make a reckoning with that boy," he told his friend.

"What're you going to do?" asked the other.

Abram put his fingers up to his busted lip and winced in pain, "I'm going to make him bleed a lot worse than me, that's for sure."

And so Abram went around that rest of that day making plans. He told his housemates what he wanted to do and one of them offered to join in. Colby, though, had genuinely started to like Emma. He had grown up hard and never had a woman be so nice to him and care for him like she did. His own mother had died giving him birth and he had been shipped around from relative to relative until he struck out on his own. Emma wasn't what most folks would call a pretty woman, but she was good to him and that meant more to Colby than looks ever would. So he listened to Abram's plans but told him he wasn't taking any part in them. And later that night when Emma and her family showed up to the dance hall he pulled her aside as quick as he could. At first Emma thought he wanted to make out some more and was going to protest as she didn't want to get in trouble and have to leave just after getting there, but instead he said to her, "Look, I've got to talk to you. It's about your brother."

"What about him?" she asked.

He whispered close to her ear, "Abram and some others are looking to get him alone tonight and hurt him something bad."

She jumped back a little with wide and scared eyes, "What've them other fellas got against Marcus?"

"Abram been going around telling some of the other whites out in worker's row about how Marcus sucker-punched him when he was drunk and nearly passed out. He's also been telling them that Marcus said they was all white-trash niggers that were stupid and lazy, and the like."

"He never said no such thing!" Emma cried.

"I know he didn't, but it don't matter. A couple of them boys believe him and when he said he wanted to teach your brother a hard lesson tonight for saying such things they said they wanted a piece themselves. There's four or five of them all told, now, and they're all liquored up, so there ain't no tellin' what they'll do if they get the chance. You got to warn your brother and get him to go on home just as fast as you can."

"I'll go and find him right now." She looked into Colby's eyes and realized that he had risked getting in a scrape himself by telling her what he did, "Thank you, Colby," she said, "I ain't going to forget it."

He gave her a kiss on the cheek and a pat on her rear, "Go on, now. And make sure don't none of them see you two leave alone. I'll go out back with the fellas and make sure that don't none of them follow y'all."

Annie had seen Emma and Colby talking furiously and before she could ask Emma why she seemed so unnerved, she was being told, "We've got to find Marcus," started Emma. She briefly explained the situation to Annie.

Annie was terrified at the very thought of it. "Oh, my God. I knew it, I just knew it. I heard the way Abram was yellin' at Marcus that night when we walked off. I knew he was going to do something!"

They found Marcus eating with Mary Jo and her folks and urgently waved him over to tell him where things were.

When they finished he just looked at them coolly and said, "To hell with them. I ain't scared of a bunch of dumb-ass, lazy fools like them boys."

"But Marcus, you gotta go. If they all catch you ain't no telling what they might do," pleaded Annie.

"What're they gonna do here with everybody watching on?" asked Marcus. "To hell with them." And with that comment he went back over to Mary Jo and sat down to finish off his chicken pot pie. She seemed to be asking him what the fuss was about but he just waved it off.

"Stubborn idiot," said Emma. "What're we gonna do now, Annie? We can't let them other fellas rip Marcus limb from limb. And you know if they do get him alone he won't have the sense to try and get away. He'll just stand there and try to take them all on like a damned fool."

Annie herself was almost in tears. "I don't know. I just don't know what to do. You reckon we should go tell Mama and Papa?"

They held hands for a second as Emma thought. "Na, Mama would just have herself a heart attack and we'd all be locked up in the house from now until the end of days. And Papa would just let Mama handle it however she wanted to, so best not to tell him, neither."

Then another idea struck Annie. "Abram likes me," she said. "At least it seems that way. Do you reckon I could talk him out of it?"

Emma's eyebrows raised and she looked at Annie. "That's not a bad idea. He does like you, that's plain enough." But the idea worried her, too. "What if he's just as mad at you, though. You don't think he'd go off and hit you or something, do you?"

Annie thought about it for a moment and imagined herself walking up to Abram and him punching the daylights out of her. She decided it didn't seem likely. "I don't think so. He's got a temper maybe but I think he'd be all right. Besides, we gotta do something."

"Well, all right, then," said Emma, "and I'll go with yah. If he does take a swing at you, though, I'll fight him just like a man. And I know Colby wouldn't let it get outta hand. That'd help out a lot. Besides them being friends and all, Colby's a lot bigger than any of them other boys. He'd make them think twice about giving us any trouble."

They set off to find Colby, who was outside with the others drinking. Abram was there, too, and when he saw them walking up he said, "What the hell do you two want?"

Annie was a little intimidated but she managed to speak with confidence. "I wanted to talk to you about my brother."

"What about him?" Abram said with a snarl.

"I don't want no trouble between you and my brother for what happened last night. He was just being protective is all."

"Yeah, well, he shouldn't have sucker punched me like he did."

She certainly wouldn't have called it sucker punching, as Abram had walked up on Marcus like he was going to throw a punch himself, but it had been awfully quick and she didn't want to agitate him further, "I know. He's my brother, though. He's supposed to be like that."

"Yeah, and what reason does he got to be going around calling us white-trash niggers fer?" asked one of the other men, who let a disgusting glob of chew fly out of his mouth.

Emma jumped in. "He didn't say them things."

Abram studied her and then glanced at Colby and figured as much. "Yeah, well I heard him say it. He's been talking to that Mary Jo girl and done told her that Mr. Wilkins hired himself nothing but a bunch of stupid and lazy good for nothing workers this year. He said how we all just like niggers. I heard him say it myself, I did." He had a smug look on his face when the other three men there besides Colby and Abram looked at each other and seemed to share a silent resentment.

Both Annie and Emma knew Marcus wouldn't have made that type of comment. Marcus was as good as color blind in his ethics. Unlike these men, he didn't care if a man was white, black, pink, or purple. To him, a man either worked hard or was a lazy good for nothing. It was one way or the other and there wasn't anything much else he deemed important in a man. In fact, he had commented more than once on the fact that the coloreds Mr. Wilkins hired on for the harvest were working harder and didn't mess around near as much as this group of slackers. The only one in the bunch who was really working hard was Colby. The rest took every opportunity to slough off, or, when they were working, put in a half-ass effort. Marcus even tried to talk Mr. Wilkins into taking on a colored or two full time, but Mr. Wilkins always seemed to believe in giving a white man a job over a black man, said it was his Christian duty. Marcus thought it backwards thinking, but didn't say as much. Annie had to admit, however, that even though she couldn't see Marcus making that particular reference, she could see him calling these boys stupid and lazy good for nothings. In fact, that's just the language he might use and Mary Jo Greenley was just the person he'd say it to. After all, he took after his father in his work ethic, and he had little respect for anyone who didn't work half as hard has he did. So instead of addressing that portion of things, Annie just responded to the one she knew wasn't true.

"Well, I've never heard him say such things," she told Abram, "and I'm his sister."

"Neither have I," supported Emma.

"What, y'all saying I'm lying?" Abram was ready to cuss them both out. He stood up to give them an earful and much to his surprise Colby, who had previously been leaning against the tin building's back wall, leaned forward and uncrossed his arms. He didn't do it aggressively, but it didn't go without notice, either.

"I didn't say you're lying, just said I've never heard it," said Annie.

"Maybe he just said that 'bout you because you kept talking to his sister during the harvest when we was working and he got mad," offered Colby, still standing ready to move if events went that way. "That's probably why y'all had that scuffle in the first place."

Abram could feel himself losing ground. Colby was taking the side of the girls and that was swaying the opinion of the other men. If Abram had differences with Marcus because they didn't agree on him talking to Annie, well that was between them, the other men would think. That was different from Marcus talking bad about all of them.

"Well, I best not hear your brother talking such things about me, or I'll have him answer for it," said one. "But since I don't know what he did and didn't say, I reckon I'll leave it alone."

Abram knew they wouldn't help him put a beating on Marcus, now. And he didn't want to go up against him alone. As much as Abram hated to admit it, he was scared of Marcus. He thought quickly about what could be salvaged out of the situation, how he could still save some face in front of everyone, "Well, maybe if you was to be a little nicer to me, you know, to make up for your brother sucker-punching me and everything, then I guess I could let him slide." He wanted to play the part of the bigger man looking the other way, "But just this once. You know, if had been anyone but your brother, I'd of already done something bad to 'em." He even tried smiling at her.

Now it was painfully clear to Colby, even if he was generally considered as slow and dullish as one could be, that Abram lost his nerve when he lost the help of the other three. But in the mind of a fourteen year old girl like Annie, who didn't understand that Abram was just trying to cover up his own cowardice, she thought she had won a victory. Here was this man, older than her brother and who was just a little while ago planning Lord knows what in the way of revenge, offering to let her brother out of a most dangerous situation with the compromise that she just act nice towards him. She took it that he was doing her a considerable favor.

"Thanks, Abram," she said. "I appreciate it."

And Abram could see it on her face, she did appreciate it. He felt puffed up knowing he had succeeded in making her see how kind and forgiving he was being. He could feel his confidence rising again. So much so that he thought this whole thing might have even bettered his chances of laying her, "And maybe I can dance with you tonight without being sucker-punched," he quipped. It was awfully bold of him considering, Annie thought, but now she felt obligated. And in addition, she felt such a weight lifted not having to worry about what they might do to Marcus that she almost wanted to dance with Abram just to say thanks. Everything could be smoothed over now. She'd have to make sure Marcus didn't come and start trouble again, though. "Okay, Abram. I think that'd be nice." With that, her, Emma, and Colby went back inside, her to go ask Marcus to let it alone tonight, and Emma and Colby to go dance.

Everyone agreed it had been a good resolution and Abram felt just like a Saint with his friends telling him how good he was to look the other way for that girl's benefit. “Yeah, that boy just doesn’t know any better, I guess. He’s lucky he’s got his sisters to get him out of trouble,” he told his friends.

Marcus was none too pleased when Annie told him she had promised to dance with Abram tonight. "What do you want to go and waste your time with that one for?" he asked angrily. "'Specially after you just said he was telling lies on me so he could get others to help him whoop me."

"I done talked to him about that. He says he heard you talkin' to

Mary Jo about Mr. Wilkins hiring good for nothings like them. But he says he ain't going to make no more trouble if'n you leave him be."

Marcus sucked in his breath and let it out with a bit of a tsk, "Well, they are a bunch of good for nothins, Annie. And here you go wantin' to mess with one of 'em. Too ignorant to know what's good fer yah." He waved her away just like he'd done with Mary Jo's questions earlier. "Go on and do what you want. I don't care if you ain't got better sense."

Now she was getting upset with him. Here she was smoothing things over for his benefit and he thanks her by calling her ignorant and waving her off like an annoying fly. Well, she would do what she wanted, then. If he couldn't see what she had done for him and how maybe Abram had a right to be mad like he was, she wasn't going to worry herself over it.

And when Abram and Annie did meet up for a dance, circumstances had conspired just right, or just wrongly enough, that she saw him as being better than he truly was. And he was so full of himself at that moment that he believed himself to be just as good as she thought he was. So they danced and had fun, laughing together and actually enjoying each other's company. And when Mrs. Stotley pulled Emma aside to ask why in the hell Annie was dancing with that man again, Emma told her happily, "Oh, they worked all that out. He's not so bad."

Mrs. Stotley was just sick with her two oldest girls. Annie was with that drunkard having the time of her life and Emma was joined at the hip with that bushy ogre. She tried to pour out her anxieties and horror to Mr. Stotley, but he was indifferent.

"Let them enjoy the festival," he said. *Let them find someone to marry and go off to live their own lives so I can have mine back,* he was probably thinking.

Chapter 5

The harvest was over and so the extra hands that had been needed around the various farms were let go. The out-of-towners found their work dried up and most moved on. Abram and Colby didn't, though. Their third housemate, Keller, had joined up with some other men that were headed East where there were more people and more jobs to be had. Louisiana had a lot of farmland that needed extra hands, they'd been told. But Emma had been so quickly infatuated with Colby that she had gone to various farmers she knew looking for work for him. Mr. Wilkins said he was full up and didn't seem to think Colby had much in the way of smarts about him, but Mr. Andrew Pyle said he could use a strong hand and took Colby on. Colby didn't want to stay by himself, though, so he asked Abram to stay since Keller had made up his mind to leave. They weren't the best of friends, but they'd walked a lot of roads together, and since Colby offered to pay the rent until Abram got himself a job, too, Abram saw it as a good deal for himself. They stayed in Mr. Wilkins' work shack and Colby paid a meager rent per week while he worked for Mr. Pyle. Abram sold his hemp cigarettes to the other field hands for a little extra spending money that went mostly to whiskey. Both were still convinced that they could get rich off of the marijuana but the selling was few and far between. The only people that would buy any were the laborers like themselves and most of them seemed to prefer a stiff drink to Abram's hemp.

After a few weeks of working like a mule Colby began winning praises from Mr. Pyle. He'd tell the other workers, "Why can't you work like Colby, there?" And brag to other farmers.. "That boy Colby is just like having two men. He's strong as an ox even if he's only as bright as one." Colby could do it all on a farm. Besides plowing and sowing seeds, he knew his way around horses and cattle and he wasn't a half-bad carpenter. He wasn't nearly as dull as people thought, either. He was just an introvert who wasn't interested in much more than the simple things in life. Mr. Pyle thanked his good luck on taking a chance on the boy. And so when Colby asked if Mr. Pyle could find a place on his farm for Abram, Mr. Pyle made room for him. He was never as pleased with Abram's work as he was with Colby. It was like night and day watching Colby sweat through the hot day working all the while and watching Abram follow along behind him doing a third of what Colby did. He would have gotten rid of Abram except he didn't want Colby to leave along with him, so he dismissed the nuisance.

Emma and Annie both walked about a mile and a half over the fields and through the pastures each day to bring lunch to the men. By this point Emma was utterly smitten. She had heard Colby's praises from Mr. Pyle, and in church on Sundays, even though neither Colby nor Abram attended, she held her head a little higher. Annie was happy for her sister. She tried to feel the same way about Abram but she felt she must have inherited her father's indifference on things. She didn't dislike him, but nor was she enamored with him. When folks got to her asking her if he was her beau, she said yes, she supposed so, but it didn't elicit the same warm and tingly feelings inside that Emma had described to her.

Time went on this way for months. Marcus got his apprenticeship with the blacksmith in town and moved out. He was a spectacular metal worker and besides shoeing the horses and repairing tools, he could also make wrought iron fence work and beautiful ornamentation. He would marry Mary Jo Greenley and they'd leave Varner Creek some years later when word of Marcus' talents spread and he was offered a job making more money than he ever imagined up in Houston working for the railroads.

But before Marcus had become a metal working marvel, and before he and Mary Jo Greenley left for the city, Emma and Colby had expressed their love for one another, both verbally and physically. Annie and Emma got in the habit of going to visit Colby and Abram sometimes at night. It was a practice Mrs. Stotley was completely against, but since she couldn't get Mr. Stotley to side with her, as he of course was indifferent on the subject, she yet again accepted defeat. Colby and Emma would immediately disappear into the one-room workhouse when they went to visit and it shook with their passion like there was a tornado trapped inside. Neither of them were fragile people, after all.

It wasn't long before Abram began pressing for a tornado of his own. He and Annie would take walks sometimes while the other two were engaged in their activities. He was always at her dress trying to get a hand somewhere inside to find a spot of bared skin. She let him kiss on her and press up against her but wouldn't permit the removal of her clothes. And when Abram started pulling out his manhood on a regular basis she'd rub it for him until he got release. It wasn't because of love or lust for him, though. She just wanted to help him get over his urges so he'd stop squirming all over her and dry humping her dress.

I had often pressed my Aunt Emma in later years about how Mama ended up with Pap, and while she never would give me all the details,

I've managed to splice together the bits and pieces. Getting Aunt Emma's recollections was like pulling teeth, but there would be a lot of confusion in my early adulthood that Aunt Emma wanted to help resolve in any way she could. She never came right out and told me I was a child of rape, of course, but all the stories I've heard seem to skirt dangerously close to that conclusion. As I came to understand it, things took a serious turn on one of the walks Mama and Pap used to take. They had lain down on a blanket in the grass that they had brought with them. The mosquitoes were biting and Abram had his tongue all over her, down her mouth, in her ear, all down her neck. He had been drinking and was in a foul mood. The rubbing had been holding him off pretty well for a while but tonight when she reached down to rub it for him he moved her hand away.

"I'm sick of that," he told her. And he clawed at her dress to undo the strings that held it tight.

She tried to politely deter him, "Abram, I don't think we should."

He pushed himself up a bit to look her in her face, "To hell with that. Every night y'all come by Colby's in there getting done right by your sister and here you are won't even let me see you without all these damned clothes on yah. I'm sick of hearing him tell how good it feels and then all I can say is you givin' me a hand job." It was highly unlikely Colby ever talked about his intimacy with Emma, but Abram knew a good pressure tactic when he saw one. "I can do that myself. What do I need you to do that for me, for?" And he went back to kissing her neck and trying to find the right button to push to get her excited. He lunged up her dress and had invaded her petticoat to find the waist strings in her cotton long pants.

"Abram, stop!" she cried in surprise. He pulled so hard on the cotton underpants that the waist gave out and snapped. He felt them give and began pulling them down with a forceful zest. "Abram, quit it! What are you doing?"

Annie could suddenly feel his hands on her bare skin and the evening air drifting along her pubic hairs. He quickly pulled them down as far as they would go and slid himself between her legs. He was so heavy Annie couldn't move out from under him. She urgently tried to reason with him, "Abram, stop. I'm not rea . . ." but it was too late.

She closed her eyes with the pain. It hurt so bad that it was like a hot poker had just been pushed inside of her. She let out a pitiful moan but it seemed to only stir him on. He grunted and groaned centered solely around his own pleasure. Annie couldn't believe this was happening.

She didn't want this to happen. She wasn't ready for this. She could feel the tears welling up in her eyes as the pain coursed through her. She wanted to be some place else. In her mind she imagined being back at home cuddled up with Candace on some cold winter night. They'd giggle and cause a ruckus until Marcus would tell them to shut up so he could get some sleep. She wondered where he was at right now. Probably at home with Candace or maybe out walking with Mary Jo Greenley. Maybe they were doing the same thing she was doing, except that Mary Jo wasn't hurting and it was a pretty thing instead of this nightmare. She bet not, though. They were really in love and Marcus and Mary Jo were both proper and good people who would wait for marriage. Not like Annie, who was dirty and shameful.

She wanted Marcus to come and rescue her, to pull Abram off and punch his lights out again. But Marcus wasn't there and wouldn't be pulling him off of her this time. 'If you ain't got better sense . . .' she remembered him saying. Nobody came except Abram, who didn't even bother to pull himself out first. Instead he spent himself inside of her and then stayed laying on her breathing hard and blowing his whiskey breath in her face. She felt the tears roll down her cheek and didn't know if they were from the pain or the humiliation. The first time she ever made love she felt like a whore.

On their way back home Annie had to stop and take off her cotton underpants, which were soiled and discard them. When she stood up again she tried to explain to Emma what had happened with tears in her eyes.

Emma put her arm around her shoulder, "It hurts the first time but then it's not so bad," she told her.

Annie sniffed up her nose drips and wiped away the tears, "That's not what hurts so much, Emma. I didn't want to. I wasn't ready and I told him I wasn't and he didn't care. He just did what he wanted and didn't even care."

Emma tried to console her but she didn't understand just how things had happened. In her mind it was natural that Abram and Annie had done what they did. She had always had a rebellious nature herself and figured Annie was just having regrets, knowing what a religious violation it was, and all, and how their Mama would condemn them both if she knew. Emma also thought Annie was really upset because it hadn't been as sweet and nice as she had imagined. "Some men just aren't sensitive in that way," she told her little sister, "Colby's not. He doesn't have hardly any sense of romance but I know that inside he's real sweet and kind. I know he loves me and I'm going to marry that man, you just see." She seemed to be missing how traumatic the night's events had been on Annie. She was blinded by the rose colored glass that was her and Colby's blossoming relationship, and too lost in her dreams of the future to see exactly what was going on in the present.

They walked on as the remaining light slowly left them. They were supposed to be home before dark but Annie was happy to see the evening shadow swallow them up. Emma walked as though she were a flame in the night immune to the darkness spreading around her, but Annie felt it creeping inside of her. She wanted to disappear into the night, to crawl under a rock and hide. Abram's not sweet and kind, she thought to herself, not a bit.

She didn't go with Emma two days later when her sister went to visit Colby. Instead, Annie got her mother's Bible out thinking she could find some solace in the good Book. She was a bit taken aback to find her mother's bible had hundreds of passages underlined and with little notes out to the side of almost every page. It seemed that since Mrs. Stotley couldn't get her husband to agree with her on issues of morals, she had sought her confirmations from the highest of authorities. Annie read through looking at all the highlighted passages, searching for something to relieve her from her emotional distress. One of the passages her mother had underlined twice read, "In case a man happens to have a son who is stubborn and rebellious, not listening to the voice of his father or the voice of his mother, and they have corrected him but he will not listen to them, his father and his mother must also take hold of him and bring him out to the older men of his city and to the gate of his place, and they must say to the older men of his city, 'This son of ours is stubborn and rebellious; he is not listening to our voice, being a glutton and a drunkard.' Then all the men of his city must pelt him with stones, and he must die. So you must clear away what is bad from your midst, and all Israel will hear and indeed become afraid." It was Deuteronomy 21:18-21. She read this and, knowing her mother had highlighted it because she wholly believed in it, Annie put away the Bible having found no relief from God's words. On the contrary, she now felt much worse and much more scared. She crept into bed early and cried to herself. What would her parents think of her having sex with a man outside of wedlock like that. "Harlot!" her mother would call her. "Jezebel!" And rightly so, for that's just what she felt like. And when Candace crept in bed with her that night she held her tightly hoping some of her sister's purity would rub off on her. When she finally fell asleep she found herself standing in the church. It must have been Sunday sermon because everyone in town was there. She dreamed she was having sex with Abram right there before the pulpit in front of everyone, and that her mother suddenly stood up from her pew and pleaded with everyone to help her cleanse her sinful daughter. Then Abram disappeared with a sly smile, and everyone in the church suddenly began gathering up big rocks that had appeared at their feet and they started throwing them at her, pelting her with them over and over again. Everyone she cared about was there, her parents, Marcus, Candace, that cute boy Gerald, even Emma had a stone, and they were all hurling them at her. She looked to Marcus and said, “Please, make them stop!” But he was angry with her and only said, “If you ain’t got better sense . . .” and then he hit her with his rock. The only one who wasn’t throwing stones at her was her parents. Mr. Stotley was sitting stoic on his pew smoking his pipe and staring into nothingness. He seemed either not to notice or not to care that Annie was being stoned to death. And finally, when she felt her insides crushed from the blows, everyone stopped and looked to Mrs. Stotley, who had finally reached down and gathered up a stone. "It was to save your soul," she told Annie. And then she threw the last rock. Annie woke up, panicked and frightened, thinking she’d just died. She looked around expecting to see the town around her, rocks in hand. Instead, she found Emma sleeping soundly beside her and Candace in her own bed, undoubtedly dreaming of Colby and love, seemingly at peace without a care in the world. Annie had never been so jealous of her sister in all her life.

As the weeks went on Annie stayed away from worker’s row. Emma would come home with pleas from Abram, or wild flowers he had picked for her. He even had Emma give her a very nice carving of a horse he’d done, but Annie didn’t want it and gave it to Candace instead.

Emma couldn't understand why Annie was acting so distant, "He’s not so bad, Annie. I think maybe he really loves you." And as the guilt and shame ate at Annie another thought entered her mind, one of salvation and repentance. What if she were to marry Abram? Then, even though they had done wrong by having sex that would at least make things somewhat right. Maybe she could even bring herself to look at her mother again without hating herself. And so she went back with Emma to the shack Colby and Abram shared and she let Abram lay with her and have his way, all the while resigning herself that she would marry Abram eventually and things would work out for the best.

I realized after putting all the pieces together so many years later that Mama had trapped herself in her own mind, and that's why she married Pap. Whether it was the threat of her own mother's moral condemnations, Emma's well-meaning prodding, or just because Mama was so young, I don't think she felt there was anything else she could do. It seems so often the case that people who think they're up against a wall don't realize it's only themselves doing the pushing.

One morning, before the early light had called even Mr. Stotley awake, Annie woke up tormented with nausea. She snuck out of the room and through the front room where Marcus slept, and out the back door. There she heaved her guts out everywhere. She was sick again that evening, and the next day. She told Emma about it and Aunt Emma seemed to know just what it meant, "Oh, shit, Annie. How have you and Abram been doing it? Does he pull out when his stuff comes out, or does he stay inside?"

"He normally just stays inside," she said.

"Oh, Lord, Annie, you can't do it that way. That's how you get pregnant."

Annie didn't say anything. The words seemed to float around her instead of being absorbed. Then slowly they crawled inside of her and ate at her heart. "You think I'm pregnant?" she asked Emma.

She seemed to think on it a bit, "The way you been throwing up and he been doing his business inside of you . . . yeah, Annie. I hate to say it but I think maybe you are." There was a long pause and Emma said, almost as an afterthought, "Mama's going to have a fit." Annie broke down into tears. Emma put her big man arms around Annie. "Oh, I'm sorry Annie. I shouldn't have said that. Mama thinks the whole world is going to hell, anyway. Don't you go frettin' what she's gonna think."

"Why didn't you tell me?" cried Annie.

Emma was confused. "Tell you? Tell you what?"

"That that's how I'd get pregnant!" yelled Annie.

"Welll, hell, Annie, I thought you knew. I thought everybody knew that. And even if you didn't, Abram knows it. It never crossed my mind that you two wouldn't have the sense to not do it that way. There's always the chance you can end up pregnant when you do it, anyway. I thought you knew that."

And the truth was Annie did. She just didn't think it was going to happen to her, at least not this soon. "God's punishing me," she cried. "He's punishing me for what I did."

"Oh, now, don't go getting all worked up. You're sounding like

Mama now. Nobody's punishing you; this is just how things work."

"What am I going to do?" she asked Emma.

Emma held her close. "Well, you'd better tell Abram. You're both just going to have to grow up a little faster than you planned, that's all. He's overdue for a little growing up, no how. And I don't say it to make you feel worse, Annie, but you still got some childish ways about you. You're going to be a mama, and that means you've got to learn to open your eyes a little more." Annie wasn't exactly sure what Emma was making reference to, but she did know she suddenly felt older than her fourteen years. She felt a great weight about her, and somewhere inside she knew she'd never giggle and skip like Candace ever again. It was as though her own childhood had just abandoned her completely.

When Annie told Abram that she thought she might be pregnant he didn't seem to take much notice of it. He sat on their blanket after they had finished their intimacy staring off in the distance. She kept looking at him waiting for a response. "Well, what you want me to say?" he asked.

"I don't know," she said. "I don't know what to do, I guess."

He continued looking off. "Me, neither," he finally told her. "I need to take me a walk and think on this a bit." And with that, he got up, buttoned up his clothes, and strolled away into the fields.

That night Abram told Colby he was thinking of leaving Varner Creek. He said he wanted to go East like the other fellas had and see what was there. He wanted Colby to come with him, but Colby wouldn't hear of it.

"No," he told Abram bluntly. "I'm staying here. And as soon as I get me enough money I'm going to marry Emma and build us a house."

Abram tried to talk him into it. "Well, I don't want to go by myself. What do you want to stay here with that girl for, anyway? She ain't much of a looker."

Colby's face immediately reddened and it was clear Abram was dangerously close to crossing a line he didn't want to cross. "I love Emma, and I'm staying." Then he followed it up by saying something most unexpected, "And you ain't going nowhere, neither."

"What you mean by that?" asked Abram.

"You done got Annie pregnant. Emma told me so. And you ain't going to leave her with a bastard child. She deserve better than that. Besides, her brother and daddy would hunt you down." He looked at Abram with intense resolution, "And I'd probably join them."

Abram was stung. He couldn't believe what Colby had just said.

"What's wrong with you!?" he exclaimed. "I thought we was friends."

"We are," said Colby, "but Annie be Emma's sister and a sweet girl. It ain't right you gone and got her pregnant and then going to run off like that. And even though we don't always see eye to eye on everything, I never figured you the type to try and skip out like you are. You done told me once you wanted to lay with Annie Stotley. Remember that? Well, now you have and she's pregnant. You going to have to cowboy up and be a man, now."

Abram took the whiskey bottle out from under his bed and sat down with his back against the door inside the little shack he and Colby shared. "Shit," he said. He thought about leaving on his own but he didn't know where to go, and the thought of being hounded by not only the Stotley men but also his own friend Colby was enough to discourage the thought. He pictured Annie and thought maybe it wouldn't be so bad. She did have a good nature and was pretty as she could be. Prettier than he thought he'd end up with. Still, the thought of settling down and having a baby crying all the time and crapping all over the place scared the hell out of him. His own childhood had been a nightmare. He never planned on having kids of his own. He was going to plant his tobacco, make lots of money, and spend his days carousing with his buddies, drinking late into the night, playing cards, having a different woman every night. He could see his dreams, or fantasies as they more accurately could be called, falling down around him. "But what about our plans, Colby? We were going to make it big with our tobacco."

"Mr. Pyle say cotton better to grow, and don't nobody want to be buying tobacco so much as they do cotton. I've got me a new plan, now. Me and Emma going to have a family and I'm going to be a cotton farmer." And that was the end of Abram's hopes of running away and being a rich hemp farmer.

"I guess I'd better start saving up, too," Abram said. "I'm gonna have to put her and that baby somewhere."

And so just a few months later, around the time that Marcus was beginning to make a name for himself in metal working, there were three weddings in Varner Creek, Marcus Stotley married Mary Jo Greenley, Colby Patterson married Emma Stotley, and Abram Mayfield married Annie Stotley. Mr. Stotley was beside himself with happiness with three children out of the house all at once.

True to his word, Colby built himself and Emma a nice, sturdy two-bedroom home that would be added on to later, complete with a separate kitchen area from the front room and a large front porch. Everyone in town was impressed with the home he built. He had purchased the land from Mr. Pyle on a payment schedule and would, many, many, years later come to own most of the farm when Mrs. Pyle left it to him after her passing.

Abram had moved Annie with him to worker's row. Mr. Stotley was happy to have her leave and start a family of her own and Mrs. Stotley was so disgraced by her pregnant child that she couldn't find it in her heart to ask Annie to stay. Instead, she took to clutching her Bible with her everywhere she went, and even seemed as though she might be talking to it on occasions. Marcus was so mad he all but disowned Annie. He could barely even look at her for marrying that man he hated so much. Candace was the only one that wept and cried miserably when she left. Annie would have cried, too, except she felt numb inside. She felt like she was paying for her sins. And when her baby arrived and didn't develop correctly, she thought that was God's way of punishing her, too. Either that or the devil had thrown in his lot on top of God's harsh will, and it wouldn't be the last time she thought that.

A lot of things happened in the early years of Abram and Annie Mayfield's marriage. Marcus, of course, moved away with his new bride. He lived in Houston up until December of 1900. Right after the Houston railroad finally reached Varner Creek, Marcus was offered a job by the GH&H railroad to help rebuild their station in Galveston after the great storm that nearly destroyed the city wiped the old one out. Colby and Emma announced that the first of four children was on the way right after moving into their new house. And, most unfortunately, Mr. Stotley died. He almost had that personal space at home he'd been waiting so long for, but fate's not without its occasional cruel humor, one has to suppose. They found him out in the field where he had apparently suffered either a heart attack or heat stroke. I imagine he was probably scared at first, but then most likely found his characteristic indifference. At least he finally got his peace and quiet.

Mrs. Stotley wrote to Marcus who was still in Houston at this point, and happily accepted his invitation to bring Candace and move up there. He had described to her all about the city, with its theaters and great churches, and told her about phones that were like telegraphs except people could talk to each other over miles and miles. He told her about the Houston Railway where he was working at the time and how he was being paid a lot of money for the various manufacturing of metal goods he was crafting. Even though he had no formal education, Marcus had the mind of an engineer and the hands of a craftsman. All anyone had to do was show him a picture of a tool or something mechanical in a book, and he could make it. Some things could be ordered from up north, he said, but others had to be handmade and the company paid him a lot to make them. The trains also brought in goods she had never seen before, beautiful things that she could use to decorate her new home with. He promised to build her and Candace their own little house near his and that when she was old enough he would personally see to it that Candace met a respectable man. I think it might have been this last part that seemed so appealing to Mrs. Stotley. She had taken to smothering Candace, intent that her youngest child not make the same mistakes as her other two girls.

Not long after she accepted his invitation Marcus came into town to retrieve her and Candace. The railroad hadn't arrived yet as it was only 1896, so Marcus arrived by wagon. He briefly stopped to visit Annie but couldn't hardly stand to see her with Abram. And Abram, for his part, left them alone to visit. He didn't want to be anywhere near Marcus. His jaw seemed to get a dull ache sometimes when it was really cold and I wouldn't be surprised if for some reason it seemed to act up on that day that Marcus came by to say farewell to his sister. Marcus tried to talk with Annie and be happy about his first niece, but he couldn't help feeling betrayed by his sister somehow. He couldn't imagine what his sister saw in this man that she would get pregnant by him and marry him. He thought she was too good for him and disappointed that she hadn't met the expectations Marcus had had for her. He'd write Annie now and then in the years after, but they never actually saw each other again, which is something he'd always lament. Marcus always meant to make it down for a visit, but everything was always so busy for him, especially when he moved his family, including Mrs. Stotley and Candace, to Galveston four years later. And so, except for Emma, Annie's former family, like her childhood, slipped away from her life.

Abram continued working for Mr. Pyle, and since Colby became more or less the manager of the farm at this time, he was blessed with a stability he otherwise would never have known. The truth was he had it a lot better in life than he had earned, but that didn't stop him from acquiring a huge resentment towards Mama. For the rest of his days my Pap would blame her for stealing his dreams and trapping him in Varner Creek. It took me a long time to learn just how Mama ended up with Pap, but in the end I discovered that things just sort of fell that way. Pap made enough money to buy a house left abandoned by a family a couple of years back and Uncle Colby helped him fix it up. That's where I was born and that's where I was on the day my Pap told me Mama had taken Sarah and left.

Chapter 6

“. . . took your sister and they gone,“ Pap had said.

What? I thought to myself. *They left? What does he mean they left?* “Where’d they go?” I asked Pap.

He kicked back his glass and emptied the last bit down his throat. “I don’t know. She just left.” I studied Pap carefully, trying to gauge what he was telling me. He didn’t look like a man who was lying through his teeth, but then again a good liar never does, and there was definitely something about Pap that made me think he was cutting this explanation short on purpose. I stood staring at him, from his head to his feet, trying to find a chink in the armor, waiting for him to say something more, something I knew to be a lie. As I looked him over I noticed his boots had mud on them and his hair was a bit wet. “I been out looking for ‘em, but they already gone,” he said, as though in answer to my querying glare at his boots.

“When are they coming back?” I asked.

Pap was getting’ angry, now, “I don’t know! I reckon she might not be comin’ back! Ain‘t you listening, boy?”

I was hearing the words but the meaning still hadn’t settled, but I didn’t want to rile him up worse by asking more questions. So for a few more tense seconds, I just stood in the kitchen staring at Pap trying to figure it out, and he just stared right back, not saying a word.

He finally broke the silence. “I think your Mama left for good. They probably done gone and went to that Galveston city with your Uncle and them, I don’t know. Point is, they’re gone, boy. That’s just all there is to it.”

Galveston? Without me? Why would Mama leave without taking me? She wouldn’t. I was sure of it, she wouldn’t just leave me here. I didn’t believe it. I stared at Pap like he was the lyingest liar I ever met, but he didn‘t flinch and he didn‘t recant. I went back into the room Sarah and I had and opened up the dresser. Sure enough the clothes were gone. Had Mama come in during the night and gathered Sarah and all her belongings without me hearing? Why would she leave me all alone with *him*? I ran into my parents' room and saw the same. There weren't any of her clothes and none of her personal items left. Even our books and Mama’s hairbrush was gone. *No. No, she couldn’t have*, I thought. She wouldn’t do that to me. *Oh, God*, I thought. Why didn’t I wake up? Why didn’t she wake me up, too, and take me with her? How could I not have heard her. She must have been rummaging all through the dresser for the clothes and even Sarah had gotten up without me hearing her. If I had woken up maybe she would have taken me with her.

My mind raced with possibilities and conjecture. What had I done that was so bad Mama chose to leave me behind? My world collapsed. I ran back into the kitchen and stared at Pap. "I told you, boy. They're gone."

Pap almost looked sad. I couldn't believe it. They really were gone. I bolted out the door and ran around to Lilipeg's pen. The chickens squawked and flapped their wings in protest of the invasion of their domain, but they were alone. Lilipeg wasn't there, and neither was the wagon. *It's true*, I thought. They really left. I stood staring down the worn path that led towards town, picturing Mama and Sarah disappearing down it while Sarah was looking back for me. I ran after them. I ran as fast as my feet would carry me down the path. I ran all the way down to where it met the dirt road and I kept right on running. Maybe if I ran hard enough and long enough I could catch them. But I didn't know which way on the dirt road they had gone so I just chose one and ran. I pounded the dirt with my feet as I went, cursing my lack of speed. My legs ached and my lungs burned, but still I ran. Past cotton fields and cow pastures I pushed myself on and on. I expected at any moment to catch sight of a black speck ahead that would turn out to be Mama and Sarah on the wagon, but I never did. Past the path that led to Aunt Emma and Uncle Colby's place, past the fork in the road that led to town, nothing. And when finally I couldn't go any further I fell to my knees, gasping and weeping.

"Mam-a-a-a!" I cried to myself. "Mama, why?" Why did she leave me behind? Quietly I sobbed to myself. My sides were splitting in pain from running and I lay down just off the path trying to alleviate the pain and catch my breath. I don't know how long I cried because somewhere along the way I actually cried myself asleep.

I woke up hours later around midday. I was covered in dirt and grass and the chiggers had made a buffet out of me. Crumbs of dirt stuck to my face and I had indentations from the pattern of dried twigs I had lain on. Everything seemed a little different when I woke up to this new life without Mama or Sarah. The sky was still blue, but not as bright, and the locusts and grasshoppers still sang, but not as sweet.

I made my way home, slowly stumbling along in a dazed march like perhaps wounded Confederate soldiers had done as they passed through these parts some forty-odd years ago on their way back home from the killing fields. Surprisingly, I wasn't oppressed by a million thoughts on the way home. In fact, I can't remember thinking about anything. When home was in sight I saw Uncle Colby's wagon outside. Ours was still missing. Joe the horse was gumming the metal bit in his mouth, no doubt wishing he could remove it to munch on the grass near his feet.

I walked inside and Aunt Emma came out from Mama and Pap's room, apparently being the only one there. She walked up to me and swallowed me in a hug with her large, man-like arms, squarely planting my face in her breasts so I could hardly breathe. "Where have you been, boy?" She asked in a quiet voice. "Had me worried sick."

She held me back to get a look at me and with the renewal of air I told her, "Pap says Mama left. He says she took Sarah and left."

"I know," she said, "Your daddy done told your uncle and me."

I looked up at her and choked back the tears threatening to fill my eyes again,

"Why would she do it, Aunt Emma? Why would she leave and not take me? Not even tell me goodbye?"

She held me close and kissed me on my head. "I don't know, honey. I don't know what's going on except what your daddy told us, and I'm not sure what to make of that."

I thought maybe she knew more than I did, "What'd Pap say? He didn't tell me nothin' except Mama took Sarah and left, and that he didn't know to where or why."

"Well," said Aunt Emma, "That's more or less about what he told us. He walked over to our place this morning and told us your Mama had packed up her and Sarah's things and left. Told us you ran out the house this morning and he wasn't sure where you had gotten off to. I want to talk to you about things but not right now, I don't think." She gave me a kind and pitying look, "Bless your heart, you look a mess, Sol. I think it'd be best if you came and stayed a while with your uncle and me, just until we get things sorted out. I think you need to go and get cleaned up and then get something in your stomach first, though. Why don't you go wash up a bit and I'll fix you something to eat?"

I wasn't really hungry, but didn't even have enough energy to say so, so I blindly obeyed. "Okay." I went out to the well and drew up a bucket while she went to the kitchen. Lilipeg's absence made it unusually quiet and I was struck with how small and empty her pen looked. I put the bucket on the edge of the well and as I leaned over it there was a strange greenish tint in the water, as though algae had sprung up in the bucket, and for a moment I thought I saw something move inside. I peered over the water and the reflection I saw staring back at me was not my own. As I looked down, Sarah was looking back at me. But as soon as I blinked she was gone. The bucket of water was its normal color and clarity, and the reflection was my own dirty face, still with a few indentions from this morning's nap. It's because I'm thinking of them, I told myself. I had imagined Sarah's face looking back toward our house as the wagon disappeared down the path and now I was seeing her reflection when it wasn't really there. I put it out of my mind and tried scooping handfuls of water on my face to clear my head. Finally I just dunked my entire head completely in. As soon as my face hit the water a horrible nightmare hit me. My head was pounding in pain and some unknown force was holding my head under the water. I was trying to catch my breath but couldn't. Every time I struggled to pull away, I was pushed further in. I tried to yell but no voice came, only bubbles of air. My mouth, too, was pulsing in pain. Then I felt my head swim with dizziness and knew no more. I came to again to the sounds of Aunt Emma.

"Sol! Sol? Come on, Sol. Take a breath." She was patting my back hard and I spit up a bit of water. "That's it! Take a deep breath." I opened my eyes and was on the ground gasping and shaking. I looked up to see the bucket still on the well's edge, and I crawled backwards as fast as I could away from it, looking all around for whoever, or whatever, might have been there trying to drown me. But nobody was there except Aunt Emma, who looked like she'd had a horrible fright herself. "Sol? Are you okay, honey? What happened?"

The air came to me in deep gasps like when I had been running earlier and my lightheadedness swirled around before settling. "I don't know," I told her. "I was washing up and then the next thing I knew I was having a terrible nightmare."

Aunt Emma was feeling my head and checking my eyes like a seasoned nurse. "Oh, honey, I think you fainted. Can't say I'm surprised what with all that's going on. You must have passed out and had yourself a bad dream. I was in there just settin' you a plate when I looked out and saw you sprawled out on the ground. You're just givin' me one scare after another today, boy."

Fainted hell, I thought. That was the most realistic dream I ever had. I thought I must be going crazy. My mind has gone damaged like Sarah's and I've lost my wits. I sat there on the ground, looking this way and that, my eyes eventually falling back on the bucket still sitting on the edge of the well. It looked plain as ever. I stared stupidly at it in disbelief. I listened and watched that bucket as though it were a snake that I expected to pounce at me at any second, but it didn't do anything. And after a little bit I started feeling foolish that I was expecting it to. Finally, I convinced myself that Aunt Emma was probably right. The day's events, and all the running I had done, had so worn me down I wasn't thinking straight. I was so distraught over Mama and Sarah leaving that I was losing it. I let Aunt Emma help me up gently. She patted the dirt off the bottom of my pants like Mama had done in such a way that there could be no doubting their relativity.

"Come on, now, I've got some breakfast over the fire that'll be ready soon. You come on in and have a bite and you'll feel much better."

After we ate she helped me pack up my clothes and things. She spent a while in Mama and Pap's room, looking for things left behind by her, I'd imagine. There wasn't hardly a thing to be found. It was almost as though Mama had never lived here at all. Aunt Emma was going through everything thoroughly, though, and I knew she was looking for anything, good or ill, that would explain Mama's sudden disappearance.

Pap never came home during this time. I could only assume he was over at their house or maybe even out working the field. It seemed impossible to me that Pap could just go to work like it was any other day, but then again Pap didn't seem too surprised this morning, as though he'd long suspected the possibility of Mama leaving him.

After a while Aunt Emma said we were ready to go and we climbed up in the wagon. "Ho, Joe! Get on now!" she called. And with a flick of her wrists on the reins we started along to her house.

Aunt Emma let Joe walk at a leisurely pace and it took a good thirty minutes to reach Uncle Colby and Aunt Emma's house. The dirt road between wasn't a straight line, but rather curved in and around the fields. We spent the first few minutes in silence, but Aunt Emma would peek over at me now and then. Finally she spoke up, "Did your Mama say anything to you yesterday?"

I had already thought back while I was eating on the very same question, "No, ma'am. Nothing I can remember, at least."

"But she seemed a bit out of sorts at dinner," she said, "you reckon?"

I shrugged my shoulders a bit, wishing I had paid more attention to everything the day before. I thought about Mama's strangeness while reading us the bedtime story, and how I should have been more interested in what was gnawing at her.

The wagon bounced along in a rutted area of the road and I shifted uncomfortably on the wooden bench. The cotton fields on either side were beginning to bud and I watched a rabbit off to our right happily hopping along. It was a long minute that seemed to stretch itself out before she asked another question. "Her and your daddy been fighting much lately?" Now she was looking me in the eye, and she asked almost in a whisper,

"Has he been hittin' on her again?"

I didn't meet her gaze. I don't know why but for some reason the way she asked me made me feel a bit ashamed, not only of my Pap, but also of myself in some odd way. Pap's old ways were like a family secret we'd all kept, though it wouldn't have surprised a lot of folks in town, I guess. I tried not to think about it and instead watched Joe's back as he trudged along.

"Sol?" Aunt Emma politely prodded, "Has he?"

"No, ma'am. Not for a long time, now, that I seen." It was the truth, but I wasn't so young that I couldn't remember what she was talking about. Joe gave an occasional swish of his tail trying to beat off a stubborn horse fly. Somewhere under this same hot sun and the sky decorated with cotton, Lilipeg was probably also swatting at flies. Mama and Sarah were probably talking about wherever they were going. Would Sarah ask about me? Would she beg and plead with Mama to go back and get me?

Whap! Joe's tail whipped around and ended one particular fly's annoyances.

Another was there to take its place, though. I watched the horsehair whip dart this way and that and those memories of Pap hitting Mama around came back to me. He and Mama could be arguing in the kitchen about something and just like Joe's tail his arm would fly out and slap her. Only when Pap did it, he did it a little faster and harder than Joe the horse.

Chapter 7

I can't say he was a kind man. I guess that much is obvious. Pap had his good and bad like anybody else, but there seemed more of the bad in him than the other. He had a hard life and just wasn't able to find the happy things in living most of us can. It seems both cruel and sad, but the only times I really remember Pap smiling was when somebody else was getting the short end of things.

When I was little and used to visit Aunt Emma, Uncle Colby used to grab me by the ankles, turn me upside down, and spin me around until I was dizzy. Then we'd both laugh as he set me down and I tried to walk in a straight line, failing miserably. I'd eventually flop down with nausea threatening, and then beg to do it again. Pap didn't seem to like me playing this game with Uncle Colby, though, so he made up his own way of playing it. He'd grab me by the ankles, turn me upside down, but then hang me over the well playfully threatening to drop me. He thought it was hilarious, but I didn't. I can't help but to remember that feeling, hanging over the darkness of that black hole, crying out for the fear of it, and then looking back to see Pap smiling. Mama would often yell at him, "Abram! Quit it, you're scaring him."

"Oh, I'm just foolin' with 'em." Then he'd put me back on my feet and said, "You know you're old man wouldn't ever drop you, now don't yah, boy?"

"Yes, sir," I told him. But the truth was I wasn't really so sure.

"Hell, if you think that's scary, you should thank your lucky stars nobody plays the games with you that I played when I was your age." I wasn't sure what he meant, but the way Pap said it, I was thankful.

I never understood why Pap picked on me like that, whether he was happy to have that kind of power over me or happy that somebody else didn't have that power over him, anymore. Maybe he was jealous . . . jealous that I didn't have to suffer the things he suffered, so he felt like giving me a dose just so I'd appreciate not having the full measure. That's just the kind of thinking Pap found perfectly rational. Whatever the reason, I was always scared he was going to take it too far.

Then there was the hitting, of course. One of the earliest things I can ever remember is of the time Pap went into a rage and gave Mama a full blown beating. I was only four at the time, but I can still remember it. I never saw my Pap the same after that. Whenever I looked at him, I didn't see my father, I saw the monster hiding inside of him. This is not to say my Pap was always mean and hateful, but he was a servant to his demons and they often ruled his nature.

Before anybody could say my Pap was truly a worthless, evil human being, they'd have to know where he'd been in life. Abram Mayfield was born into hardship. The term hardship I've heard used many times to describe poverty, lack of love, neglect, what have you, but I use the term here in its most basic of meanings, which is to say all of the above and then some. He was an unwanted child, one of several children, and was sent to live with his uncle at the age of eight as his father died. That's when things really went bad for Pap. His uncle had no love of children, and saw his nephew Abram as only an extra hand in the field and another mouth to feed. He agreed to take the boy on as long as Abram pulled his own weight. That's what he told Pap's mother, at least, but his idea of what constituted pulling ones own weight was distorted to say the least. I heard a lot of this from Pap's own words growing up, and the rest Aunt Emma had gleamed from Mama.

Pap's uncle worked him more than twelve hours a day, every day, in the fields at hard labor. If Pap failed to meet his uncle's requirements and expectations, he'd go without food for that day and could expect a good beating. Or his uncle might be in a foul mood and decide to make a point. Pap told me once that he had been sick all day, but still working, and when he sat down to dinner that night his uncle put a plate in front of him with pig shit on it.

"You do a shit day's worth of work, boy," his uncle had told him, "you get shit for dinner." Pap tried to push the plate away but his uncle grabbed him by the neck and told him, "Eat it." Pap had to eventually take a piece in his mouth, and when he threw up his uncle laughed and was satisfied. Then there was the time Pap stole a bit of moonshine from his uncle and got caught. His uncle tied him to a fence post at midday and told him that if Pap managed to untie the rope and wasn't there when he came back he'd find and beat Pap to within an inch of his life. He ended up leaving Pap there until the following evening. I can only imagine what went through Pap's mind as his body tried to sleep standing up, no guard from the elements, or the ants and bugs, no food or water, and not being able to do for himself when he needed to urinate. And even those weren't the worst of it, I don't think. There were other things Pap's uncle did to him, things that don't bear going into detail over, but suffice it to say his uncle was an alcoholic, just like Pap would end up being, and until Pap's arrival, his uncle had lived by himself with no intimate contact with others. He saw Pap as his property to do with what he wanted. Aunt Emma and I had a long talk about it years later, and while Mama had never told her outright what Pap had gone through, we both could imagine some pretty terrible things. Pap never was a well-adjusted man. He didn't get any love growing up, so I guess it shouldn't surprise anyone that when he had a family of his own, he didn't really know how to love us, either. Pap struck out on his own when he was thirteen and drifted from place to place trying to eke out a living before he wandered into Varner Creek several years later and into Annie Stotley's life.

I can't say exactly when Pap first started hitting Mama. Before I was even born, as Aunt Emma remembered it. It first started with a slap here and there after Sarah was born. She was generally a very quiet baby who hardly ever cried, but as she got older and her differences became more pronounced, she started getting sick a lot. She had trouble sitting up on her own and wouldn't take to solid foods, so Mama spent more and more time with her. That made Pap mad and he started pushing and shoving Mama around to get some attention. Kind words and the occasional flower probably would have worked a lot better, but he wasn't wired that way. He'd been taught you get your way by overpowering the other person, so that's what he tried to do.

Then I came into the picture just over eleven months later. I was not the quiet baby that Sarah was, I've been told. Two babies in one house and my constant crying drove Pap to the bar in town where he hid until late at night. Somewhere in there he climbed into a bottle and never came out again. He was heavy on alcohol before being a family man, but I finished the job, I reckon. Mama tried to keep him happy, but when a person wants to be miserable, there's nothing that can be done. He had a beautiful and kind wife who did everything around the house and never said a word about his drinking, but Pap treated her like she was the cause of all his ills anyway. I think he did love her in a way, but again, he just didn't know how to love the way most of us think of it. And as she doted on us, he got resentful towards everybody. Mama did her best to take care of Sarah while having to meet the demands of a very demanding baby, that being me, but it all took its toll. She lost interest in sex all together, not that she had much to begin with for what I imagine to be obvious reasons. More and more she tried to discourage it without setting off Pap's anger, but the more she pulled away from him the angrier Pap got. I suppose he was feeling abandoned in a sense. So he did the only thing he knew to do and started forcing Mama. Almost always drunk, he would take her when the urge came over him, and if she pulled away from him he'd grab her and pull her back until she'd silently allow him to have his way with her. She simply accepted.

Like her father, she learned to live with certain things by just being indifferent about them.

Every now and then Pap would come home drunk and find something Mama had done to upset him. Either his dinner hadn't been put out for him or she was neglecting the house. Whatever it was he'd go and pick a fight with her about it and it would lead to something physical. Mama told Emma about it and Colby intervened on her behalf more than once. He'd pull Pap aside and tell him to quit hitting on Mama. Then Pap would back off for awhile until he had another excuse. It was never as bad as that one night, though.

After some years of their marriage, something happened to Pap that would bring him to cross the line into an all out wife beater. Uncle Colby had heard the story and relayed it to me in those later years. The anger and hate Pap had always felt about his unfair childhood was always buried inside him, and when it finally broke completely out, it brought hell with it. Pap had been drinking beer and cheap whisky steadily for over an hour in the town bar, and had taken to bellowing profane curses at everything and everyone as well as stumbling into everybody. When he fell over into the man drinking next to him, the man rose and pushed Pap back against the bar counter yelling, "Get off of me, you sorry drunk, before I knock you toothless."

Pap was barely able to pull himself up again, but when he did his face went flush red and he glared like a mad bull, "Push me will, yah?" With that he lunged at the man, who easily dodged the blow. The momentum took Pap right down on top of an empty table, flipping it over and crashing beer to the floor. He looked up again just in time to see the other man's boot crashing down upon his face. The blood came pouring from his nose, but he was so drunk the pain was numbed for the moment. It was a throbbing that slowly multiplied in his skull. Again he managed to get up and tried to tackle the man, who delivered a fist right to Pap's cheek.

The bartender, Jack Alders, had seen enough. He didn't like Pap to begin with, and now he'd gotten a damaged table and some broken glasses because of him. He grabbed Pap roughly by the cuff, "Come on, Abram, I've had about enough of you," and led him to the door.

Pap cursed him and everybody else in the room trying to get free of Jack, but it was all in vain. The few patrons of a weekday's crowd only laughed and cursed him back. When Jack got Pap out into the street, he pushed him forward and Pap lost his balance, hitting the ground with a thud much to the delight of the onlookers who had come out of the bar to enjoy the spectacle. Unfortunately, Pap had been tossed right towards a mess of horse manure, which ended up smeared on his face and down his shirt. The men in the bar thought it was hilarious and whooped and hollered in laughter. The bartender was laughing, too, but he yelled out, "If you ever come into my place again, I'll beat you into a bloody pulp and then have you arrested. And I'll feed you some more horse shit, to boot!"

When Pap came back home that night he had changed a bit. He was a little more broken than when he left and his bitterness consumed him. I think maybe some of his own old memories with his uncle had come back to haunt him, and it was Mama that became the emotional punching bag. And then a physical one.

A few nights later Pap was working on a bottle of white lightning and in a particularly nasty temperament. I reckon it must have been somewhere around 1900 because I think I was four, and just like the great storm that was about to demolish Galveston, a great storm was brewing in our small home. I don't remember why, of course, being so young and all, but something in a child's nightmare set me to crying late that night. Sarah was still sleeping in her bed and Mama was in the kitchen quietly cleaning up the few dishes we owned. Pap sloshed the bottle to and from his mouth, sucking like an eager calf at its mother's tit. "Annie. Can't you shut that damned boy up?"

Mama didn't say a word, she just put down her dishes and went into the other room where I was crying. She picked me up and held me gently in her arms comforting me, but whatever had frightened me so much in my dreams left me still crying terribly.

Pap yelled from the other room. "Shut up you little shit! Before I give you something to cry about!" Mama began shushing me and trying to quiet me down. She had been watching Pap all evening, and she knew that if he lost his temper while he was this drunk, he'd get physical. Up until this point, he had never hit me and I can't recall seeing him beat Mama, either. I just have foggy recollections of slaps and shoves. I kept crying and even grew louder, probably sensing the tension in the air. I just remember crying and then the horrible fear that surged through me when Pap came storming into the room. He snatched me from Mama's arms and began shaking me violently, "I said shut up, dammit! I've put up with your hollerin' fer long enough. Shut up! Shut up!" He half lowered and half dropped me on the ground and then his hand went up, and it seemed to linger up there for bit before it came back down and struck me across the face. It doesn't matter that it was so long ago and I was so young because I tell you truly, I remember the pain from that blow. It stung like a whip across my face, and immediately I thought the left side of my face had just engorged to twice its normal size. My face clenched in a horrible cry that had no sound at first. It's the type of cry that only babies and little children can make, and when the wail did find its way out, it became loud and deafening, and it angered Pap even more.

Mama was shocked by the horror before her eyes. She couldn't believe she had just seen such a thing. Her husband had picked up their son, nearly shook his head off, practically slammed him on the ground like a sack of flour, and then slapped the hell out of him. She just couldn't believe Pap had done it. He'd hit her before, but never hurt one of the children so badly. I sat there, stinging and wailing on the floor, and Pap's hand went up again ready to give me another one. Mama shouted with all her might in terror, "Abram, no! Please, stop it! He's just a little boy!"

"Boy or no! I told 'em to shut up his hollerin'! This young un's goin' to learn early that when I say something, I mean it. I'm going to get some respect in my own house!" Pap's eyes were like fire as he placed them on me, "You understand me, boy? When I tell you to shut up, you bes' shut up! You'll do what I'm tellin' yah or you'll deal with the punishment. You hear me, boy? Huh!? You best answer me!" He grabbed me off the floor and again and again he shook me, so hard I thought I might break into pieces. It's a wonder my brains aren't scrambled.

Mama couldn't take it anymore. She let a shrill scream, "Stop it! Stop it! You're going to kill him!" She snatched me from his arms and ran back into the front room of the shotgun style house, Pap hot on her heels.

She carried me into the kitchen just as Pap grabbed her elbow, "Where do you think you're running to, huh? Think you're so much better than me, don't yah? I've had enough of your high and mighty ways, Annie! Maybe I should be learning you, too." He pushed her back against the wall and she hit her head sharply as she fell. I fell with her but crawled quickly under the table to get away from him. He stood over Mama slapping down at her again and again with brutal force as she tried to block with her arms. He started ranting at her. "It's because of you I's got to live in this shitter! You went and got knocked up on purpose so I'd have to go an' marry yah! Didn't yah? Didn't yah?"

Mama kept putting her hands up and begged him to stop, but he didn't. He just pulled her hands out of the way and kept slapping her. Then the slaps became fists and right there in front of me he was pummeling her. "Stop! Stop! Please stop!" cried Mama, "I'm sorry, I'm sorry." She didn't even know what she was apologizing for. She just hoped he would accept it and stop hitting her. When finally the blows did cease, the room reeled as she sat dazed. If my face felt swollen, Mama's must have felt like watermelon. Pap stepped back and seemed a bit surprised at what he had done, but he didn't try to help her up and he didn't apologize. Mama could feel a warm liquid running down her face, and when it reached her mouth she could taste the salty substance. She didn't know if it was tears or blood. I could see her from under the table, and I can tell you now that it was a mixture of both. Seeing Mama there, bloodied and nearly unconscious, was one of the worst things that I've ever seen in my life.

Aunt Emma told me later that that night, when Pap left Mama lying there in the kitchen as he went to go pass out in his bed, Mama actually debated about killing him. Her face hurt so bad she couldn't touch it and she could barely see out of her eyes because they were swelled almost shut. Remarkably, Sarah had slept through it all. I had stopped crying out of the sheer shock of Pap wailing on Mama. I forgot all about whatever nightmare I had in my dreams, because the nightmare I'd just seen was far more frightening.

Mama was lying there with her back against the kitchen wall, crying as quietly as a person can cry. She looked over and saw me watching her and she didn't want to be seen by me like that, so she picked herself up and took me back to bed. Then she went out back and got some water to clean herself up, which undoubtedly ran red with blood as it streamed off her face. When she went back into the kitchen she was shaking from the turmoil within her, and when she heard Pap's snores coming from their bedroom she opened the drawer and snatched up a kitchen knife, the one she used when she cleaned catfish or cut up vegetables. She held it in her hand and wondered if she had it in her to cut his throat as he slept. Would he wake up before she could do it and see what she meant to do? Would she be able to keep pressing the knife deep into his flesh when the blood came? She stared at the metal blade and wondered what it would feel like, both to cut him with it or to be cut by it. The idea of it piercing into her own flesh, seeing it slide along like it did when she filleted the fish, unnerved her so much that she dropped the knife with a slight shudder and wiped her hands on her dress. No, she decided, she didn't have the courage, not for that, at least. She could leave, though, and that much she could do and right now.

Mama gathered quickly a few clothes for her, me, and Sarah. We didn't have a wagon then, so she had to pack light. She came in to rouse Sarah and me, but I was still awake. I'd been listening to her walking around, wondering if she was okay. Sarah was so sleepy she didn't take notice of Mama's face by the lamplight. I had an idea of what Mama was doing and tried to help her carry our things as we quietly slipped out of the door with nothing but the dim lamp to light our way. It was November and a cold snap was in the air. We had to walk slowly because of the clothes we carried and because Sarah and I were so little.

It took us twenty minutes to reach Aunt Emma's house on a straight route between the fields. When we did finally get there all their lights were off. Mama started banging on the door loud as she could. At first there was no reaction, but after she banged again someone lit a lamp inside.

Aunt Emma opened the door and when she saw us standing out there she held out the light and said, "Well, what in the world are y'all . . . Oh my God. Annie!" She saw Mama's face, broken and battered. "What in the hell happened?" She pulled us all inside and her eyes were red and wide, "Annie, what's happened to you?"

Mama couldn't say anything, she just looked at her sister and started crying again. That made Aunt Emma lose her tears but it also seemed to answer her question. "That son of a bitch!" she declared. "I'll kill 'em! I'll kill 'em my damned self." She hugged Mama and then yelled out, "Colby! Colby, get up!" Uncle Colby had slept through the banging on the door but Aunt Emma was raising the whole house now with her hollering.

Amber was too little at the time but George and Francine came out to see what the alarm was. George was rubbing the sleep out from his eyes, "Mama?"

"Hush up and git you back to bed," she told him. "Both of you," and she waved her hand at Francine, too.

The little girl disappeared in her room but George, who was younger than me, stood innocently staring at me, Sarah, and particularly at Mama, who at this point was trying to hide her face as best she could.

Aunt Emma had started to her own room to get Uncle Colby but she wheeled back around when she sensed George was still standing there, "What'd I tell you, George? Get back in bed right now!" And she said it with such intimidation he instantly ran back to bed, his feet pit-patting on the hardwood floors as he went.

Uncle Colby was still snoring away. "It's like trying to wake the dead," Aunt Emma whispered to herself as she climbed on the bed and started poking at him. "Wake up, honey. Annie's here and she's hurt real bad. You've got to get up."

Colby rolled over and groaned, "Huh? What's all the fuss?"

"I said Annie's here and she's been hurt real bad."

Uncle Colby had started rolling over again to go back to sleep but he leaned up a little when the words registered, "She's hurt? What's wrong with her?" He got out of bed and started putting on his suspender pants.

Emma waited until he had his buttons done to make sure she had his full attention, "Abram. Abram done gone and beat her into a bloody mess, that's what's wrong with her."

Uncle Colby was pulling up his last strap over his shoulders and paused, "Abram?

Abram done beat Annie?"

"That's what I'm trying to tell you, hon. Yes! He done gone and beat her worse than I ever seen anybody get beat. You go on and have a look at her and see for yourself."

He came walking out of the bedroom and saw us all huddled together like refugees. He brought the lamp with him and when he held it up, Mama raised her hand because she didn't want him to see. "Annie," he said, "Go on and let me see what he done."

She reluctantly lowered her arm and he let out a long exhale. "God damn that boy," he said. "I don't know what the hell's wrong with him."

Emma walked out from behind him and looked at Mama's face. "Something's going to have to be done about this," she declared. She was getting redder by the minute. She looked Uncle Colby in the eyes and said, "Do you hear me, hon? Something's gonna have to be done about this."

He lowered the lamp and looked at his wife, "Well, what you want done, Emma? You want me to go and fetch the sheriff?"

"Hell, no, I don't want you fetch the sheriff," Aunt Emma said incredulously. "What's he gonna do? Not a damned thing, that's what."

Uncle Colby was upset at what Pap had done but he was also tired and didn't want to have to make guesses at what Aunt Emma wanted to do about things. "So what you want me to do?" he asked poignantly.

"I want you to go over there and beat him like he did my sister, that's what," she said. "Let him know what it feels like. Hell, if you don't, I will," she let him know. And none of us there doubted that she meant it.

Mama didn't want to stir things up between Emma and Colby so she tried to calm Emma's spirits a little, "It's okay, Emma. This ain't none of y'all's concern."

Aunt Emma just let it roll off, though, "Oh, the hell it ain't, Annie. Ain't no man got no right to beat up a woman, specially one that's as small as you, and specially if that woman is my blood. He's going to answer, by God. One way or another he's going to answer."

And such was her determination that Colby agreed to take action so that she wouldn't. "Where's he at now?" he asked Mama.

"He's home sleeping off the drink," she said.

Uncle Colby told Aunt Emma, "Ain't no good doin' nothin' about it tonight when he's still drunk. It'd be bes' to catch him tommorra when he's sober and got his wits about him."

Aunt Emma really wanted to see something done tonight, and if she had it her way it'd be to see Abram strung up by his balls, but in the end she accepted her husband's advice. "Fine then. But first thing tomorrow when you see him, all right?"

“All right, Emma. I will.” Aunt Emma gave him a look like she wasn't quite sure to believe him. “I will, Emma. I promise.” And when she finally seemed content he went back to bed.

Aunt Emma took some quilts she had stored in her bedroom and some extra blankets from out of the children's room and made us three a big square of blankets in the main area to sleep on. We cuddled up with one another and slept, Sarah on one side of Mama and me on the other.

Pap always walked to Mr. Pyle's farm on a specific route. It led him to enter the farm from the Northwest corner that bordered a thicket of trees. It was under one of these trees that Colby decided he'd wait for Pap the next morning. He was later than usual, no doubt nursing a hangover and possibly worried over the prospect of whether or not there'd be trouble waiting for him, but he was still on his way. He knew that since Annie wasn't there that morning she must have taken the kids over to her sister's house. He remembered beating her up, but through the fog of intoxication couldn't remember how bad. He wondered if his old friend was going to be waiting for him, ready to tell him how wrong he was for doing it, but he didn't have to wonder long.

Colby stood up to greet him when Pap came popping out of some trees. When Pap saw Colby he froze. For a split second he thought about running. Colby was a big man, after all. He had known him for years and couldn't imagine that he was going to have any real trouble with him, but the sight of him standing there with that serious look on his face gave Pap pause. Surely he wasn't here to start a fight, Pap thought.

"Annie and the kids walked over last night," Uncle Colby said.

He had some chew in his mouth and spit out a bit, "Figured. How bad was she?"

"About as bad as I've seen. Why'd you go and to that that to her for?"

Pap was a little scared of where this was going so he chose he words carefully. "She's been giving me lot of trouble for some time now."

"What kind of trouble that she deserved that?" asked Colby.

Pap stared down at his feet with his hands in his pocket. "She ain't been doing her wifely duties, for one. She been actin' high and mighty, like she's too good for me." Colby didn't look satisfied, "Hell, Colby, you know I ain't never want to marry that girl. Only reason I did 'cause she got pregnant. But I stayed, didn't I? Not like I had much choice. You remember?"

"You got her pregnant," Colby said. "You can't be hatin' her for that."

The talking had allowed Pap to regain some of his nerve, "I can hate her for that and then some if I want. She's my wife. And what business is it of yours if we get to arguing?"

"She's my wife's sister," he told Pap. "And that means I gotta look after her since her daddy's dead and brother ain't here no more." With that he started towards Pap with his fists up.

Pap didn't have much time to be surprised. By the time he realized that, indeed, Colby had come to start a fight, he was already in it. Colby's arms were like tree branches and the first hit nearly knocked Pap out, but he wasn't drunk now and was able to counter with some of his own. It was never really a fair contest, though. The years of hard work had made Colby fit as a prizefighter and strong as a bull. He could've ripped Pap limb from limb if he'd really had a mind to, but as it was, he didn't have it in him to put the kind of beating on Pap that he had given Mama. In fact, he took a few good licks himself because of his restraint. He told me once he pitied Pap in a way, and just wished Pap would find a way to get right with himself. He still left Pap with something to think about, though. When his last punch flattened Pap out on the ground with a busted lip and a terrible black eye, Colby decided Pap had had enough.

As Pap lay there trying to catch his breath, Colby sat down to do the same. Pap told him, "I never did think we'd end up like this. I thought we'd have ourselves lots of land and be rich."

Colby opened his mouth, but finding nothing worthwhile to pass through his lips, closed it again.

So Pap kept talking, "I should have left. I still could. I should just up and leave 'em all."

Colby was tired of listening to Pap constantly complain about the sour hand he'd been dealt in life. His hadn't been much better but he'd made the most of it. "You should quit yer belly achin', is what you should do. And don't be beatin' on Annie no more. I mean it. I don't never want to see her looking the way she does right now again. It ain't right. Now come on and let's get to work." And with that he got up and walked off into the fields nearby. Pap lay in the thicket a bit longer. Eventually he hauled himself up, though, and since there was nothing else to be done about things, he went to work, too.

Right about the time Pap and Colby were having their man to man, Mama and Aunt Emma were in the kitchen fixing us kids something to eat. Normally, Aunt Emma would make her own kids get up at dawn with her and Uncle Colby to eat and start the day's chores, but today she decided it'd be easier to have them sleep a little later and make a separate breakfast. She didn't want them staring at Mama over their eggs, either, so she made a mental note that she would pull them aside and tell them as much before they sat down to eat.

We stayed at Aunt Emma's for nearly a week that winter back in 1900. Aunt Emma stayed in contact with Uncle Marcus via letters and Mama was tempted to write one herself and ask if he couldn't help her by moving us all like he had done with their own mother and Candace, but she couldn't bring herself to do it. She and Marcus hardly ever corresponded themselves. Besides, Marcus was apparently in the middle of relocating down to Galveston to help rebuild the rail lines from the great storm. He had distanced himself from Annie and even though she realized her mistakes now, she didn't think Marcus would excuse them. He'd been so hurt when she married Pap.

I don't know what it was in Pap that made him decide he missed and needed Mama after all, but after a few days he came over and begged her for her forgiveness. It seemed sincere enough as they sat outside for privacy and he poured his heart out to her about how horrible it had been for him as a child and how he had stayed in Varner Creek trying to become a better man by taking care of her and the baby they had, and about how he needed his family to keep himself sane. Mama never really forgave him, but she knew she couldn't stay in Uncle Colby and Aunt Emma's house forever, and Pap made promises.

"You're going to go back to him?" asked Emma that night when

Mama told her what she'd decided.

"There ain't much else I can do, is there?" said Mama.

Aunt Emma told Mama she could stay with them, but Mama had already made up her mind. Aunt Emma told me years later she'd always wished she'd handled those days differently. "I should have seen then just how bad he was," she had told me. "You're Mama had tried to tell me back when she first met your daddy about some of his ways, but I didn't listen. I just didn't see him doin' the things he did."

I told Aunt Emma that she couldn't have seen what was to come. I know it always bothered her, though, wondering if she didn't have some blame for not doing more.

So a few days after Mama told Aunt Emma her decision, we went back home.

Things were much better for the next few months. Pap drank less and kept his voice down. I was still scared of him from what'd I'd seen that night and tried to stay out of his way as best I could, but it's tough when you're in a small house and there's not much to do in the country. Mainly I just tagged around after Mama helping her with her daily chores or going to pick pecans and blackberries. Sarah normally came, too, but she was limited by her condition a bit. And on those occasions when it was just Mama and me, I must confess I enjoyed that stolen time.

Things seemed like they had finally settled down for us all and might work out okay, but after a while they took to arguing again. Pap didn't beat her like that one night but he did slap her on occasion. When Aunt Emma found out she was furious. She had Colby talk to Pap again, not the fist-fighting kind of talk, but one where Colby would warn him repeatedly about slapping Mama around and let him know that if she showed up on his doorstep again looking that way she did that one night, he'd do the same to Pap and then some. After a while, though, Mama stopped telling Aunt Emma when Pap hit her. It wasn't doing any good except to cause a rift within her and Colby's marriage, Emma always getting on to Colby to get on to Pap, so Mama left it alone. When Aunt Emma saw Mama with bruises or red marks about her, though, she knew where they were coming from, but Mama wouldn't let her get Colby involved. "It ain't gonna do no good, Emma, and he ain't bad like he used to be."

"But Annie, he ain't got no right! I can't stand by why my blood's gettin' beat on."

"Just let it be, Emma. He ain't beatin' me no more. He just loses his temper now and then and pushes me around, but it ain't nothing to be worryin' about. He's just like that, and he ain't never gonna change." Aunt Emma was still skeptical and didn't like things a bit, but Mama said again, "Just let it be. Things is fine." It was Mama's indifference again, and while I don't think it really didn't weigh on her, pretending like it didn't is how she got by. Aunt Emma was always watching, though, and now that she understood what Mama had told her all those years ago, she wasn't about to let Pap pull the wool over her eyes again.

Things went on like that for the next few years until it seemed like one day Pap just stopped striking out at Mama completely. It must have been about 1905 or so. Nothing special happened, at least that we could figure. He didn't find religion and he didn't suddenly give up the drink, he just completely stopped slapping and pushing Mama around. None of us knew why, particularly Mama, but when they argued and he got mad like usual he'd think twice when his arm went up, and never let it fall on her again. I didn't fare as well, but at least it was something Mama wasn't getting hit on anymore.

Chapter 8

That was years before the morning Mama and Sarah disappeared, though. Now here it was, 1909, and I was twelve years old standing on Aunt Emma and Uncle Colby's doorstep as a refugee again, except this time I was all by myself. Mama and Sarah were gone and had left me behind to live with Pap. I was glad Aunt Emma had come to the house to take me home with her. I couldn't imagine staying under that roof just Pap and me. I was scared of him, always. He might not hit Mama anymore but he was still quick to lay one on me when he felt the inclination, and I never could forget what he'd done that night. The only one he seemed to have any affection for was Sarah.

Aunt Emma's house was a bustle of activity. It was just what I needed in order to get through the difficulty of thinking Mama had taken Sarah and left me. George and I had to share a bed but it wasn't too bad. I kept my mind off things for the first week or so playing pranks with him on Amber and Francine as often as possible. We put frogs in their shoes during and lizards in their beds. George showed me how to fill Amber's hand with Uncle Colby's shaving lather while she slept and tickle her nose with a feather from the pillow to make her smack her own face with a handful of cream. We tried dipping Francine's hand into a glass of water to get her to pee, but for some reason she was immune. We ended up improvising and it worked better than we'd hoped. Both Amber and Francine were thick as thieves and constantly whispering to one another and giggling at George's expense, which also became my burden as well when I went to stay with them. All day long they'd go around whispering and laughing at us in their secret taunts. But George found a way to divide and conquer, even if it was just temporary. Francine and Amber shared a bed, and since the old hand in water wasn't working, George decided to just pour some water in the middle of the bed while they were sleeping. When the moisture woke them up, each blamed the other for peeing in the bed. Neither of them would admit it, though, since both were innocent, of course, but since each knew she hadn't done it that could only mean the other one had, and so both accused one another of peeing the bed and then trying to blame it on the other. To give George credit, it certainly ended up being the best of pranks. The next few days were bliss. Amber and Francine were so busy being upset at each other that they lost all interest in their private jokes at our expense. Unfortunately, Francine suddenly realized the possibility that we had scammed them. And when she told Amber about her theory, they immediately agreed and fell over each other in apologies. Well, they had it in for us after that. George and I were the butt of jokes worse than ever, but it was worth it. I congratulated George on the grand success he had achieved, however short-lived, and promised to aspire to his level of perfection when it came to pulling off pranks. To show my appreciation, when we went looking for an armadillo down its hole to haul out by the tail, I told George I'd let him have it all by himself. I coached as we walked, "Always make sure you get them by the tail," I told him, "'cause they have sharp claws that'll get yah, and they'll bite, too. But as long as you get 'em by the tail they can't get at yah." I was enjoying the teacher's role.

"You ever been bit?" asked George as we trudged along looking in holes for one.

"Sure have," I boasted with the pride of a wounded war veteran, even if had only been a nip once.

"What'd you do?" he asked.

I let him go and screamed like a little girl is what I did, but I wasn't going to tell George that. "I pulled him out and bit him back, right on his tail!" I said.

"Tsk!" he scoffed, "You're foolin'. You can't bite one of them things."

He caught me. "Can if you shuck 'em first. Armadillo's are good eatin, ya know," I informed. That much was true.

"You've eaten an armadillo?!" he asked with disgust.

"Well, shoot yeah. Ain't you never had two-bean armadillo?"

"Nu-uh," he said, "Mama ain't never cooked one of them."

"Well trust me, it's good. My Pap makes it with hot peppers and it's right fine." Maybe saying it was right fine was a bit of a stretch, as Mama, Sarah, and me only had it the one time and figured that was enough, but Pap sure seemed to like it.

George and I tromped off in the woods on a regular basis. We'd climb trees after squirrels or try to cram ourselves down holes to see what was inside. We were the masters of the woods and all creatures feared us. Or so we told ourselves. A few days into our regular adventures proved things otherwise, though. We were kicking through the brush one early morning when we heard clucking. Around the house that was perfectly normal, but clucking out in the woods was a novelty. And when we followed the noise into a small clearing there were a good dozen hens pecking at the ground all around. We were surprised to find them out there by themselves. I had never really heard of wild chickens before, but since I was there looking at them it made sense to me that there must have been wild chickens in the world if there were farm chickens. That had to come from somewhere. There were parts of the country that had wild horses, after all, so why not wild chickens? It was certainly the first time I'd ever seen any, though, and apparently George, too. I suggested to him that it would be great fun to give them a chase and take a few home. I could just see the surprise on Aunt Emma's face when we arrived back home each carrying a couple of chickens. She'd gush over what fine hunters we were, catching them with our own hands and all, and probably be pleased as punch to fix them up for dinner. I could see it all in my mind and I painted such a pretty picture of it for George that he immediately agreed. We both proceeded to pick out the chickens that each of us thought we could most easily catch. My first choice was a fat hen that seemed like she'd be slow. George was eyeing another of his own, and once we had it clear who was going for what, we took off after our prey with the speed of mountain lions. I got within five feet of that hen, though, and she started squawking and flapping up a storm and flew a few feet away before thumping back to the ground. I was just about on her again when out from the right of me shot the biggest rooster a man ever saw, let alone a twelve year old. He was two feet high if he was an inch and had talons like an eagle. And he wasn't hopping his way over to me, or even the ugly type of flying a chicken can do over short distances. No sir, that rooster was flying at me at head's height and with the speed of a darting blue jay when you invade its nesting area, and he was coming right for me. I went to throw my hands up in defense and that thing clamped down on my arms like a razor-wire lasso pulled tight. Its heavy wings batted me about the head, its beak tearing at me like a wood pecker gone mad, and it held tight to me with one leg while slashing about with the other. It was the devil's chicken. The Satan of poultry, the Lucifer of Leghorns, and that damned bird was ripping at me with its hell spawned claws that burned like the whips of fire that I imagined only the devil had. He was just evil, big, bad, feathery evil. I turned and ran blindly screaming back into the thickets hoping my retreat would satiate the bird's bloodlust and finally, after an eternity of seconds, the bird did let go and headed off back into the clearing. I was just about to thank God in heaven for my life being spared from that wicked creature when I heard George let out a blood curdling scream. A few seconds later I spotted him darting off into the woods not far from me. That Leghorn rooster was atop his head like a hat come to life, pecking, scratching, and pounding poor George with its wings like they were fists. A few moments later I heard the beating of wings and the chicken came flying out from the woods back towards the clearing.

I yelled out for George in the general direction I had seen him running, "Hey, George! You all right?"

I could hear a moaning noise and marched towards it. George was sitting on the ground with one leg stretched out and the other tucked in under him. He was crying and trying to wipe his eyes with his sleeves when he heard my footsteps in the brush. It was then I realized that I kind of felt like crying, too. My arms and face were stinging. Blood was soaking through my own sleeves and something very smelly was slowly oozing down my cheek. I wiped it with my hand and held it up to see what it was. It was chicken shit. George wasn't much better off. He had scratches all over and blood was trickling down from his temples where that demon bird had clamped itself. I sat down by George and we both licked our wounds. All the while we listened intently to make sure that rooster didn't come back to finish us off.

After a bit George said, "You won't tell nobody I cried, will yah?"

"Hell, naw," I said. "I had some tears myself just cause it stung so bad. I ain't never seen a rooster that mean," I told him.

"Me, neither." He dropped his head and stared at the ground. "I didn't never think I'd get whooped by a chicken."

I couldn't help it, then. I laughed. I looked at George and remembered how funny he looked with the chicken on him, "That thing was stuck on you like a rooster hat," I told him. I held up my hands in the air like he had done and gave him an impression of himself running into the woods. "You was running and screaming, 'Ah-h-h-h!' All the while that thing stuck on your head flapping at yah."

He laughed a little bit, too. "Well, what about you? I had that hen I was chasin', had her right by her hind feathers. Then I heard you yellin' bloody murder and there you was with that rooster pecking at yah like you was a big corn kernel, and you run off same as me. I figured I had that hen since he took off after you, but the next thing I know that bird was flying at me goin' plum crazy." He smiled, though. "That chicken's possessed," he finally decided. "Ain't no way a normal chicken act like that. We ought to get the preacher out here to do drive the devil out of it or somethin'," he suggested.

We both had a good laugh, but not too loud. We didn't want him hearing us and coming back for seconds, so we went ahead and pulled ourselves up off the ground and headed back to the house. We had a dandy of a time convincing Aunt Emma that a chicken had attacked us in the woods. She was convinced we'd snuck over to someone else's farm and been up to no good. She didn't believe in the whole wild chicken attack story, not until Uncle Colby backed us up. "There's chickens in them woods," he said bluntly over dinner. Not a chicken dinner, by the way, just a plain dinner with a carrot and potato stew. "Don't nobody know how long they been there, but they're there. I've heard them a time or two myself." Henry Mullins could have told us how those chickens came to live and breed out in the woods, but none of us knew. His old fighting roosters had spawned the granddaddy of cock-fighting roosters.

That night neither George nor I slept very well. Our scratches hurt and no matter how much I had washed earlier, I could still smell the chicken crap on me. Finally the thought of it sliming down my face like it had drove me out of bed and back outside to the well. I had to make sure it was all off and get the smell gone, otherwise I'd never get any sleep, so I crept out the door quietly so as to not disturb everyone else still sleeping.

Outside a cold chill had settled along with an accompanying misty fog. Aunt Emma must have put the soap and bucket back at the well, and I hesitated to approach the well remembering what had happened back at my house. The eerie quiet of a half gray, half black night wasn't encouraging, either. Still, I told myself that I was acting like a baby, plus my cheek was remembering the texture of chicken crap along with the smell that I thought I could still detect emanating from me, so I went ahead and drew up the bucket. There was an old lye bar of soap we used earlier and I grabbed it and began scrubbing away. My arms were scratched up a hundred times worse than my face, but the soap still stung in my cuts on the cheeks and neck. I threw another handful of water over my face and some of the suds crept down into my eyes causing them to burn. Lye soap could be excruciating on the eyes, even in small doses. I shut them tight to block the invasion of soapy water and bent over close to the bucket to cup water into my hands. I dipped my hands along the surface of the bucket like I was holding a hymnal in church, a V- shape to catch a nice little puddle, but as they slid just beneath the water I had the sudden sensation that I was looking for something. Yes, there was definitely something I was trying to find. My thoughts seemed to run away from me and I just started feeling over and over again, I'm looking for something, I'm looking for something, I'm looking for . . . someone. I have to find someone. I have to find . . . Sol! And at that moment something grabbed my hand in the water. It gripped me tightly and I had to jump back to get it to let go. My eyes opened wide. The lye immediately stung them horribly, but I was just able to make out a small hand disappearing back into the water with barely a ripple. My first instinct was to run, but then I wondered if I hadn't had another waking dream. Surely, that didn't just happened. I crept cautiously towards the bucket, leaning back just in case that hand came thrusting out of the water to grab me again. When I got closer, I pushed the suds from my eyes and squinted to see the water. The first thing I noticed was the water. It was black with the night sky's reflection but it had suddenly taken on that same greenish tint. It just didn't make sense. I stayed where I was a few moments, still frightened a hand might rise again, but when it didn't I got a little closer to the water and tried to see what it was making the water tint that way.

All of a sudden, as though rising from a deep abyss, I saw something pale white rise up. It was a face, Sarah's face. Her head seemed to float towards the surface as though the bucket were much deeper than possible, and then her eyes opened and looked right at me. Terror rose up in me from somewhere deep in my belly. It amplified as it jumped into my chest and froze me from the inside. Her face was dimly lit in a green luminescence, and then she said my name. I didn't hear anything, but her lips clearly mouthed "Sol . . ." But then, as though someone had grabbed her by her ankles and pulled her back down, she disappeared quickly into the depths. Within seconds she had vanished inside the bucket. I still wanted to turn and run back inside the house, but I felt compelled to look into the bucket deeper to see where she might have gone. It was like trying to see through to the other side of a mirror. Nothing was there except the shadow I was casting from the moonlight, creating even a blacker surface than the night alone could manage. I poked the water and little ripples danced on its surface, but nothing else stirred inside. Slowly, and with a lot of caution and fright, I put my right hand all the way into the bucket. I half expected to be pulled inside down into some underworld, but there was nothing there except the bottom of the wooden bucket and the water between.

"Sarah?" I said. "Sarah?" There came no answer. I picked up the bucket and dumped the water out, then looked back inside as though there was some hidden door within. But all I saw was the bucket, emptied and shallow.

The coldness of the night and the empty lonely feeling of being out there in the dark with nothing but the image of my sister's head in that bucket was too much. I dropped it and took off back into the house, furiously wiping my eyes as tears cleared away the lye that had stung them. As I went I questioned myself if I had just seen what I thought I had. *What's happening to me?* I thought. The house was still quiet inside. George was asleep but I could tell he had changed positions yet again since I'd been outside. Obviously he wasn't in the deep slumber that's so hard to wake people from. I thought about shoving him a little to wake him up and tell him what had just happened outside, but I didn't know how I'd tell anyone. Even just thinking it to myself was making me think I might be a crazy person. George would think I'd cracked or made it up. Maybe I had cracked. So instead I just climbed into bed to think on everything. I wasn't crazy. That had been Sarah's head out there, just like the time before at my house when I'd seen her reflection, except this time I know I didn't black out. Something grabbed me and I knew it was her that had I seen in that strange glow. And she said my name. When her lips had moved there was nothing else they could have said but my name. I just knew it. This time, it was real. I wasn't a dream, I told myself. That was Sarah. I resigned myself that the next day I would tell George what I'd seen. I'd tell him that I was beginning to think Mama and Sarah didn't go to Galveston. I'd tell him that I thought I had seen Sarah's ghost.

I was laying there thinking about her, about the way her face had looked there in the water surrounded by that eerie green glow when I fell asleep. George and I had slept back to back in the small bed and I woke up while it was still dark, feeling something wet against me. Immediately I noted how cold the room was, too cold even for the chilly night outside. I felt like I'd been dipped in icy water from head to toe. Goose bumps riddled my body, particularly the back of my neck and chest. I thought I could feel someone else in the room. I lifted my head enough to look over the curve of my shoulder to see if there was anyone there. I couldn't see anyone, but the little half-moon of mattress left between me and the edge of the bed was slowly being pockmarked with invisible droplets that were magically appearing as though someone was standing there dripping on the sheets. Perfectly dry parts of the blanket suddenly broke out with droplets like it had caught the measles. Although I couldn't see anyone, I knew it was her. I pulled back the sheets and looked at the floor by the bed. Little wet footprints spread out before me in a perfect path out of the room I was sharing with George. But they weren't headed away from the bed, they had been made by someone coming into the room and there weren't any leading back out. Someone had recently walked into our room and something in my gut said that they were still here. I sat up and looked over the edge of the bed and could see a puddle of water slowly accumulating on the hardwood floor. I thought to myself, if she is here, she's there. She's standing right there.

I felt like I was freezing from the inside. I sat looking into the empty space where I thought she must be, intently listening for any sound and looking for any sign of her physical presence. Suddenly a puff of air as though someone breathing caressed my cheek. I cringed backwards quickly, but a moment later I leaned forward and in a whisper I said, "Sarah?"

And as though I had called her to form, there she was. Light sprang forward and it was surrounding her. She appeared just inches from me, staring right at me in that same green mist wearing her pink dress. She was wet all over and reached out for me. I had jerked back in fright again, but after I paused for a moment I found the courage in me to reach out for her hand. I looked at her eyes and felt strangely happy. I felt like I'd just found what I had been looking for. Our fingertips connected and then she was gone. A small breeze of air manifested from where she had been and blew itself over me and George. He stirred a little in his sleep but nothing more. He had no idea what had just happened.

The room suddenly felt empty again except for us. Sarah was gone. The water remained, though. There it was on the floor, her footprints into the room, and the puddle where she had stood. I had proof, I thought. I wasn't crazy. I could tell people the things I'd seen now because there was the proof right there on the hardwood floors. Everything seemed to bubble up in me at that moment, the terror of seeing what I could only assume was my dead sister's ghost, the elation that the water had remained proving that I wasn't a nutcase, and an absolute necessity to tell someone. "Aunt Emma!" I yelled. It was a sudden outburst and louder than I had intended. I jumped out of bed and ran towards her and Uncle Colby's bedroom. I pushed open their door and yelled for her again, "Aunt Emma! Aunt Emma, wake up!"

Uncle Colby was snoring loud as ever but Aunt Emma leaned up quickly in the bed, her bird's nest of hair silhouetted by the slight light of the window. "Sol? What's wrong? What is it?"

"Come quick, Aunt Emma, come quick!" I felt around for her arm and when I found it I tried pulling her out of bed.

She came stumbling after me, "What is it, Sol? Somebody hurt? What's going on?"

"I saw her!" I said, "She was in my room!"

Aunt Emma was trying to get her mind out of bed, too, "Who?" she asked, thinking she must have missed something and needed to get caught up on things.

"Sarah!" I yelled. "She was here, right here in my room!" I dragged her into the room by the bed.

By this time George was up, too. He had heard the noise and was looking around frantically trying to figure out who had been in the bedroom while he was sleeping, "Who's here?" he asked frightened, "Where? Where?"

"She was right here," I told him and Aunt Emma, both. I pointed at the puddle on the floor, "See, Aunt Emma, right here. There's her footprints right there."

Aunt Emma looked at the water on the floor. "Well, where'd she go, Sol? Is she in the house?" She took a step towards the door like she was about to search the house.

"She's gone, Aunt Emma. She disappeared," I told her.

Aunt Emma stopped and gave me a queer look, "What do you mean, disappeared?"

"I saw her earlier, too, Aunt Emma. I went outside to wash up again and I saw her in the bucket."

Now she was kneeling down beside me, "In the bucket? Sol, honey, what in the world are you going on about?"

I knew she'd think I was cracked, but I had my proof. "I'm trying to tell you, Aunt Emma. I think something's happened to Sarah. I think maybe she might be dead and trying to tell me something. I saw her, I swear I did."

"Calm down, Sol, just calm yourself okay. Now, your sister's fine, you here me?

What makes you think something's happened to her?"

"Something has happened, Aunt Emma. I think Sarah's dead and I've seen her ghost."

"Ghost?" cried George. And he pulled the sheets up tight around his neck and started scanning every inch of the room.

"Quiet down, George," Aunt Emma told him. "There ain't no ghosts here." And she had looked back at me when she said it. "Now, Sol, I want you to listen to me. I know you're scared and worried about your Mama and sister, but you didn't see her ghost, now, yah hear me?"

"But Aunt Emma, the footprints . . ." I had proof!

"I think I know where they come from, Sol. And I'll take care of it, but right now I want you to calm down and think for a sec. Your Mama and Sarah took all their things and the horse and wagon. Now, I don't think anything bad has happened to either one of them. I think someone's pulled a bit of a mean joke on you is all, so don't go getting yourself all worked up. We're going to figure out where they went soon enough and everything will get settled. You just gotta wait and let things find their course. But I don't want you thinking bad thoughts, okay, sweet pie? Ain't no cause to be thinking like that, and there ain't no such thing as ghosts." She gave me a hug and I could see little tears hiding behind her eyes. I didn't think she wholly believed what she had just told me about finding Mama and Sarah in due course. She was worried, too. And I knew what I had seen.

Aunt Emma did her best to calm George and me, but there was no way either of us was going back to sleep. It was a bout four or five in the morning anyway, so we agreed to get back in bed just until the light said it was time to get up again. Aunt Emma went out of our bedroom right into Amber and Francine's room. George wouldn't let her close our door and we could both hear her storm into their room, "All right!" She yelled at them, both of whom were peacefully sleeping despite my outburst earlier and blissfully unaware of the commotion around them, "Which one did it? Don't play asleep with me girls; I'll tan your hides."

I could just imagine her shaking them both awake in the other room. Then we heard Amber's voice, "Mama?" It sounded sweet and innocent and I felt bad for her because I knew she was innocent of this one.

"Don't Mama me. Whose bright idea was it?" She asked both girls as they groggily awoke.

"What are you talking about, Mama?" I heard Francine ask.

"One of you or both of you have been messing around with George and Sol. Traipsing around my house with wet feet and dripping water on my sheets while they're sleepin'. Which one was it? huh?"

Both the girls looked at each other dumbfounded. "Mama we ain't been outta bed, I swear," said Amber.

Francine went into a rant, "It's him, Mama! Him and Sol! They done it and now they're trying to blame it on us just to get us in trouble. They pranked us something just like it the other day, Mama, when they poured water in our bed."

"Uh, huh," said Aunt Emma, "and I suppose neither of you thought it'd be funny to play a similar prank on them to get them back, huh?"

"But we didn't, Mama, honest," whined Francine.

"Well, look here," said Aunt Emma, "In any case I've had enough of the practical joking around here. Sol's going through a tough time and things like this just making it worse, you hear?" Both girls were about to be up in protest again, but she cut them off, "Now, I don't wanna hear it! You just do as I say and no more messin' around. Understand?"

They both must have looked like a couple of pitiful martyrs, but since they didn't want to risk getting in more trouble, they just said, "Yes, ma'am," in that automatic way they were used to using.

The next morning they both approached me and George as I was telling him everything that had happened. His eyes were big and although he didn't seem to care much for the idea of ghosts standing in our room at night he didn't seem to think I was crazy, which I appreciated more than I could say.

Amber and Francine strolled up on us with that girlish swagger that said trouble, "Think that's real funny, don't yah?" asked Amber. "Mama coming in and getting on to us like that for a prank you faked on yourselves just to get us in trouble."

"Yeah, real funny, you shit-heads. We'll see how funny it is when we tell everyone in town how you both still pee the bed," added Francine.

"We don't!" I yelled at her.

"George does," said Amber, "And it don't matter. Everyone will believe it, anyway. Maybe that'll make y'all think twice before y'all try to get us in trouble again."

"We didn't do it," said George. "It was a ghost."

Amber squinted her eyes, folded her arms, and shifted her weight to one leg and puckered her lips like a soured fish, "Oh, shut up George. Like we're going to fall for that."

"Yeah," said Francine. "A ghost poured water in your bed just like you did ours. You're both just stupid." And with that her and Francine walked off with the same swagger as before, except a little more triumphantly.

George looked at me and said, "I don't wet the bed. They're just trying to embarrass me."

"It's okay," I told him, "I wouldn't care even if you did, but I know you ain't since I been here. Besides, I think maybe something real bad's happened, George. I know what happened last night and I know it was Sarah that I saw and her in that was in our room." The more I thought about what it might mean, the worse I felt. And before I knew it I was crying. "I think maybe they're dead, George," I told him. "I think they're dead," I said again.

George put his arm around me, "It's all right," he comforted, "Maybe it ain't like you think. Maybe Mama's right and somehow Francine and Amber been playing some kind of joke on yah without us realizing it. I wouldn't put it past 'em."

"It ain't them," I told him. "It was Sarah!"

George took a deep breath, "I believe you. But maybe she ain't dead. Maybe it's something else."

We talked together all day, he and I, not wanting the day to end because we were both scared of what the night might bring. I didn't want to see or feel Sarah's ghost again.

Besides scaring the daylights out of me I didn't want to believe she was dead. Because if she was, where was Mama? Wherever Sarah was, Mama was sure to be. And if they were both dead, I know who'd done it. It was the most evilest thought I could have imagined of him, but it wasn't impossible to see him doing it in my mind. I thought about that one night years back when he had beaten Mama so bad. I also remembered his muddy boots that morning when he told he'd already been out looking for them. Maybe he hadn't been looking for them at all, but doing something else. The more I remembered the guiltier Pap started looking to me, and before I went to bed that night I told Aunt Emma all of it. She assured me Mama and Sarah were okay, and that everything would work out okay, just wait and see, but she was shaken by what I told her, I could see it in her.

Chapter 9

It was nearly impossible falling asleep that next night. George kept the blankets so tight I couldn't move, and I could feel him searching the room in the dark, his head jerking with every little creak the house made. I wasn't much better. I thought something might happen at any second, but the hours ticked by uneventfully and somewhere along the way he and I both fell asleep. The following day was Sunday and that meant church. True to their word, Francine and Amber set out in the whispers only young girls can master to spread the rumors of George and mine's fictional bedwetting problem to all the other kids. By the time Reverend Monroe finished his sermon and church was let out, it seemed like everyone our age was pointing and laughing. Francine and Amber were as proud as they could be.

We didn't go immediately home. Aunt Emma and Miss Thomas stood off by themselves in discussion. George and I couldn't hear what they were saying, but I knew Miss Thomas had grave concerns regarding my mother's sudden departure with Sarah, especially when she learned that I hadn't been taken along. And by the look on her face now, her and Aunt Emma were talking about what I had told Aunt Emma the day before. They talked for a few more minutes before Uncle Colby went to retrieve Aunt Emma. It was dinner time and he was hungry, which was one of the few things that could make him impatient with her. The three of them walked back towards us and I heard Miss Thomas say, "I'm going to talk with him today, Emma, and I'll let you know how things go." They said their goodbyes and we headed home.

I didn't know at the time who "he" was, but I'd put enough together later to figure Aunt Emma and Miss Thomas had been talking about the sheriff. The next day Miss Thomas went and had a visit with Sheriff Covell. She baked him up a nice apple pie first to bring to him so he'd be a little more easy to sit down and have a good talk with. "Sheriff, I think maybe there's something fishy going on here with Sarah Mayfield's suddenly being gone."

Sheriff Covell was an ample man in his fifties who looked like he could easily be bribed by a mass murderer to look the other way with an apple pie like the one Miss Thomas had brought him. "I know, Hetta." That was Miss Thomas' first name, though I had never heard anyone call her by it. "But there ain't no signs of foul-play over there. I've been out and visited Abram Mayfield and everything he's sayin' seems to check out fine."

"Well, Sheriff, I think he'd hope everything he says sounds fine, but that doesn't mean it is. I don't think I need to tell you what kind of a man Abram Mayfield is."

"Miss Thomas," he was back to being formal again, "I know you mean well in this, but I have to have more than people's thinking something bad mighta happened before I can go invadin' people's lives. I need something to prove it has. You catch my meaning? They horse is gone, her and the child's things are gone . . . it all looks to me like they up and left, just like he says they did."

"I know, but I want you to hear me out, Gus." That was the Sheriff's first name. She must have decided formality wasn't the way to go about things on this particular occasion, "I've known Sarah Mayfield for years and her sister knows her better than anyone, and we both think something just doesn't sound right. I don't doubt that it's possible she did just up and leave town, 'specially being married to that man, but I can't see Annie leaving without her boy. She just wouldn't do that. Those kids are everything to Annie and she would have told her sister, or even me for that matter. She wouldn't just up and disappear like this."

The sheriff helped himself to a third piece of pie while secretly unbuttoning his top pants button under the table and giving his round stomach a little pat. "Well, what you think I ought to do about it, Hetta? I can't arrest Abram because his wife left him, and unless something says otherwise that's how the law sees things. There ain't no other way for me to see it, even if the whole town thinks it funny the way she left. There ain't no facts that say she didn't and lots that say she did. That's all there is to it."

Miss Thomas knew this all too well. The purpose of her visit was primarily to see what the sheriff thought about the situation, as he had visited Abram at Emma's request, and to make sure the situation was still in his mind. She didn't want him forgetting that there was still some things he needed to be aware of going on around him besides his appetite. "Just promise me you'll stay on top of things, Gus, and that you'll keep an eye on that Abram Mayfield. Everybody knows that man is trouble, and if anything bad has happened to those girls it's him you need to keep in mind."

"Believe me, Hetta. I got my eye on things. If Abram Mayfield so much as take one step outta line, I'll be on him like fleas on a dog. You have my word." The last bit of that third piece of pie disappeared down his gullet. "Bud I Dink Eferybody might be gettin vorked up fer notn," he mumbled. Swallow. "I feel fairly confident that Annie Mayfield and her daughter did up and leave. From what I know of Abram, it was only a matter of time. I 'spect before too long someone will get a letter or telegram from her. I do feel bad for the boy, though. I know his daddy ain't much of a man. Maybe wherever she went, Annie went ahead just to get settled before sending for him. You wait and see, though, we'll hear from her soon enough."

It wasn't the type of perspective on things Miss Thomas would have liked to have seen from the sheriff, but about as much as she expected. Sheriff Covelle was a good man, but he was like an old guard dog who'd taken to sleeping on a porch since nothing every happened. Varner Creek was usually a quiet town, and it took a bit to get old Sheriff Covelle roused into action.

Miss Thomas came out to Aunt Emma's place on Monday and they sat on the newly finished wrap-around porch drinking iced tea and discussing things. Aunt Emma had made a point to ask George and me to go have a nice play away from home for awhile, so we decided we'd go have another whack at the wild chickens. Except this time we carried big sticks with us and knew to be on the lookout for that crazy rooster, who we'd named Lucifer the Leghorn between ourselves, since we were convinced he was part devil. We stole a little of the chicken feed from the henhouse and struck out into the woods. George carried the wooden crate we'd brought and I carried the rope we'd borrowed from Uncle Colby's tool shed.

It took us a long time to find the chickens. We had marched back to the clearing and they weren't there, so we started tromping around until after a while we heard their clucking away in some brush. We stealthily crept up on them with our sticks at the ready. I kept my eyes peeled for the rooster.

George pointed out a nice sized hen that was off a ways from the rest. We figured that one would be the safest one to go after, and there was still no sign of Lucifer the Leghorn. We got to about ten or fifteen feet before she started clucking and pacing about a bit letting us know we weren't too welcome. "She's calling him," warned George.

We both paused and listened quietly. There was no sudden attack, though.

"Naw," I said, "she's just nervous about us is all. These here wild ones ain't used to people like the ones at home." It seemed a good enough explanation and George calmed a bit, but he was still looking every which way. "This here's about as close as we're gonna get," I told him. "Let's go ahead and spread out the feed and try to get her interested in it." So we proceeded to spread out the corn and mash, adding a little pile between two small trees. Then we put the crate over it, propped it up with a stick that George had tied one end of the rope to, and we crept off as far we could go with the rope without it getting tangled in the brush.

"You think she'll go for it?" asked George.

"Sure she will. She's a chicken, ain't she? And it's chicken feed. Better than they probly been eatin' out here. She'll think it's a meal fit for a queen." Sure enough the hen bobbed over and started pecking at the corn. It must have carried a scent, though, or the other chickens must have heard her pleasurable pecking, because within a minute or so a few more chickens showed up. Then *He* showed up. Out from our left came Lucifer the Leghorn. He was just as big and ugly as he was in my memory from a few days ago. I could feel George tense up next to me, and I have to admit, I did the same. I clenched my stick tighter and my knuckles went white.

"He's going to see us!" said George.

"No he won't," I said, "He's too busy cramming his beak. Look at him." And I was right. Ole Lucifer the Leghorn had a heck of an appetite. He was practically stepping over the hens pecking away frantically. Then he did something we didn't expect. He went straight for the pile under the crate box.

"What are we going to do if he goes for it?" asked George. "He's too big to fit under it, ain't he?"

"Yeah, I think so." I wasn't too sure, though. And I had an idea of what to do if he did get under that crate. "Let's catch him," I said, both to George and myself.

"What?" George grabbed me by the arm, "Are you nuts? He'll slice us to Sunday if we catch that thing."

"Not if he's under the crate, he won't. We can just drag him home if we gotta."

George pondered on it and his eyes got real big with the thought of bringing home Lucifer the Leghorn. "Yeah, maybe we could . . ."

He didn't get a chance to finish his sentence, though. Because while we were fantasizing, the rooster had squeezed himself under the crate. His red comb smacked the top of it, knocking it loose from its prop, and the box came down around him. Before either one of us could go on planning the strategics involved in how we'd get him in the crate, he did it for us. "We got him!" screamed George.

"Holy shit!" I yelled in excitement. We could see his beak poking out from the bottom of the crate and it was bouncing up and down. "He's gonna get loose!" I yelled. I jumped up and ran for the crate full speed. My plan was to throw myself on the crate and let my weight do the job, but I wasn't quick enough. Right about the time I went airborne the crate flipped over backwards, and the rooster side-stepped my body as I came crashing down. I flopped on my belly and looked over at him and it was probably the first time a chicken ever stood taller than a man. He looked at me with his beady eyes and I swear I thought I saw him smile. Then it was all a flurry of feathers. He came at me with a vengeance. I thought for sure George's omen might just come true, and I might lose an eye. But before I went sightless I heard George yell out.

He came charging forward like one of the soldiers in Pickett's charge, screaming his own battle cry, "Ya-a-a-a!" He held his stick up with both hands directly over his head as though it were a sword. Lucifer the Leghorn heard him coming, and instead of flying straight at George I could see hesitation in those beady eyes of his. It was momentary, though, and he gave me one last hard peck on the nose and then went for George. It was a clash of titans. George was swinging frantically as though fighting off a swarm of bees. Lucifer the Leghorn, for his part, was beating his wings like thunder and dodging George's stick in an awkward sort of dance. Despite George's best effort, I could see that the rooster was beginning to get the better of him. George was panicking and swinging wildly, allowing Lucifer the Leghorn to dart in and scratch and peck, then dart back out, moving like a seasoned boxer. George's charge did take the violence away from me, though, and I was able to jump up again and yell for George to run with me. I had left my own stick on the ground when I went for the crate, and when we both ran by it I picked it up and tossed it at the rooster that was right on our heels. He had to move to miss it and we made good our escape.

"Damn!" I said to George when we were in the clear. "We had him!"

George bent over to catch his breath, "You mean he nearly had us."

I laughed, "Maybe, but he was scared of you, boy."

He smiled, "Not half of scared as I was. I thought he was going to peck your face off if I didn't do something."

"Well, you sure charged in there like you was just as crazy as him. That was great!" George appreciated the encouragement, and I appreciated still having my eyes and nose intact. "Thanks, George," I told him.

"Lot of good it did. I didn't even hit him one good time, not one."

"That's all right, it was enough for me to get up and gone."

We hung our heads in defeat yet again and headed home, but somehow it didn't feel like a total loss. On the way we talked about what had gone wrong and how close we had come to bringing home the big one. We also talked about Sarah and Mama. He asked if I really thought Sarah's ghost had been in our room. I said yes, and he wanted to know what I thought it was all about. It was hard talking about it, though. I still had that image of Sarah's living head in the water bucket. Aunt Emma had told me not to think such things, but I couldn't help it. *What else can it be but Sarah's ghost*, I thought. And that could only mean she wasn't alive anymore. I hoped I was wrong, but nobody had heard from them yet, and my suspicions were growing stronger.

It was nearing dusk when we finally came out from the woods. Miss Thomas' buggy was gone and nobody sat outside, but there was a strange horse I hadn't seen before in the pen. It looked like it had been ridden hard that day, a sweat lather covering its hairs. It must have been here for a while, though, because it was contently munching on an oat bag that had been strapped to it and its saddle had been slung over the railing of the pen. It was a beautiful horse, gray with white spots, and very well groomed.

"I wonder whose horse that is?" I asked George.

"I don't know. Never seen it before. Pretty one, though."

We went on in the house and Aunt Emma was sitting with a strange man at the table. He had black hair and blue eyes that were a bit startling. They reminded me of Mama's eyes, except bluer than even Sarah's. As George and I walked in we heard Uncle Colby come in the back door. He put his hat and coat on a set of deer antlers he had hung near the door for just that purpose and then came into the main room. He was about to say something to us, probably ask us what we had been up to given I had some new scratches, but his eyes passed over us to the table when he noticed the man sitting with Aunt Emma. There seemed a brief moment of recognition before he walked over to the man. "Marcus," he said as he held out his arm for a handshake which the man returned. "Been a long time."

"Yessir, sure has," responded the man.

"What brings you out our way?" asked Uncle Colby.

"I reckon you know the answer to that," voiced Aunt Emma.

"Annie didn't show up in Galveston?" asked Uncle Colby.

Aunt Emma gave him a warning look. She didn't want him to say it out loud in front of George and me, particularly me.

"No. I haven't heard from her, neither. Reckon I would've by now, even if she got lost. Probably someone would have heard from her by now," said the mysterious man.

Aunt Emma was nearly beside herself with frustration with the two men who so openly discussed things clearly not meant to be heard by a child in such a precarious situation as myself. "Less'n she wants it that way. She's probably trying to make a fresh go of things somewhere," she added. "Ain't no good speculatin' just now." She glanced over at George and me. Francine and Amber were also listening in. Their heads were poking out from their bedroom, no doubt where they'd been sent when the strange man arrived so Aunt Emma could have a private talk. "What've you boys been up to?" she asked us. It was probably half to change the conversation and half genuine curiosity.

"We went chicken hunt'n again," George said. The strange man gave us a strange look. I suppose it did sound funny to someone who didn't know about the wild chickens in the woods.

"Well, it don't look like y'all fared none too better," she said.

"It was that Leghorn again. He's meaner than a cornered bobcat," I said. "But George nearly walloped him good. We almost caught 'em. Had him under the milk crate and everything, but he was too big. He knocked it over and had at us again. Ole George gave him a good run, though."

She gave a half-hearted smile, "Well, I think you boys need to leave them things be before you lose an eye. And speaking of which, where is my good crate?"

George and I looked at each other. During the melee, neither of us had thought to grab the crate. Aunt Emma saw it on our faces, though, and didn't seem too upset. "If'n you boys do go messin' around out there again, I expect my crate to be returned. Anyhow, now, why don't y'all get cleaned up and ready for supper. There's some fresh water already out by the back door."

I wasn't too keen on buckets these days, but thankful I didn't have to go near the well. After two bad experiences, I was beginning to acquire quite the phobia about them. We got cleaned up, stinging some more with that lye sap, and then went inside. Aunt Emma had slaughtered some of her own chickens and two of them were laid out with cornbread and butter milk. An extra place was set for the mystery guest. I still didn't have any idea of who he was until after we had finished eating and cleared the table.

He came over to me and said, "I reckoned we'd have us a talk outside."

And then he proceeded out the front door to the porch. I wasn't quite sure what to make of him, but when I looked over at Aunt Emma she gestured that I should follow him.

We occupied the two wooden chairs Uncle Colby had made himself. They were sturdy, being both made of oak and big and wide. When I scooted myself all the way back in the chair my feet barely touched the ground. The man pulled out a stick of tobacco from his pants and a pocket knife. He cut himself a big chaw and placed it between his lips and gum.

"I'm your Uncle Marcus," he explained. There was a good pause after that as though he expected some kind of an answer.

"Mama's told me about you," I finally said. She didn't tell me much, though. Just that she had a brother who used to live in Houston but now lived in Galveston, and that her own Mama and sister lived there, too. He worked for the railroad or something like that. I knew that most folks in town figured Mama went to live with him. "My Mama and Sarah ain't gone to Galveston, have they?" Would he be here if they had? I asked myself.

"They hadn't shown up as of yesterday when I struck out to come here," he told me. He had been looking off in the fading sunset but turned his attention directly on me,

"Caught me a train to Houston last evening and then come in on y'all's this morning. You reckon your Mama and sister intended to go all the way to Galveston in that wagon 'stead of the train?" he asked.

I could feel my legs start to bounce up and down on their own.

"Dunno. Mama didn't say nothin' to me before she left. Nothin' at all," I said. I was half-tempted to tell him what I really thought, but he was kind of intimidating and I just didn't feel comfortable enough with him to start talking about ghosts and things.

He gave a spat that cleared the railing of the porch. It sailed clear over it onto the ground beyond. It was a heck of a spit, and a twelve year old notices things like that. "I know I ain't been much of an Uncle to you," he said. "Last time I saw your sister, she was just a baby. And truth be told I ain't never seen you when you was younger." It didn't seem the kind of thing I was supposed to respond to, so I didn't. "How's things been over at y'all's place? Before your Mama left, I mean."

He kicked one leg over the other and grabbed George's stick that had been placed by the chairs before George and I had gone into the house. He started whittling a curving line at the top of it with his knife like I'd seen Pap do so many times.

"I reckon things was fine," I told him.

"Your Mama and daddy been fighting much?" he asked.

It wasn't too difficult finding the answer for that one. "Sometimes. Pap got a temper on him, but Mama ain't much for starting arguments, or nothin'."

"Your daddy been hitting' on her any?" he asked in the same monotone voice, as though asking about the weather.

"No, sir," I answered.

This strange uncle of mine gave me a looking over as if trying to gauge the honesty of my answer, but he seemed content. "What about you?" he asked, "Does he hit you around?"

"Sometimes, mainly when he's drinking or I act out of hand," I told him. From some weird place within myself I suddenly felt the need to stick up for Pap a bit. I didn't have a clue where Mama and Sarah had gone off to that night, and certainly had come to believe they probably didn't go of their own accord. None of it made much sense, except that the strange things I'd seen led me to believe the worst may have happened. But as bad as Pap was, it was hard to image him doing what my thoughts said he might have, so I didn't want to come out and tell this man what I really believed. And part of me was still in denial, maybe. I told myself, the horse and wagon were gone, and so were all their things. It's not impossible they just left somewhere and the things I'd seen were just some weird workings of my mind. If Sarah hadn't been born quite right, maybe neither had I. I knew I was just trying to talk myself into believing those thoughts, though, and it wasn't working.

"You talk to your daddy, lately?" he questioned.

"No, sir. I've been stayin' here near on three weeks now, and only seen him once. Aunt Emma had George and me take some lunch over to Mr. Pyle's place for Uncle Colby, and I seen Pap then, but he didn't say much to me, though. He just asked how I was over at Aunt Emma's house and whether or not I was behavin'. I told him I was and he said that was good. That was it."

Another long pause came and went before he asked me, "You love your daddy?" I didn't expect him to ask me that. That was a hell of a question for some stranger to just come right out and ask me, but now that he had, I realized I wasn't quite sure.

"He's my Pap," I said, as if though that answered sufficiently.

I guess it did, because the man kind of nodded a little and then changed the subject, "How'd you get all those cuts on yah?" he asked, pointing to all the scratches, new and old, that I had received from

Lucifer the Leghorn.

"Chicken," I told him. I saw his eyebrows raise as though he thought I must be the weakest boy there ever was to get covered in cuts like that by a chicken. "Meanest rooster in creation, I reckon," I added quickly. "We call him Lucifer the Leghorn. He's wild and out in the woods with some other chickens. Me and George been trying to catch some of them, but only times we've gotten close he come at us. We nearly caught him, himself, today, though. But he got loose and scratched me up again."

My uncle didn't smile, and didn't frown. He pretty much didn't react at all, but something about his mood seemed a little lighter. I think if things with Mama might have been different, maybe he would've laughed, but things were as they were. Instead, he said something I wouldn't have guessed he'd say in a million years, "I'm in town for a bit. I reckon tomorrow I'll show you boys how to catch that rooster." He stood up and said, "If you want, I mean."

"Sure," I told him. "That'd be just fine."

And with that the conversation ended. He went back inside and he and Uncle Colby brought out some of the whiskey he had stashed away from Aunt Emma's judgment. She knew he had it, of course, and even dipped into it herself now and then when she had a cold. She reckoned they could use a drink, anyhow. Neither of them were big drinkers, not like Pap, but it might ease some old tensions between them and help the conversation a bit. They stayed up late talking into the night while the rest of the house went to bed.

Chapter 10

The next morning Uncle Marcus wasn't at breakfast. Aunt Emma told me that she had sent him a telegram just a day or two after Mama left to let him know she might be on the way and to ask for some word if she should arrive. Since Mama and Sarah never did, Uncle Marcus thought it best he make a trip to Varner Creek. He was staying over at Miss Thomas' in town seeing as how she had a large home and a room to spare. There aren't many people she'd of done that for, but she was fond of all the Stotleys, and Uncle Marcus was unquestionably an acceptable occupant, especially under the circumstances.

Not long after breakfast he showed up at Aunt Emma's again. He came riding up on the same glorious horse that had been munching on oats the night before. Francine made a comment on how handsome he was. I thought she meant the horse but Amber knew better, and she teased her about it, "Eeeeew, he's our Uncle," she said.

"So?" answered Francine, "Just 'cause he's handsome don't mean I want to kiss him or anything. He's just a nice looking man, is all." And Amber had to agree with the assessment.

Uncle Colby had expressed the need for a bit more quiet that morning at breakfast, obviously nursing a slight hangover as it had been a while since he'd drank so much. It probably hit him harder than he expected, I guess. I was used to being quiet in respect of hangovers, anyway. And Uncle Colby was much better with handling his than Pap was. Pap would curse and complain, and if I was being too loud, give me his backhand upside my head to shut me up. Uncle Colby just downed about three glasses of water while nibbling on two pieces of bread. He couldn't even seem to look at his eggs, so the rest of his breakfast sat untouched when he left for work.

When Uncle Marcus arrived, though, he looked no worse for the late night and strong drink. He told Aunt Emma he had intended on spending some time with George and me today and asked if it'd be all right if he borrowed their rooster. She thought it a bit of an odd request, but said that as long as he brought him back like he took him, it'd be fine.

"Come on, boys. I'll show you how you catch that chicken what's been giving you all the problems," he told us.

George and I were both excited. We couldn't for the life of us figure out how George's rooster was going to help us catch Lucifer the Leghorn, but Uncle Marcus seemed so nonchalant about the whole thing, we figured he had some kind of chicken wisdom we lacked. We all three went outside and Uncle Marcus put George's rooster in a burlap sack with his feet sticking out. Then he carried him upside down like his feet were handles. The rooster was none too happy about it, but he couldn't do anything but cluck and complain, since he couldn't find himself a way to get upright again. One of his chicken legs kept kicking and he was trying in vain to stretch his wings inside the sack. Uncle Marcus then took some more of Uncle Colby's twine and George's stick from yesterday, the same one he had whittled on a bit last night to keep his hands occupied, and we set out.

"Y'all go ahead and show me about where those chickens are at," he told us. So we led him through the woods. This time George and I were optimistic. There was something about having Uncle Marcus' quiet strength with us that led us to believe victory was assured. It took a good long time to find the chickens again, though. They had crept back even further into the woods. No doubt Lucifer the Leghorn had decided to put some more distance between his harem and the invaders. Hardly any words passed between us and Uncle Marcus. George quietly whispered his curiosity about what Uncle Marcus and I had talked about. "Did you tell him about seeing you know who?" he asked in a barely audible voice.

"No, I reckon he'd just think that crazy talk," I told George. Although I hadn't seen Sarah since that night I roused the house, she was never far from my thoughts. I looked for her in the night and thought about her nearly all the time, but still hadn't seen her again.

While we walked Uncle Marcus had me carry the rooster, who was still loudly protesting. He seemed preoccupied in his own thoughts and walked quietly. He was making use of his hands, however. He had taken out his pocketknife and was cutting some of the twine into three foot sections. When he had four of them he made each one into a slipknot noose. We were walking along, George and me whispering, Uncle Marcus tying, when we heard a loud crow. Our own rooster answered back in a half-hearted attempt and we stopped in our tracks.

"That must be him," I told Uncle Marcus.

"All right then," he said, "George, gimme your stick."

George reluctantly handed over his only defense from the evil rooster, figuring Uncle Marcus must be getting ready to go after Lucifer the Leghorn himself. Instead, though, Uncle Marcus kicked a little hole in the dirt with the heel of his boot and then jammed the stick into it. He pressed all his body weight against the top of the stick and then twisted it around until it sank down several inches into dirt. Then he had me fetch a rock off a ways and used it to knock the stick down even further. He tied one end of his little nooses to the stick all around it. George and I looked at each other dumbfounded. We had no clue what in the world he was up to. Lastly, he took George's poor rooster and with the last bit of twine tied him to the top of the stick, just about two feet off the ground, letting him hang there in the bag. "That'll do it," Uncle Marcus told us.

"Do what?" asked George.

"Y'all come sit over here with me and watch," he said.

We backtracked with Uncle Marcus about twenty yards away from George's rooster that was now miserably strung up, still squawking and complaining. He let out a little crow and immediately from up beyond in the denser trees came a blasting answer from Lucifer the Leghorn. Uncle Marcus took out his tobacco and cut off a piece and placed it in his mouth. "Roosters don't like any competition," he told us. "When I wasn't too much older than you boys I went to work for a man name Mr. Wilkins. He's passed on now, but he used to fight roosters for sport. But don't go repeatin' that. He taught me this little trick here on how to catch a troublesome rooster." We sat in awe trying to imagine how George's rooster was going to catch Lucifer the Leghorn for us. For a few minutes nothing happened. Just some more clucking from the one in the bag, and occasionally a much louder and stronger answer from somewhere in the distance. Abruptly, though, a big feathery thing with huge wings came darting in towards the rooster on a stick. Even Uncle Marcus seemed startled at the speed of his approach. Leave it to Lucifer the Leghorn for a grand entrance. Again, there wasn't any tentative hopping in or cautious curiosity. Personally, I think he knew we were invading his territory yet again, this time bringing in another rooster, and he was pissed off. He shot in quick as a snake ready to inflict his vengeance for the invasion, but he never noticed George and me crouching by the bushes, and a bit behind Uncle Marcus if I'm to be perfectly honest, he went straight for the burlap sack with George's chicken. Lucifer the Leghorn was nearly twice the size of our bagged rooster who was bleating like a pig being slaughtered. It was something to see. That devil chicken was going absolutely berserk trying to get at poor George's rooster, furiously attacking at the bag again and again.

"What do we do now?" George asked Uncle Marcus.

"Nothin'," he responded, "Just watch. He'll get himself tangled nice and good, and then he's caught."

Sure enough, that's exactly what happened. Somehow or another

Lucifer the Leghorn managed to get one of his wings stuck in a noose. The more he hopped and pulled, the tighter it got. Then one of his feet got stuck. And before we knew it he was caught up in twine fighting like mad. One second he was fighting to get at our rooster, and the next he was fighting to get free of the nooses, then back to trying to get at the bagged rooster again. He was just about as mad as I've ever seen a critter, but it wasn't no good. Before long he was exhausted and completely tethered to George's stick. He'd almost managed to pull it free from the ground, but got tired out before finishing the job.

"Got to let him wear hisself out before you go trying to manage him," Uncle Marcus explained. "But he looks good and tired now. We'll use them other two nooses to tie his legs and wings so he doesn't get free and can't scratch."

George and I were beside ourselves. There he was, the king of the woods, our captive. Uncle Marcus had made it all look so easy. He'd done in ten minutes and without hardly any effort what George and I had spent all day yesterday trying to figure out how to do. And Uncle Marcus didn't have so much as a scratch on him. By the time we got to Lucifer the Leghorn, he could barely hop at us to attempt a good slash. He was still mad as ever, but the fight was out of him. Uncle Marcus used his pocketknife to cut the other two slipknots loose and bundled up the angry chicken. George's own rooster stopped squirming around like it had keeled over and died, but Uncle Marcus said it was fine. And when we carried our prize back through the woods towards home George's chicken started clucking and crowing again. He had nerves of steel once it seemed obvious the much bigger rooster couldn't get at him anymore.

It was quite a contemplation to figure out the fate of Lucifer the Longhorn. When we got him home that day Aunt Emma was shocked. She had never seen a rooster that big in her entire life. "Well, we ain't keeping that thing," she announced right away.

Both George and I protested. He was our captive, after all. Even if it took Uncle Marcus to make him that way. "But Mama, look at him. He's the grandest rooster there is," whined George.

Francine and Amber both agreed with Aunt Emma. They had a couple of puppies they had gotten from the Radtke farm down the way, and they didn't like the new rooster one bit. "Mama, that thing will kill Boots for sure," cried Amber, speaking on behalf of her own puppy, named so because of his white paws.

"Not if we keep him in a pen," I said.

"What good is a rooster you can't let out?" said Aunt Emma. "And besides, I don't want to have to worry about that beast tearing me and the girls up. I'm with child if I need to remind you all. I can't be botherin' with a thing like this here rooster lookin' to get at me any chance it gets. You boys may enjoy such things, but personally I'd rather not have to fight a wild chicken like that every day just to get clothes out on the line or feed the animals. Nope," she said with conviction, "he most definitely goes."

Uncle Marcus suggested making dinner out of him, but George and I both couldn't endure the thought of it. As much as we wanted to keep him, we both had rather let him go than see him served up for dinner. He was too fine an example of a rooster for that and probably would've been tough as a boot, so it was decided that we'd keep him that night, and the next day George and I would let him free back in the woods.

Uncle Marcus stayed around that afternoon talking with Aunt Emma. Around five or so he headed to town saying there were some other folks he wanted to visit with. I wondered if the sheriff was one of the individuals, but I didn't ask.

When Uncle Colby came home that evening for supper he asked Aunt Emma, "Where'd that rooster come from?" Lucifer the Leghorn had been penned up by himself in the chicken coup. George's rooster was taunting him from a safe distance and Lucifer the Leghorn had been crowing so loudly in anger that Uncle Colby said he could hear him clear over at the Pyle's farm. Aunt Emma replayed the day's events for him and he immediately had the solution, "Well, I know someone who'd love to have that thing."

"Who would want that monstrosity?" Aunt Emma asked.

"Mr. Pyle," Uncle Colby said. "He's always looking for the biggest roosters." He caught himself saying a little too much. Mr. Pyle was a respected member of the community, and even though cock-fighting was a common practice, good Christian folks weren't supposed to indulge in such barbaric past-times. Mr. Pyle, however, had a weakness for the betting and excitement. He had himself had a few short-lived cock-fighting winners, but nothing special. Lucifer the Leghorn, however, could be just what he needed to rectify that. Aunt Emma didn't pry into why Mr. Pyle was always looking for roosters like the horrid one outside, though. She respected him too much to acknowledge such moral weaknesses in his character.

The next morning broke out in a ruckus of crowing. It was like the two outside were having a competition. Aunt Emma and Uncle Colby's family rooster let out his routine morning cry, only to be severely outdone in volume and intensity by Lucifer the Leghorn. And remarkably, when Uncle Colby spread out the morning corn and mash for the chickens on his way out to work, there seemed to be a number of more additions. Hens they'd never seen before came scratching and pecking along just like the ones that had been born and raised there. Uncle Colby went back inside and fetched Aunt Emma. "What in the world?" she said when she came out the back door. "Where'd they come from?"

George and I came out and recognized them immediately, "They're the ones from the woods," George said.

"Well, what in the Sam hell are they doing here?" she asked.

"Reckon they heard him hollering," Uncle Colby said, gesturing towards the extremely perturbed rooster in the pen. "I heard him all the way from the fields yesterday. I don't wonder that they did, too."

"Well, God bless," said Aunt Emma, "Ain't no telling what infestations they done brought with them." But she seemed pleased at suddenly having a dozen more full size hens to get eggs from. She threw together some concoction to kill whatever the wild chickens had spread to her good ones, as she was convinced they had, and as they pecked away at the ground she ran around singing, "Here, chick, chick, chick . . . here chick," trying to douse all of them, hers and the new ones, with the powder. Even after Uncle Colby took Lucifer the Leghorn out of the pen, earning himself some deep scratches in the process, the hens stayed at Aunt Emma's house from that day forward. I guess the easy food was too much temptation to leave even after their great leader disappeared yet again.

Uncle Colby took Lucifer the Leghorn to Mr. Pyle, and the present only served to deepen his good graces. "That's the finest cock-fighting rooster I did ever see," he told Uncle Colby.

And from that day on, Lucifer the Leghorn became known as Pyle's Pride. He fought thirty-two cock-fights in his life, at least official ones with bets and all, there was no telling how many he truly fought in his life, and he won every one of them. People talked about that rooster, years after he was gone. And whenever a particularly large and fierce rooster fought and won, someone would say, "Like Pyle's Pride that one is." And pride is exactly what the rooster gave Mr. Pyle until the end of his own days. He always seemed to walk around with a little smile, privately enjoying the thought of the next cockfight and his impending victories.

Chapter 11

After the experience with the chickens I'd started feeling better about Uncle Marcus. He was still a stranger to me, but now that he'd managed to reach heroism in my eyes, I was less intimidated by him. If he'd of pulled me aside to ask me about things again, I would have at least told him my suspicions, even if not the reason for them. As it was, though, Uncle Marcus wasn't around after that day.

I hadn't heard much about Pap during the past weeks up until Pyle's Pride began his new life of glory. Aunt Emma had told me Uncle Marcus hadn't visited Pap and didn't want anyone to mention to Pap that he was in town. It seemed peculiar to me, though, seeing how Uncle Marcus was willing to question everyone except Pap, the one person who might actually know something he wasn't sharing, but I didn't know anything of their history together, yet.

A few days after Uncle Marcus had come to Varner Creek he left again. Not for good, though. He took the midday train that went back up to Houston on that day, some travel once there. He wanted to see if maybe Mama had gone to Houston and he might find her. Perhaps she had gone there to catch a train to Galveston, he thought. Maybe she even forgot he didn't live there anymore and was up there looking for him.

Once there he sent a message to his wife, Mary Jo, via telegram. There was the phone system, the state's first line being from Houston to Galveston back in 1883, but he wasn't fond of phones with everybody listening to everybody, so he didn't have one at home. Instead, he liked the tried and true method of telegrams. He knew he'd have to get a phone sooner or later, though, because Mary Jo and the kids were complaining about living in the dark ages, but he'd just as soon put it off as long as possible.

He had told his wife to expect the message on that day and wanted to know if she had heard anything from Annie. By this time we had a station in Varner Creek, too, but he mainly made the trip to look around the city for Mama and Sarah, just in case. He went by the telegram station and then and had an early supper in a nearby restaurant. The telegram station was still open when he finished and there was a return message waiting for him:

Sister not here. (Stop) No news. (Stop) Will send word if changes. (Stop) When will you return? (Stop) Love, Mary Jo. (Stop)

He read the message and crumpled it in frustration. He had been hoping Annie arrived just after he left and his concerns had been completely unjustified, but he knew his wife would have sent word to Varner Creek if that had been the case, and his worries were mounting. After reading the telegram he began going over the possibilities again in his mind. Did Annie make a fresh start somewhere else? No, if so she still would have written Emma, at least. And leaving her son behind was not the sister he had known in childhood. So what else could it be? If Abram had done something to her and was trying to cover it up, he was doing a remarkable job. He couldn't have just stashed the horse and wagon somewhere. By now somebody would have noticed, unless he manage to sell them in a town nearby and gotten rid of Annie and Sarah's belongings. But if he had finally crossed the line with Annie, what about Sarah? Things just weren't adding up. What was he missing? Annie didn't just fall off the face of the earth. Where was she? Why hadn't anybody heard from her in over three weeks? He knew he couldn't stay in Varner Creek forever. He had a family at home and work that needed to be done. He had always been frugal and had plenty of money saved, but every day he was gone was a day he risked his reputation with the railroad company and the others in town who came to him for specialty items. He had spent years building up a reputation as a reliable and excellent craftsman. He'd be doing wrong as a provider for his own family by turning his back on that reputation. Still, he blamed himself for the situation. He remembered his own father being content just to have the kids gone as soon as possible. He felt like it had fallen to him to protect his sister from making the mistakes that had led to this, and he had failed her. And even now, their own mother was practically disinterested in the mysterious disappearance of her middle daughter. She was worried and wanted word of events, but all her attention and devotion was placed on her grandchildren, both Marcus' and Candace's, who had married an architect there in Galveston the year before, 1908, and just had her first baby. His were bright and beautiful children, proper and respectable, the kind of children Mrs. Stotley had always wanted. She was worried for Annie, but she'd always felt like her two daughters had done wrong in the eyes of the Lord, and that kept her at a distance.

Marcus contemplated all these things as the telegram operator attempted to politely encourage him to leave. It was dusk and time to close the office. "Had a bite to eat at the inn, eh?" he asked Marcus,

"Reckon I'm ready to get home and do the same. Been a long day." He smiled encouragingly at Marcus, who wasn't paying him much attention. "Well, sir? Anything else I can do for yah before I close up?" asked the man.

"Yes," said Marcus, without much more attention than before, "Please send the following." And Uncle Marcus dictated a return telegram to his wife:

Miss You. (Stop) But must sort things here. (Stop) Will return in a few days. (Stop) Marcus. (Stop)

He wanted to tell his wife he loved her and for her to tell the children the same, but it wasn't in Marcus' nature to express such things to the stranger who was tapping out the telegram for him. He knew it went without saying, anyway. He and his wife had never been apart before now, not for more than a day or two, at most.

Marcus stayed the night in a hotel and the next day rode Geronimo all around the city asking about Annie and Sarah. Nobody had seen a little retarded girl with a woman at the train stations, or the hotels he went to, or the churches. He looked everywhere he could think to look but it was the same no matter where he went. "No, sir, haven't seen nobody like that," or "sorry, not been here." It was all the same chorus. A city full of people and yet to him it was an empty as a ghost town, because Annie and Sarah weren't among them.

As the next day ended he decided to go back to Varner Creek, but not to take the train. He'd follow a line of travel Annie might have taken if she had come this way in the wagon with Sarah. He'd check all the towns from here to there to see if anyone remembered their passing through. So thinking this, he left that very same evening.

It'd take two days to get back if he stopped at all the towns on the way, but it was the last thing he could think to do. He'd camp out under the stars tonight. He wanted solitude to think as he slowly trotted out of the city. He had become accustomed to the modern things in the world. The telephones in the hotels and the automobiles here and there humming along the streets weren't the first he'd seen. Model T's were just now gaining popularity from the Ford Company, but Galveston always had the newest things. But as much as he was used to them, tonight he felt bothered by them all.

There was something like a maggot in his stomach, a small thing, but one that was making him sick thinking about it moving around inside himself. It was a feeling of guilt eating at him from the inside. He had abandoned Annie to that man, he thought. He should have done more, but at the time he was so preoccupied with the metal working and courting Mary Jo that he had made the decision he would worry about his own life and let her worry about hers. If she was stupid enough to get mixed up with the likes of Abram Mayfield, let her, he had thought at the time. Now he was the one who felt stupid. Stupid and selfish, he admonished himself. He was the older brother and she was just a child at the time. He had failed her. If she did arrive in Galveston, he wouldn't give her the cold shoulder anymore, he told himself. He'd welcome her, Sarah, and Sol all in with open arms, even help them get their own home like he had done with mother and Candace. He'd take care of all of them, by God. If she came. If she was still okay and could come. The maggot in his stomach squirmed. He sat atop Geronimo at a trot, and then gave him a prod in the ribs so the horse took off into the night at full speed, away from the city, away from his guilt.

All the next day he heard the same song he'd heard in Houston. Nobody had seen someone like that come through. She hadn't been here, they all said. It was like Annie and Sarah had fallen off the face of the Earth. And on the second day out from Houston, that last thirty miles that was the day's ride home, he'd hear it all again.

Chapter 12

My nights after Uncle Marcus first arrived at Aunt Emma's house passed without incident. Sarah did not visit me, and part of me was beginning to wish she would. If she and Mama were alive and well somewhere, just making a new life for themselves, then it would have meant I had imagined her face that night, her footprints beside my bed. It would mean that truly I had been left behind and Mama simply didn't want me in her life anymore. Maybe she looked at the son and saw the man who had robbed her of her innocence and hope. Was I my father's son? I had always thought of myself more like Mama, of course. I didn't see myself as having a mean streak. I never went into rages like him. But maybe it was there, hiding under the surface and she could see it when she looked at me. I couldn't help questioning myself. I didn't want to believe they were dead, but I didn't want to believe she'd left me behind on purpose. There was just no way things were going to come out right, I thought.

But on the night before Geronimo was walking those last thirty miles back to Varner Creek, my dreams were dark. Since things had been quiet again for a bit, George was back to sleeping peacefully. His deep breath was in rhythm and untroubled. I, too, fell into sleep easily enough, but as I slept I felt myself going into a dark place. I felt cold again, and scared and lonely. In my dreams I felt myself being placed somewhere under water. I could feel it creep in around me. It soaked in through my skin and wherever I was, something held me down, sinking me to the bottom. I felt my face against the silt as my body came to rest. When I opened my eyes I was face to face with Sarah. Again there was a dim green illumination, not a real light, but something manifested and unnatural. At first I didn't recognize the person next to me. All I could see was black hair swirling about a white fleshy face. The skin was nearly picked off her features and her eyes were hollowed out. There were no lips, only her teeth and the bottom of her jawbone poking out from spongy tissue. I noticed one of her front teeth was badly chipped, almost all the way down to the root. There was little human about what was in front of me, but as the light moved about her I could see, like an overlapping photograph, her face as I'd known slowly emerge. First came the eyes. From somewhere within the empty sockets they grew and appeared, their blue the only color except for the green shining in this black place. Lips came in, then flesh over the muscle of her cheeks, and then the face became animated. She had been lifelessly resting on the silt like me until then, but as she came back to herself, the neck twisted and the eyes opened to meet mine. I could feel her hand, the bony hand of a corpse at first, close around my own. As it did it became plump and real. She clenched me urgently and her lips made a word.

"Sol," they said.

She was so happy to see me, and I felt happy, too. We were together again. We'd found each other in the blackness.

As we held hands I felt her being pulled away from me again, and I held on tight to keep her with me. Her blue eyes pleaded with me and I was taken aback at how piercing they seemed. They had never had such expression. They had always been happy and somewhat oblivious. Now they were directed and keen. They were like Uncle Marcus' eyes when first I saw him sitting next to Aunt Emma.

"Where are you?" I asked her. "I don't know where you've gone," I practically cried.

She said something, her lips moving, but I had trouble making it out.

I could feel myself losing her. "Where have you gone?" I asked. "Where's Mama?" Her eyes still pleaded with me. She was being pulled back into the darkness and didn't want to go. I felt her fear like I felt the cold water about me, but as hard as I held on to her, I couldn't keep her with me. "Sarah!" I said. "Sarah!"

George woke me up. It was still night, but he was shoving me and calling out to me, "Sol, wake up!"

It was like being pulled out of a hole by the back of your neck, a quick yank.

Everything I had seen and felt was gone. Sarah was gone, the water, the green glow, nothing was here but the small room and George sitting up in the moonlight. "What?" I asked.

"You were calling out to her in your sleep," he told me.

"She was trying to tell me where she was," I told him.

"Sarah?" he asked with a quiver in his voice. "She was here?"

"I don't think so," I told him. "I think I was wherever she is this time."

"But you were here," he told me. "You were just having a bad dream."

"I know," I said. "But in my dreams I was wherever she is. I can't tell it right, but I was with her even though I was still here."

"Where's she at?" he asked.

I thought about the place again, the black water. My hand felt clammy and I held it up to the moonlight that arched over the bed. The tips of my fingers were pruney as though I'd been sitting in a tub. It was somewhere very dark, where not even the faintest light by stars could reach, and somewhere under cold water. Then I had it. "I think I know where she is," I told him. "She's at home," I said. "She's been there the whole time."

The next morning after breakfast I pulled Uncle Colby aside. I waited until he was outside about to go to work and followed after him, "I think I gotta go home today," I told him.

"Hmmm," he said, "I'm not sure that's such a good idea, Sol. Things ain't so good with your Pap just now. He ain't been showing up to work regular, and when he does, he's been in an awful mood. He's taken to drinking more than usual. I done had to warn him Mr. Pyle's gettin' unhappy with it, but I reckon it's hard having your Mama gone and people talking and all. I don't think your Aunt would be keen on the idea you moving back jus' now, neither."

"I don't mean go back to stay there," I said. "I've been having feelings, lately." It was difficult figuring out just how to explain things so I didn't seem out of my gourd, "Been having dreams, you could say. I think sumthin' bad done happened to Mama and Sarah."

There was a look of awkward pity on his face like he wasn't sure what he was supposed to say or do, "Your Aunt done told me you've been thinkin' so. But I reckon ain't none of us should have them kinds of thoughts," he said.

"It's not like that, Uncle Colby," I tried to explain. "I've been seeing Sarah. I mean really seeing her, like she's there. I think she's been trying to tell me something."

Have you ever had somebody say something you just wished they had never said because it made you feel so uncomfortable you wanted to just run off and pretend you'd never heard it? That was Uncle Colby at that moment. He seemed to shift uneasily in his own skin before saying, "Not too sure what to say, Sol."

"I know how it sounds, Uncle Colby. And I swear I ain't gone crazy or nothin'. I'm only tellin' yah 'cause I want you to come with me."

"And do what?" he asked.

"I think maybe Sarah's in our well at home," I told him. "I think she's there under thc water."

His eyes looked over me like he was taking measure and he shuffled his boots in the dirt for a bit, "Well, look here, Sol. It ain't that I think you're crazy, but maybe this has all been kind of hard for a young 'un," he said. It sounded like a no and he could see the disappointment in my eyes, which I guess had some affect. "But if it'll make you feel better, we'll go. I'll go with yah." Then he added quickly as though it had just struck him, "I don't see a need to be telling your Aunt, though. Let's just you and me have us a look. I reckon your daddy will be in to work today, least he's 'sposed to, and I'll come home round noontime if he is and we'll go out there when he's not home. That way the sun'll be directly up and to our advantage."

"Okay," I agreed. I looked at him with genuine gratitude. I couldn't have gone out there by myself, I don't think. And George would have been just as afraid as me if we had gone out there and found Sarah in the well, especially if Pap ended up being home and drunk as a skunk.

When Uncle Colby had left, George and I decided to go down by the creek for a bit. We found a spot under a heavily wooded area and watched the fish pop up here and there, the rings of ripples expanding outward sporadically in the calm waters. "So you're gonna go see if she's there?" he asked me. I had told him about my conversation with Uncle Colby.

"Yeah," I said. "Reckon I need to."

"You really think that's where she is? This whole time she's been down the well?"

"I don't know for sure, but it seems like the mostly likely place from what I remember about my dream." I looked up and watched a buzzard circling in the sky.

"I hope you don't find nothing," George said. "I hope Aunt Annie and her found some place nice and are just waiting to get settled before they come and get you like Mama says." His eyes showed the truth of his words, "I'd miss you if you went away to live, though," he said. "It's been like having a brother. Francine and Amber always give me a hard time."

"Thanks," I told him. "You've been like one, too." I tried not to dwell on what may or may not be down the well at home, so I pointed up at the bird in the sky and asked, "You reckon Mr. Pyle's Pride could whoop that buzzard?"

George was quick on the subject, "No contest!" he said, "That buzzard would be a meal for some of his kin if'n Lucifer the . . . I mean Pyle's Pride got a holt of 'em." We had a nice what if conversation to pass the time.

I was back at Aunt Emma's helping out with the chores when Uncle Colby came home. George and I were sifting the bag of chicken feed trying to get the little weevils out of it. It seemed to me the chickens would be just as happy to eat the bugs as the corn, but Aunt Emma insisted that left on their own they'd spread to everything and before you knew it the whole house would be crawling with them. She was outside hanging laundry when she saw Uncle Colby coming from across the way. At first she held one hand over her eyes and the other on her hip as though she were trying to figure out who was coming for a visit. It was unlike Uncle Colby to come home in the middle of the day. Normally, when he was working at Mr. Pyle's, he stayed all day until the light was lost.

"What're you doing back at this time?" she asked him when he was within earshot.

"Sol wants to go get something over at Annie's," he told her. It wasn't entirely a lie. It just happened to be my dead sister I wanted to go and get from out of the well. Uncle Colby had called my old home Annie's place simply out of habit, even though Mama hadn't been there in nearly a month.

"What's he want from over there?" she asked disapprovingly.

I had heard the conversation from the henhouse and answered for him. "A book," I told her as I walked over to them. It was the first thing I could think of. "One of them that Miss Thomas brought for me and Sarah."

She looked over at me like a skeptical mother, "A book? Well, Sol, honey, I don't reckon I remember seeing any books when we was there. Looked to me like your Mama took them with her." Aunt Emma was still stuck in eternal optimism, or denial one.

"I think I saw one in the kitchen next to the stove," I entirely lied. I supposed a fib was inevitable and it might as well have been me that told it. Aunt Emma had made me a quick meal in the kitchen that day she came to get me, but it was one of the only places she hadn't gone over with a fine toothed comb, so it seemed the best place to put an imaginary book that I knew wasn't there.

"Well, I declare I would have seen such a thing," she said, "but reckon maybe not." She looked like she was trying to see the kitchen again in her memory. "Is your Daddy gonna be home?" she asked me after failing to remember every nook and cranny of the kitchen in her mind.

"Naw, he's at work," said Uncle Colby flatly. We were officially conspirators, now. I scratched his back and now he scratched mine. At least he was still fib free, mostly.

That's how we won Aunt Emma over without even a battle, "Huh," she said, "Well, I guess there ain't no harm, then. But make sure y'all leave things like they is 'ceptin that book if you finds it. Ain't no sense lettin' Abram know y'all was in there when he not home if it ain't there. He might think we was trying to spy on him or somethin'," she told Uncle Colby. Besides, I think another thought must have struck Aunt Emma about a possible benefit to us going home because she snuck up close to Uncle Colby and said in a whisper, "And if anything looks funny over there, you make sure to take note of it."

He promised her he would and I promised we wouldn't ransack the house and risk having Pap fly off at the handle. Uncle Colby could handle him well enough but there wasn't much sense in any unnecessary confrontations. We walked along over the empty fields towards my home, or my old home as things were. Tobacco used to grow in the fields here, but they hadn't been tended or worked in years. Uncle Colby didn't say much as we walked, and the silence was too loud for me.

"I do appreciate you coming with me, Uncle Colby," I said. "Reckon I'm a bit scared."

My walk fell in step with his, but his stride was long and I had to stretch to keep pace. "Might not should be thinking such things, Sol, but I understand you got an itch needs scratchin'. My guess is ain't nothing' there, but if it helps you feel better, I don't see no harm in it."

I knew he didn't believe me about seeing Sarah. He probably thought I had either imagined it or talked myself into believing it. It didn't matter, though. He had come with me and that was enough for me to be in his debt in my mind.

When we reached the house it looked a little bit different than it did just a few weeks ago. Mama used to have a little cluster of flowers by the back door, but they were overrun with weeds now. It seemed as though they knew the keeper of the garden was no longer on duty. So was the vegetable garden. Little stalks of weeds that barely nipped at my ankles before were now over my waist. Dandelions were assaulting the squash and had nearly conquered the tomatoes.

We walked over to the well and Uncle Colby put both hands on either side and looked down into it. He had brought a thick and long rope with him. Looking carefully he seemed to take stock of its depth and width. "Well, ain't but one way to know what is and ain't down a well, and that's to get down in it. I reckon I could tie one end to that fence post over there," he said pointing to one of the posts of Lilipeg's old pen, "should hold me fine."

I looked at his broad shoulders and the well that would barely fit him.

"Naw," I said. "Uncle Colby, I'll climb down. I'm a lot smaller and if you was to get stuck or somethin', wouldn't be nothing I could do but to go fetch somebody. You could just yank me out quick as you please, though."

He poked his head back over the well, "I guess that'd be fine," he said. "Only 'cause I don't think there's anything down there to worry over."

We didn't need the fencepost with Uncle Colby holding fast. It was like tethering to an oak tree. I took off my clothes down to my cotton whities, and we tied the rope around my waist leaving a good ten feet off the end, which we put over the edge into the well. Then I climbed in and Uncle Colby began lowering me down without effort. It was spooky how the light faded so quickly. Just above it was midday and the sun was shining directly overhead as Uncle Colby had planned, but somehow the bottom of the well ate most of the light up, just as I'd imagined it would. It was precisely the reason I thought of the well . . . somewhere pitch dark and under water. When Mama and Pap bought the house the well had fallen in on itself. They had to have it dug out again and the black boys who had come to do it had put brick up the inside to keep the hole from collapsing again, but as I slowly went down I could see roots of various kinds poking out here and there and the bricks becoming slimy the lower I went. It wasn't a very deep well, really, but it was enough to make me feel like I had fallen into the earth. I felt the water kiss my toes as I slid into it. Goosebumps jumped up from my skin like a plucked hen in winter. The water came up just below my neck but before it reached any further I felt the bottom beneath my feet. It was an icky, gooey mess down there. My legs sank a few inches into a thick muck that sucked at me when I tried to move around. I looked up and could see Uncle Colby standing over the well when he felt the slack in the line. "You all right, there, Sol?" he called out.

"Yessir, I'm fine." I tried to peer into the water but it was too dark and murky to see anything. Instead I used the tried and true method of just walking around to see if anything was at the bottom, kind of like the noodlers do when they're looking for a catfish holed up. But I didn't feel anything. Just sticks, mud, and a build up of leaves and whatever else had found its way in. I made three or four good passes over the bottom making sure I covered it adequately. "You findin' anything?" Uncle Colby asked at length.

I had been so sure. My near drowning experience in the very bucket hanging next to me, seeing her head at Aunt Emma's well, the dreams. I thought for sure it had been her trying to tell me she was here in the dark water of this well. But she wasn't. "No, sir. She ain't here," I called up finally. "Sarah ain't in here." I felt relief, of course. Better that I should be a little crazy than my sister be drowned down a well. But at the same time a speck of me felt loss. I had been so sure the night before. What was she trying to tell me?

After satisfying myself that there was no way a person's body could be in that well without my having felt it, I called out to Uncle Colby to pull me up. The rope tightened around my waist uncomfortably and I went back up just as smooth as I had gone down.

We hadn't the foresight to bring anything to dry off with, so when I reached the top I just used my hand to try and press the water off of me. It worked well enough and I knew the Texas sun would finish the job before I walked back into Aunt Emma's kitchen. No book, we would tell her. Must have been mistaken. I took a few steps towards my clothes and felt a pinch beneath my left foot. I looked down as I pushed it away with a sweep of my leg and noticed it was smooth and white. I bent down to pick it up and then turned it around in my fingers. It didn't look like any of the other pebbles or small rocks strung about. And then it dawned on me. It wasn't a rock at all. It was part of a tooth. I remembered my dream and seeing the face torn from flesh before it became alive. Her left front tooth had been chipped down to the root. That's it! I thought.

"It's her tooth!" I cried out to Uncle Colby.

He was busy wrapping the rope back into a neat little circle, through his palm and around his elbow back again. "What'd you say?" he asked.

"Here! This is Sarah's tooth! I saw her in my dream and her left big tooth was cracked in half. Here it is, too, the other half." I held it up so that he could see it.

He walked over and took the foreign object in-between his thumb and index finger like I had, turning it over and around. "Sol, this here could be from anything."

There was no convincing me otherwise, though. I remembered that dream vividly, "No, that's it, Uncle Colby, I know it. She ain't in the well but somethin' sure enough happened out here. That's her tooth, I swear it is."

He gave it one last glance and handed it back, "Well, maybe we'll have Doctor Wilkins have a look at it if it'll make you feel better. But look like from an animal or somethin' to me." And I could see there wasn't going to be any persuading him to a contrary opinion. He had already humored me this far today, and been proven right in the process, so I didn't think I should be pressing my luck. "We bes' be getting on home, though," he said.

I got dressed and we started back, but as we walked I held the object in my hand pondering how it came to rest by the well. Maybe she had been in the well, her and Mama both, but maybe after the sheriff went and talked with Pap he got spooked and pulled them back out of there and did something else with them. That would make sense, I thought. If Pap had done it, he couldn't very well leave them there. The water would go bad, let alone the smell of death all around. They'd be found for sure. But if that was the case, what about all their things, and Lilipeg, and the wagon? Where could he hide those things?

As we walked I looked up into the sky and could see one of those buzzards gliding around on a breeze. I held the piece of tooth in my hand trying to imagine how it came to be there and what Sarah's ghost had been trying to tell me. I thought about those moments I'd seen her. What was different about those moments than the other times I was waiting for her? It was the water, of course. I thought she had been hinting at the well, but maybe it was something else. What was that odd feeling of searching I had when she had grabbed on to me? It was as though I was sharing her thoughts, or she was somehow putting hers in my head. She had been searching for me. Had I tried truly searching for her during these weeks? I'd thought of her often, but realized I hadn't actually sat down and tried just concentrating on finding her, not in the well or wherever she was physically at, but in that strange black place where the green light was. I hadn't tried looking there in my own thoughts. So as we walked I held on tight to the tooth, pressing down on it like it was my way into that other place, and I thought over and over again in my mind, Sarah, Sarah, I have to find Sarah. As my thoughts centered around her the piece of tooth in my hand suddenly seemed to get cold. I looked down at it thinking intently about Sarah's face with the chip in her tooth as I'd seen it in my dream, and all of a sudden a blinding light seemed to strike inside my head. It wasn't exactly painful, but it was like an egg had just hatched inside my brain. I saw the creek again, just like this morning, except this time I was a little further south on it. I recognized the spot immediately because Pap and I used to set out traps in the water there and catch the little blue crabs that would crawl in after a dead fish or chicken gizzards, whatever we had baited them with. It sat on a curve and there was a large willow tree that hung heavily over the creek. And under it the water had eroded some of the under soil, so that it created a big shelf over the water. Across the creek I suddenly had an image of Sarah, standing there in that green aura and pointing towards the bend in the creek at the natural shelf. She was mouthing something again, and it looked like "There," to me. Then she hovered right off of the riverbank, out over the water, and disappeared into the water beneath the overhang. Then I felt cold and I was under the water, too, looking into Sarah's eyes again as she pleaded with me. I understood. I knew now what she had been trying to tell me, and I tried to tell her so but the words wouldn't come. She seemed to understand, though, and as she faded away this time, she didn't seem to fight it. She'd finally done what she'd been trying to do all along. I knew where to find her now.

I felt myself being shaken roughly, and suddenly my eyes snapped back into reality to see Uncle Colby standing in front of me. He had his hands on my shoulders and was saying something. "Sol? You all right, boy? Sol? What's wrong with yah?"

My heart was racing and I turned my head to look southward where the creek was some mile or so. "She showed me," I said. "I know where she's at, now." And I slipped right out of his arms and took off at a run.

Uncle Colby stood dumbfounded for a moment, then he yelled out "Sol! Sol, where you running to?"

"The creek!" I yelled. "I know it, now!" And I kept running. I must have looked like a madman, but I didn't care. I was so fired up at finally understanding what had been going on that I felt like I was flying. I didn't know if Uncle Colby was behind me or not, and I knew that even with his long strides he wasn't going to be keeping up with me, but it didn't matter. I had seen it all clear as crystal in my mind, and I went as fast as I could go. As I ran I began to think about the consequences of my vision being true, and I realized I didn't want to be right. *Let me be crazy like Uncle Colby thinks*, I told myself. *She won't be there.* I ran out of steam three quarters of a way to the creek, but kept on at a quick walking pace. Part of me didn't want to take another step towards what I might find, but the rest of me was being pulled like an obsessed person. I had to know. A cramp in my side felt like someone had reached in and was yanking on my guts, but I kept going. I had to know if she was there, if everything I'd seen been real or not.

I reached the spot I had remembered from crab catching. There was the tree on the bend, and the shelf that jutted outward a few feet. I had to scramble through a bit of thickets to reach the tree and looking back I couldn't tell if Uncle Colby was coming or not. I didn't bother stripping down this time. I started down the steep embankment off to the side of the tree and slipped in some clay mud. My feet slid into the creek and I began wading around to the secret hollow. It was deeper there than I had thought, about five feet. I looked in through the overgrown grass and weeds that cascaded from the riverbank into water, and inside the hollow is was very black, but not very big. I took a deep breath and went in under the natural roof. My arms were stretched out before me and my eyes were shut tight. Immediately I felt something like wire down near the bottom. Then I felt a big stone. I followed the wire running from the stone and hit on something squishy and bony. It was the ankle of a leg. I could feel the panic in me overflowing. I pushed myself all the way into the hole-like place and with my other hand felt more debris. It seemed like rolled up wire mesh with some material like a blanket floating around. I tried grabbing it to pull, but it barely budged an inch. Whatever else was in there, it all seemed tangled up together. I swam back outside and came up for air. I didn't know if the salt I tasted on my lips was from the creek or the tears that began flowing down my face. My eyes were burning and I could hear myself making a high-pitched moan that was getting louder. I had worked myself into a frenzy, what with suddenly realizing I'd just found Sarah's body and the frustration of not being able to get it out. I tried to get some control over myself, but my emotions were all over the place and my breath wouldn't come despite being able to breathe air again. My chest was clamped and my throat wouldn't let air in. I was grief stricken and furious at the same time. I managed to make a few swallows to clear my throat and then let air fill up my lungs again. Then back into the black I went, this time determined that she would come back with me. I felt the cloth material again as well as wire, and this time instead of trying to pull up I pushed myself down and used my feet against the silt to pull her along. I could feel the stone move, now, and started sliding it out from under the shelf with me, but it was still so heavy I couldn't free whatever else she was mixed up with down there. Silt ran through my hands as I changed grip and I remembered my dream again. Of course it hadn't been the well. We were lying side by side facing each other in a cradled position. The well wasn't wide enough for that. And the clay silt was of an entirely different consistency than the muck at the bottom of our well at home. I popped my head out of the water again gasping for air, getting madder and madder at myself for not being strong enough to free her from that watery tomb. I was just about to dive again when I noticed legs standing at the side of the creek out of the corner of my eye. Uncle Colby was standing by the tree looking down at me with startled eyes.

"Sol, what the hell are you doing in there?"

"I got her!" I said, both in a yell and an angry sort of sob. "She's here, right under me, but I can't get her out!" I was going to prove to him I wasn't crazy this time if I had to haul him in myself to see.

His expression became wildly confused and he started into the creek. I got the sense he was probably coming in more to pull me out than because he believed me, but I wasn't leaving without Sarah. When he lost his balance right where I had and his legs fell in, I didn't wait on him to get back up and dove back down. I went back under again and pulled with all my strength, but still it just barely moved an inch. I was about to have to come back up for air again, but then I felt a big arm come down next to mine, groping under the water. It grabbed on me and I could tell he was going to pull me out of the water, so I grabbed the wire mesh. I felt his arm slide down to where my hands were, probably to undo my fingers, but then they hit the wire. He patted it once or twice to feel what it was, and then pulled. Finally, I came out of the water for the third time, coughing and breathing hard. I watched as Uncle Colby ducked under and a moment later he pulled the big rock out onto the bank with the strength I'd lacked. Sticking out of the water near the edge of the wire bundle was the end of a leg, pale and mostly just bone, the ankle portion I'd felt when I first reached her. Whatever else there was left of Sarah was still hidden by the bundle that fell back into the water. Where it went or what else was attached to it was still hidden by the muddy water. Uncle Colby had a look of horror on his face. He looked at me and then pulled the rock until the rest of the mass slid out of the creek. And then there she was, or at least what was left of her. Around her midsection was another stone, though not quite as big as the first, and she was wrapped around completely with chicken wire and barbed wire, the same kind we had put up around Lilipeg's pen back at home. The cloth I had felt under the water wasn't a blanket. It was the same dress she had gone to bed wearing that night nearly a month ago. Hardly any skin was left on her arms, legs, and face, and the only reason she held together when we pulled her out was because of all the wire wrapped around her. Her torso seemed mostly intact, though bloated and mushy under the dress. It was amazing that much was left considering what carnivorous things were in the creek. All the wire and fabric must have insulated her from their probing appetites. We'd also had some good rains over the past few weeks and the influx of fresh water must have sent the blue crabs a little further south down the creek where it was saltier. If it hadn't been for that, she might well have already been picked clean.

Uncle Colby fell back on his rear in the muddy clay, wiping his face with his sleeve. "Jesus Christ Almighty," he said.

I was still crying but it wasn't the wailing moan as a few moments ago. Most of that had been just shear frustration. I'd known she was dead, really. It was certainly different, though, between slowly coming to believe a thing and having it confirmed beyond a shadow of a doubt. There aren't proper words to describe what I was feeling at that moment. I was sad, angry, and I also felt a horrible sensation of guilt because a very small part of me was glad that she was actually there and that everything that had been happening to me suddenly seemed validated. It had all become a slow and steady kind of crying, sadness and relief that at last, I'd found her. I had thought something terrible had happened to my sister, and now I knew. At first I just looked at her, at what had become of her. Someone had wrapped her up in the chicken wire, then threaded barbed wire on the ends and tied them around and around the two heavy stones. They weren't taking any chances on her floating back to the surface. They'd wanted to make sure the creek's inhabitants would leave no flesh there at the bottom, but in doing so they'd actually made it too difficult for her to be completely consumed yet. They'd hid her well, though. If it hadn't been for her showing me, I don't think anybody would ever have found Sarah. Even Noah's flood wouldn't have pulled her out from under that overhang, not the way she had been stuffed inside with the rocks.

I started pulling on the barbed wire, trying to unravel it so I could pull the rest of it off of her. Uncle Colby sat awestruck at seeing Sarah's body before him, but after a minute or so had passed, he started helping me as well. Neither of us spoke as we tugged and pulled. Down at her legs the wire had been twisted several times around and I found the end of it and began reversing the twist. I nearly gagged with the terrible smell.

When we had her free of the two stones Uncle Colby stopped me from undoing the rest of the chicken wire. "No, we bes' leave that for now, Sol," he said. He knew that if we completely undid everything her body might literally fall to pieces. He took off his shirt and placed it over Sarah's mangled head, which looked just like I'd seen in my dream before she filled back into herself, and then he used the rope we still had with us to tie it so it stayed put and covered her face. He carefully picked up the mass of flesh, bone, and wire, and we started walking. Uncle Colby used both hands to carry her and I don't know how he kept from gagging from the smell of her decayed corpse. I watched her legs bounce with each step. The skin left on her feet was black and it sagged as though it had been pulled and separated from her like a pair of socks.

We walked along in a silence for a time. Finally Uncle Colby spoke, "How'd you know, Sol?" he asked without looking at me.

"She told me," I said. "She was scared there by herself."

He tilted his head down and looked at me like I was something foreign to him, but he didn't say anything else. It seemed that he had always been holding out hope for Mama and Sarah, and now that optimism had been crashed to pieces.

"You reckon my Mama's in the creek, too?" I asked him.

He took a deep breath. "I dunno, Sol" he said, "But I'm going to make sure it gets looked over real good. If she's there, too, we'll find her," he promised.

The tears kept coming as we walked. Even Uncle Colby had to stop for a second to wipe his eyes with his shoulder. Each time I thought I was about to be able to stem the flow, I'd think of some other time with Sarah, us picking berries or pecans with Mama, me skinning fish out back and chasing her around with guts while she squealed. And then I pictured that day on her birthday, dressed like the littlest princess. My heart broke and broke again. Uncle Colby changed his grip on the chicken wire so he could carry it with only his left hand and he put his other arm around my shoulder for a bit as we trudged our way through some of the wooded area and then over the old tobacco fields.

When we reached the house Aunt Emma had finished hanging her laundry and was back inside. George saw us first and was going to walk out to meet us before noticing what Uncle Colby was carrying. As we got a little closer he saw our faces, mine still with fresh tears and Uncle Colby's knotted with grief, and he yelled out, "Mama!" There wasn't an immediate reply, and he turned and ran into the house yelling out "Mama!" again at the top of his lungs.

She was sitting at the kitchen table shelling peas, "Boy, what are you on about hollerin' in my house like you don't know no better?" she scolded.

"Daddy and Sol are comin' back," he told her.

"Well, Saints be praised, ain't that a wonder?" she quipped at him

sarcastically. "Did you think they was gone for good?"
"Daddy's carrying something," George told her with a shaky voice.
She stopped snapping the peas, "Boy, why are you actin' queer? What's he carryin' that's so special?"
George had walked over to the kitchen window, and as he looked out he said, "Looks like it might be somethin' all wrapped up." She didn't seem to be catching the possibility he was pointing out for her, and of course she wouldn't as she didn't know the real reason I had wanted to go home on that day, so George just laid it out for her. "Looks like maybe he's got Sarah," he said.
He heard Aunt Emma nearly fall over with trying to get up so fast, "What?" She darted over to the window, too, and by this time Uncle Colby and me were nearly at the house.
She came out the back door just as we arrived, George directly behind her. She walked out and looked at the bundle Uncle Colby had in his hands. She saw my tears and Uncle Colby's solemn face and said, "Oh, God, no, Colby. It ain't . . ."
He put Sarah down on the ground and went to hold his wife. When she saw his shirt wrapped around the little head and the bony legs sticking out of the bottom, she lost it, "Oh my God! Oh, Lord, no, no, it can't be." I looked down at Sarah and felt fresh tears welling up. George came out from behind Aunt Emma and he started to cry, too. He just stared at the bundle on the ground letting the weight of what it meant sink in. Then he walked over and put his arm around my neck, "You was right," he said. "You found her."
"Yeah," I told him with a choke. "She weren't in the well, though. She was down yonder in the creek, sunk down with rocks."
Aunt Emma heard me and she pulled herself free of Uncle Colby and knelt down by Sarah. She examined the chicken wire and the way it had been threaded together by the fence wire. She pulled Uncle Colby's shirt off a little and stroked a piece of black hair that was poking out, all the while shaking her head as if to say no, not Sarah, not like this. She knew what it meant. We all did.
Francine and Amber hadn't been home that afternoon when we brought Sarah back. They had finished their morning chores and Aunt Emma had let them walk into town to visit with friends and buy themselves a coca cola at the general store, the new fizzy drink everyone liked so much. Mr. Padgett, the storeowner, had bought a whole bunch of crates of the stuff from Houston and it was quite the sensation around that time.

Aunt Emma and Uncle Colby put Sarah in the back of the wagon and we all headed into town. It was a long, solemn journey, like a funeral march that it more or less was. Once we reached town, Aunt Emma went off to find Francine and Amber at the store while Uncle Colby, George, and I all went into the sheriff's office.

Sheriff Covell wasn't in as usual. But when we went back outside to get ready to go look for him we saw him walking up from the same direction Aunt Emma had just gone. He had a piece of fried chicken in one hand and a mason jar of iced tea in the other. He saw us come out of the door to his office and gave us a grin and wave merrily while he kicked up the pace a bit to a waddling trot. "Miss Thomas down the way fried up some chicken and invited me for a taste, and y'all know I ain't one to pass up some of her cookin,'" he said jokingly. "And old widower like me's got to take his home cookin' where he can get it." His humor fell on deaf ears and when he saw how solemn we all looked he changed his demeanor, "Something ain't right, is it?" he asked Uncle Colby, "Y'all ain't looking yourselves. What's wrong?"

Uncle Colby told him, "You'd best be having a look over here, Gus," and walked over to the back of the wagon.

Sheriff Covell followed him over and looked in as Uncle Colby pulled back the sheet Aunt Emma had placed over Sarah's bundle. He gave her a long look over, then leaned back away from the wagon, tossed the rest of his fried chicken off to the side and wiped his hands on his pants. "Hell's bells," he said. "I reckon I shouldn't've been so believing after all. I really had it in my mind they had gone off somewhere and we would of heard from 'em any time now. Which one is that, Annie or her young 'un?"

"It's Sarah, my niece," Uncle Colby told him.

"Where'd you find her?" asked the sheriff.

"Down at the creek, near a bend in a little hollow weighed down with some rocks. Didn't find Annie, but she might be somewhere in there, too, I reckon."

"Lord oh mighty," said the sheriff. "Well, I'll get some boys down there and check for Annie soon as I can. What with these rains, though, might be she's been washed down to the Gulf by now." He looked over at me and said sincerely, "I'm deeply sorry, Sol. I mean that. Ain't nothin' I can think to say 'cept how sorry I am any of this has happened."

He turned back to Uncle Colby and said with his back to us in a whisper neither George nor I could hear. "You reckon Abram done it?"

Uncle Colby hated to admit it, but there wasn't any other way of seeing things, "Seems like. I gave him some chicken wire just like what's here while back when we was making a little pen for the horse and wagon they had, and he kept the leftover."

"Well," said the sheriff, "I don't see much point in holding out for any silver lining in these clouds here anymore," he told Uncle Colby. "I'm just about done hoping for the better of things in this here situation. I think if the young 'un here was killed, so was the Mama. I'm awfully sorry for y'all's loss, Colby, but I promise I'm going to take care of this. How'd y'all manage to find her anyhow?"

"Sol says he knew where to look. We checked the well back at Abram and Annie's, but didn't find nothing 'cept what he said was part of a tooth. I reckon him and his daddy have been down there at the creek times past and it struck him that's where she might be."

Uncle Colby didn't mention anything about ghosts and dreams. There wasn't much point in stirring that pot.

"Well, I reckon I best be off to find Abram. It's judgment day for that boy. I'd better get a holt of him before Marcus finds out, though. He ain't back is he?"

"I ain't seen him yet," replied Uncle Colby, still in a hushed voice.

"That's good, I reckon. If he finds out before I have a chance to bring Abram in I bet we'd be needing ourselves two caskets 'stead of just the one, and I've got to try and keep things from gettin' out of hand when folks find out," said the Sheriff. "It ain't gonna be easy, though. Folks ain't gonna take this too well. And the last thing we need is a lynch mob."

"Might serve him right," said Uncle Colby as he looked back at the bundle under the sheet. "I didn't think he had it in him." Despite their whispering, I could just make out that last line. He'd tell me the rest of the conversation years later, but even then I already knew who he was talking about, and everybody in town would know pretty soon.

"I guess you'll be wanting to talk with Doc Wilkins," said the Sheriff. The town doctor served as both physician and mortician. There was a carpenter in town that put together the caskets, but Dr. Wilkins walked the families through their time of need.

"Yessir. And I reckon you got your own work to do," Uncle Colby told him with a bit of suggestion. He knew Uncle Marcus was due back any time, not to mention what somebody else might do. Even he was having very violent feelings about Pap at the moment, and he was one of the only people Pap could consider a friend, yet despite himself he didn't want to see Pap lynched. Of course even if somebody did go vigilante and shoot Pap dead, it'd probably just be cutting out the formalities. Anybody who killed a child, especially a retarded child, and sunk the body in the creek for the crabs, wasn't going to get any leniency out of the Christian people of Varner Creek. Even those that weren't such good Christians would become ones on the day they went into the town hall in witness of a trial like this one would bring. They'd be clean, sober, and full of the word. An eye for an eye and death for a death. Uncle Colby knew Pap didn't have a chance in front of judge or jury.

Each man went to his own tasks. The sheriff ducked into his office for a moment and emerged again wearing his sidearm and holding a rifle. He normally didn't go through town with his guns, but he was no slouch with a firearm. Varner Creek was just too quiet for that sort of thing, and the women had grown a habit at frowning at any man who came to town with guns attached. It just wasn't a socially acceptable thing to do here. Besides, the only trouble the town really knew was the occasional barroom fight that got out of hand, and only once in a blue moon would somebody turn up shot. They'd never had a child murdered before.

The Sheriff walked down towards a group of houses in town. He lived in one and a few doors down lived the mayor. He'd tell him the news and ask the mayor to find a few strong fellas to accompany the sheriff over to Pap's place. Uncle Colby left the wagon sitting in front of the sheriff's office with the brake on and went looking for Dr. Wilkins in the same direction. He asked George and me to sit tight so that nobody walking by would peek under the sheet and cause a scene. As they both walked off George asked me, "You reckon the sheriff goin' to go after your daddy?"

"I'm pretty sure," I told him. "I didn't want to think he'd done it, but looks like he did."

We sat up on the seat of the wagon and George looked back at Sarah under the sheet, "I can't believe that's her," he said. "I reckon that means you really did see her that night out at our place, huh?"

The face in the bucket of water, the footprints by the bed, "Yeah, it was her."

"Damn," he said, "I've heard all them stories about ghosts but figured they was just meant to scare people. I didn't never think they was real as that. I believed you and all, but damn . . . it's just so, so . . . well it just don't seem like it could be real."

"It was real," I told him. "She found me, and that's how I found her.

I went looking for her like she had done, and she showed me where to look."

George felt the hairs go up on the back of his neck. It was creepy enough thinking Sarah's ghost had been right there next to him while he slept that night, but now he had an image of her murdered and hidden there in the creek. The idea of it sent chills down his side. "You reckon he's killed Aunt Annie, too?" he asked.

I thought about her and whether or not she'd been sunk like Sarah, but maybe had floated up and was carried away. The thought that she, too, had suffered like Sarah and was somewhere lonely with no one to find her brought more tears to my eyes.

"I'm sorry," said George quickly.

"It's all right," I told him. "It ain't you. It's just that Sarah's gone, and Mama, too, but I don't know where she is. And it looks like Pap's what done it, and I just don't know what's going to happen no more."

"It'll be okay," said George "You can come and live with us. You'll see, it'll all work out." His effort at comforting me touched me. These were good people, my Aunt, Uncle, and cousins. Why couldn't we have ended up like them, a real family?

Aunt Emma came walking up with Francine and Amber. The two girls looked at the wagon with trepidation. They had been told the day's events in a quick summary and were both afraid to come near to where Sarah was. Amber started crying and holding on to Aunt Emma as they came closer. Francine looked like she wasn't sure how she was supposed to act. She stared blankly at the wagon and us. "Where's your daddy at?" Aunt Emma asked George.

"He went to go fetch Dr. Wilkins," he answered. "Sheriff gone down that-a-ways, too." He pointed off in the direction both men had headed.

After a while Uncle Colby returned with Dr. Wilkins, a slender man with thinning black hair that was immaculately waxed back on his head, and a pair of wire-rimmed glasses sitting on the bridge of his nose. He came walking beside Uncle Colby and pulled the sheet back a bit when he reached the wagon. Francine and Amber both instinctively looked. Amber clutched Aunt Emma even tighter and Francine let out a gasp. "Let the little children come unto me, and do not hinder them, for the kingdom of heaven belongs to such as these," said the Doctor quietly. He was apparently as well versed as Miss Thomas. Before he decided to become a physician he had considered seminary school, but he'd found his true calling in medicine. He turned to Uncle Colby and said, "We'd better get her in my office so we can get her cleaned up." Uncle Colby walked the horse and wagon down towards the Doctor's office and once there carried the bundle inside. Aunt Emma went in with him and told us children to wait outside.

A few minutes passed when Miss Thomas came hurrying up towards us. She lived just a few more houses down and it seemed that somehow word had reached her. I was leaning against the wagon looking towards the doctor's door, wondering what they were talking about inside, when she rushed up to me and threw her arms around me saying, "Oh, darling, I'm so sorry. I just heard, dear. Gus . . . I mean the sheriff, he just dropped in and told me." Her cheeks were moist and her powder rubbed off on me as she held me. "Everything is going to be okay, child," she said. She let go of the hug but continued to hold me by the shoulder saying, "Are you all right, dear?"

Hell, no, I thought. "Yes, ma'am," I said.

She stroked my hair and asked, "Where's your Aunt and Uncle gone to?"

"They inside," said Francine "talking to Doc Wilkins." Her lack of an "are" in her sentence didn't get corrected, for once.

Miss Thomas walked up to the door, helloed the house, and entered. A minute or two later she and Aunt Emma came out. They came over to the wagon and Aunt Emma climbed up. "We're going to go on home," Aunt Emma told us. "Uncle Colby's gonna stay and make arrangements with Dr. Wilkins, who'll give him a ride back later on this evening."

"If y'all need a thing in the world, Emma, you just let me know," said Miss Thomas.

"We will, Miss Thomas, and I do appreciate it." They reached out and held each other's hand for a moment before Aunt Emma slapped the reins, "Come on, Joe."

He started with a grunt and we headed home. Francine and Amber were both unnerved at the idea of sitting in the back, and Amber was latched on to Aunt Emma again, so George and I sat in the rear of the wagon as we went along. Francine kept looking back at me like she wanted to say something, but wasn't sure what.

"Quit yer gawking," George finally told her.

"Sorry," she said, and didn't look back anymore.

As I learned later, over the next few hours while we were home getting ready for supper, Uncle Colby was back at Sheriff Covell's office having a discussion with him. "You wouldn't have any idea of where he'd be likely to go, would yah?" he was being asked by the sheriff.

"No sir, far as I knew he was still at work today."

"Well, that was the first place we went," said the sheriff, "but Mr. Pyle said Abram skinned out early, not long after you left for the day, he said. We went over to his place but couldn't find hide nor hair of him. I reckon we'll try again tonight, though, and he'll probably be there. All his belongings were still in place so I don't think he's gone anywhere without meaning to return soon. Not unless he's somehow found out we got a body, but that doesn't seem likely. I'm trying to keep it quiet for now, but come tomorrow it'll be out."

Uncle Colby just looked at the Sheriff. And he thought about what was going to happen to Pap tomorrow if they caught him. "I just didn't think he had it in him," he repeated.

Chapter 13

When Uncle Colby returned later that night we were all asleep except for Aunt Emma. I had cried so much during the day that I felt spent, and I was out when my head hit the pillow. Crying, as we all learn in life, is an exhausting thing that wears one out, both emotionally and physically. My sleep was deep, and no dreams of dark places came to me. I was awakened in the night by Aunt Emma, who was gently hugging me and whispering, "Sol? Sol, you awake, now, baby?"

"Yes ma'am," I said, rubbing the sleep out of my eyes.

"Sol, I need you come on into the front room, we've got to talk to you."

She held me by the hand as we walked into the big room. She was in her nightgown, but Uncle Colby and Uncle Marcus were there as well and they were both fully dressed. I remember wondering when Uncle Marcus had come back. I had no idea what time it was, but it felt like the middle of the night.

"Hey, Uncle Marcus, guess you heard," I told him.

He looked at me with softness and pity. "Yes, I've heard. And there's been some other things that've happened we got to tell you 'bout." I wasn't sure what more could have happened after the day I'd already had, but it didn't sound too good.

Aunt Emma asked me to sit down next to her on a sofa Uncle Colby had bought for her some years back for her birthday. Uncle Colby sat in a nearby chair he'd made by hand, and Uncle Marcus pulled up one of the kitchen table chairs. "What we've got to tell you about ain't easy," started Aunt Emma, "especially considering all what's happened. We was goin' to wait 'til morning, but decided it'd be bes' to do it while the others are asleep." She looked over at Uncle Colby for strength, but when she started to speak again she either couldn't find the words or couldn't find the nerve.

It was Uncle Colby who spoke for her, a rare thing indeed, "It's about your daddy, Sol. He's done shot himself."

What? I thought. "Shot himself . . ." I repeated. "When did he shoot hisself?"

Aunt Emma found her voice again, "Today, Sol, this very evening. They found him in town. Apparently he had got his hands on a pistol and, well, he shot himself with it."

I couldn't believe this was being added to everything else. How was a twelve year old supposed to deal with all these horrible things happening at once? In one day I'd found my murdered sister's body, and now the man who most likely had done it, our own father, had killed himself. And God only knew what had become of Mama. I waited for the tears to come again, but they didn't. Whether it was because I was out of tears by now, or simply couldn't make myself spend them on Pap, I didn't know. It was all like some cruel joke fate was playing on me. The weight of it all pressed down on me like a ton of stone. "Why?" I asked, without really thinking about the awkwardness of the question. Two seconds of reflection would have been enough for me to figure it out, but the question had come automatically.

The adults in the room all looked at each other thinking the same thing but nobody wanting to be the one to say it out loud. Aunt Emma lent her delicate touch, "We don't know, baby. But I reckon it might have had something to do with Sarah today. But don't nobody know any particulars," she added. "There's going to be plenty of speculatin' about, but right now don't nobody know anything for sure, you understand?"

I did. I understood Pap shot himself because he had been found out about killing Sarah, and probably Mama, too. I understood that I didn't have a family anymore, that they were all dead. I understood I was an orphan, made so by my own evil Pap. *Ignorance is bliss*, I thought. Because the more I was understanding things the more that I wished I didn't.

Aunt Emma explained to me what would happen. Tomorrow the town's carpenter would be busy making two caskets, one big and one little, and they'd both be buried in the cemetery. I was sure Sarah needed to be in the ground quickly. When we pulled her out of the creek the decayed flesh had smelled horrible. "I'm going to ask that they be placed apart, though," said Aunt Emma. "I just think given things that would be best, unless you think otherwise."

"No Ma'am," I said. I was sure Sarah wouldn't want to be buried next to Pap.

"I reckon we'll bury her in one of Amber's dresses if that'd be alright."

"No," I told her. "She'd want to be in her princess dress." I knew it was filthy, and they had probably had to cut it off of her, but I felt that was what Sarah would have wanted.

Aunt Emma looked as though she'd protest, but when she saw my eyes she just said, "I'll see what can be done."

"So what's going to happen to me?" I asked.

Uncle Marcus spoke up, "We've been talking 'bout that. Your Aunt Emma and Uncle Colby say you're welcome to stay here with them, but

I'd also like to have you come and stay with me and my family," he told me. "You ain't never met your Aunt Mary Jo nor your other cousins, but I think you'd be real happy down that way. Your granny lives there, too, with your Aunt Candace and her family. We've got plenty of room and there's a good school for you, lots of kids your age and things you've probably never seen here in town. I'd make sure you didn't have to worry about anything a boy needs."

Aunt Emma also spoke, "We think it best if we let you think about that, Sol. We all love you and would be happy to have you as our own. And you don't have to decide tonight, not after all that's happened. You just think about it, okay?"

"Yes, ma'am," I told her. I was surprised Uncle Marcus had invited me to come and live with his family. He didn't even know me, nor I him, really. And his wife and kids had never even laid eyes on me before. It was strange to think that he'd be so willing to bring me home and into his family like that. But I guess blood is thicker than water and he seemed sincere about not only being willing to have me, but also wanting me. My immediate reaction was that I'd stay with Aunt Emma and Uncle Colby, though. I'd grow up here with George and stay in Varner Creek, the only home I'd ever known.

I went back to bed thinking about what had happened. I imagined Pap in my mind holding a gun to his head and pulling the trigger. I wondered if he was drunk when he did it, and if so, would he still have done it if he had been sober. It didn't matter, though. They'd have hung him anyway even if he hadn't done himself in. *Why'd you do that to them, Pap?* I asked the stillness. *What possible reason could you have had to kill poor Sarah?*

The next day after breakfast we all put on our Sunday clothes and headed back into town. Uncle Marcus had gone back to Miss Thomas' the night before and promised that by mid-morning he'd have everything set up. He paid the carpenters and paid for the plots in the cemetery, and wouldn't take any of the offers of cash from either Miss Thomas or Aunt Emma. A lot of folks wanted to chip in but he wouldn't hear of it. It was the least he could do, he told them, the only thing left he could do.

We got to town around ten and the second hole in the cemetery was already being dug. Sarah and Pap had already been nailed in their caskets. Neither one was fit for a viewing. Sarah was decayed and eaten up beyond recognition, and Pap's skull was lopsided after losing its left side. He had put the gun to his temple instead of in his mouth, I heard someone say during the burial, and half his head went flying. Most all of the town turned out. It was one of the biggest things to happen in Varner Creek since time remembered, and word had spread fast. How that many people knew about it in just twenty-four hours was beyond me, but small towns are like that. I knew everyone would find out pretty quickly, but this must have been like a wildfire spreading through town.

I got more hugs and apologies than I knew what to do with. People I couldn't remember ever talking to before were calling me by my first name and extending their deepest sympathies. Miss Thomas hugged me every time I got within arm's length of her. Her arms were like a frog's tongue chasing flies, unexpectedly flying out at me when her cup of pity runneth over.

We buried Sarah first and I cried as I watched the small wooden box being lowered into the hole. The preacher said some nice words, quoting the Bible a lot. Something about how the Lord brings death and makes alive, takes down to the grave and up again. I wasn't paying attention, really. I kept thinking about her in my dream, lying next to me hand in hand, pleading not to go back into the dark alone. I hoped I had accomplished what she wanted. Maybe she could rest now that she wasn't in that hole back at the creek, wrapped in metal and held down by stone.

Pap's burial didn't have quite as many patrons. A few thinned out here and there, but most still walked over since they were already there and their curiosity wouldn't let them leave the show until the final curtain. It was a quite a different speech from the preacher. He did the same ashes to ashes, and still quoted the Bible a lot, but instead of verses about children in God's hands and the beauty of heaven, he spoke about repenting of one's sins and the Lord's judgment. "And Job tells us, 'What will I do when God confronts me? What will I answer when called to account? He repays a man for what he has done; He brings upon him what his conduct deserves.'"

It was probably the most accusing eulogy anybody would ever hear in Varner Creek, but the people expected it. Everyone knew what'd he done and they couldn't see the salvation of his soul. Miss Thomas tried to let God have his judgment and put hers aside, but it was evident on her face as she watched them put him in the ground the way she felt. She couldn't help but to nod approvingly with the preacher's words. She'd cared a lot for Sarah, and Mama, too. And the expression was the same everywhere. Well, almost. Everyone there hadn't come to pay their respects to Pap, they were there to wish him a merry one-way trip to hell and to see that he was on his way, but Uncle Colby had some mixed feelings. He remembered just wishing Pap could have gotten right with himself, he'd tell me later.

As for me, it seemed eternal watching Pap go back from whence we all come. The preacher's eulogy droned on, "For God will bring every deed into judgment, including every hidden thing, whether it is good or evil." And in this way Pap ended up facing the jury after all. Even in death he couldn't escape the town's condemnation. The preacher was handing down the sentence with every word and all the people seemed to applaud his sentence with their nodding heads and Amens. Truth be told, I found myself agreeing with everything I heard, too. He had done such a horrible thing. I knew his own childhood and life had been rough, but he'd taken so much from me, and was never really nice to me, not in all those years. And Sarah was as sweet and innocent as a human being can be. And lastly poor Mama, they hadn't found her at the creek. At least not yet, anyway. She was probably drifting down to sea as the creek's inhabitants slowly consumed her. She had only ever tried to make the best of things. They didn't deserve what he had done; nobody could ever have deserved that. I thought about those things as he disappeared into his grave and I found myself furious at him.

"Guess you'll be findin' hell," I heard myself say. It was quiet, a private condemnation from me to him, but Uncle Marcus standing close by heard me. So did Miss Thomas, and neither one tried to dissuade my anger. They felt it, too, and figured if anyone was entitled to it, it was me. I walked away before the preacher finished. Let the worms have him, I thought. I hope they chew him up and crap him out for a hundred years. A quick bullet to the head by his own hand was better than the way Sarah and Mama went. I knew it wasn't right to think such things, but my anger stirred with memories of Mama and Sarah.

When all was said and done we went home. Uncle Marcus came with us, and so did Miss Thomas. All that afternoon, well-wishers stopped by extending their condolences. We had pies, casseroles, cobblers, and just about every confection known to man delivered to our door. The preacher came and wanted to know if I needed spiritual guidance in my time of need. Luckily Aunt Emma said she was seeing to that. Miss Thomas told Aunt Emma that if they were tight on space she'd be willing to take me in and see to it that I had a happy home to live in. Aunt Emma thanked her but said she was determined to have me under her roof if I was willing.

I went walking through the woods with George for a while that afternoon mainly to escape all the looks everyone was giving me. We talked about the rumors Francine and Amber had told us they heard in town, about how really Uncle Marcus had shot my Pap but nobody would say so. "I don't think he did," said George. "He doesn't seem the type of man to lie about such a thing if he didn't do it."

"I don't know," I told him. "Mama was his sister. And from what I gather there weren't any friendship between him and Pap." Nothing had been directly told to me yet, but all one had to do was look and listen to get a feel for things.

"I heard my folks tellin' Amber and Francine to hush up with such rumors, and that there weren't any truth to them," said George. "So if they say Uncle Marcus didn't shoot him, then that's what I'm gonna believe, too." Did it really matter? I wondered.

When we went back home Uncle Marcus was sitting on the porch. He looked like he had been waiting for us with his pocketknife out and George's old chicken stick, the one he duplicated Pickett's charge with, being whittled upon again by his skillful hands. He looked like he was carving chain links into the wood. I imagined that given enough time, he would have turned out something uniquely artistic. It was absolutely the only thing about him that reminded me of Pap in years to come. They both had that way with wood. He saw us coming up and asked if I'd join him on the porch. "Why don't you go get washed up, George. I want to have a talk with Sol for a bit."

"Yessir," said George, and he disappeared into the house.

"Your Uncle Colby told me 'bout what some folks said today there in town, 'bout how I might have shot your daddy," he said. "You hear any of that?"

"Yessir," I told him, "Francinc and Amber told me about it, but I don't reckon I believe it."

He stopped whittling, "Well, I want to tell you, Sol, as your uncle and as one man to another, I didn't shoot your daddy." He took a breath and organized his thoughts, "Truth is I might have after I heard about Sarah and the state she was in." He seemed to catch himself saying more than he meant to, "About how she'd been wrapped in the same kind of chicken wire y'all had at home, and how she'd been sunk down like she was. And the sheriff told me he suspects the same thing might have happened with Annie, I mean your Mama, but the rains probably carried her off." He looked out over the fields and watched some cows not too far off munching away, "Your daddy and I never got along, you see.

Even when we was younger, we didn't think much of each other." He looked at me and realized I didn't need the history lesson. "But after I talked to your Uncle Colby and the sheriff I went back to my room at Miss Thomas' house. She was out talkin' with Dr. Wilkins and the preacher, and when I went into my room, there was your daddy." He looked at me with his intense eyes. I hadn't heard this part of things. All I'd been told is Pap had been found shot in town, but nobody told me where or by whom, and I didn't think to ask. Unbeknownst to me Uncle Marcus made a decision at that moment. "Your Pap was there, already passed on. I don't know why he was in my room, or even how he knew where to look. Might be he thought of shooting me, might be he wanted to talk, I can't say. But I opened the door and found him in there, dead by his own hand." I suppose his hand went back to carving the stick out of lack of anything else to do with it, "It's been an unfair lot that you've been given, Sol, but I wanted you to know I didn't shoot your daddy."

"I believe you," I told him. I knew he didn't have to say any of this to me, and since he did I trusted in his words. George was right, he wasn't the type to lie about doing such a thing or not.

"I know you've been living here all your life, and that your Aunt and Uncle want to see you stay," he said. "—but I'd be real pleased if you would come with me and at least try it out for a while. I ain't been there for you, nor your sister and Mama, neither, and I'd like the chance to try and make amends in some way."

It was then that I saw the guilt he had been carrying since his arrival in town, but it didn't make sense to me. Pap was the one who had done the wronging, and in my opinion, whether or not Uncle Marcus had been around wouldn't have made a difference. I was obvious he thought different, though. "Ain't nothing to make amends for, Uncle Marcus," I told him. "Pap's what done it all."

He kind of nodded appreciatively, but he still seemed to think different. "Still, I think it'd do you some good to get away for a bit. I'm heading out tomorrow, and if you're willing I'd like you to come, maybe for just a visit at first. You don't have to stay with me if you don't like it there in Galveston, I'll bring you right back if you don't, but what say you come and try it out for a while?"

Galveston, I thought to myself. I could go fishing in the ocean and meet the grandmother and aunts and cousins I'd never met. And as much as I'd miss George, Aunt Emma, Uncle Colby, and even Francine and Amber, it suddenly felt like the right thing to do. "Okay," I said, "It might be good not have everything staring me in the face here for a while."

He gave me a smile like he knew just what I meant, "I'm glad, Sol. Tomorrow I'll buy you a good horse that you can keep for yourself, so you'll have one to ride for your very own, and we'll load them up with us and catch the train up to Houston and see the city. Then we'll head down to Galveston." He looked at me like he was about to tell me a secret, "It really is a pretty place, Sol. And the ocean is so big it looks like it goes on to the edge of the world. That's how your Aunt Candace describes it, anyway." And for the first time I saw him smile.

George took it kind of hard when I told him. "You ain't staying?" he asked. "But why not? Why don't you just go visit for a while but come back?"

"I might," I told him, "I'm just going to go and see it is all. Uncle Marcus says he lives right near the ocean and that there's fish ten times as big as us there."

"Naw, ten times?" he asked. "You'd have to have a hell of a cane pole for one of them," he joked.

I laughed, too. "Seems like I could just jump in myself and wriggle around and be my own bait."

"Don't go gettin' eaten by some sea monster," he warned.

"I won't," I promised. "And don't you go trying on anymore rooster hats while I'm gone, neither." We both laughed at that one.

"Lucifer the Leghorn," he said.

"Meanest chicken ever," I finished for him.

The next day we all prepared to say our goodbyes. Uncle Colby and Aunt Emma rode me into town on the wagon with George, Francine, and Amber. Uncle Marcus had gotten up early to go into town and find a horse and riding gear. He met us a little while later at Miss Thomas' house with a beautiful brown horse that couldn't have been more than two or three years old. "What's his name?" I asked Uncle Marcus.

"He's your horse, Sol. You can call him what you want," he said.

He had a lot of spirit, the young horse, and I worried that I might not be able to stay on him. He was tied up next to Geronimo and his hoofs were dancing this way and that with frustration from being tethered to the pole like he was. His feet danced around trying to back away, much to Geronimo's aggravation, who had enough slack in his reins to get at the soft grass by the base of the fence post, but kept getting bumped by the young horse next to him. "Quickstep," I decided. "I'll call him Quickstep because he fidgets like that."

"That's a good name," said Miss Thomas.

"Get on 'em and try him out," suggested Uncle Marcus.

I gave Miss Thomas and Aunt Emma a last hug, wished George and the girls the best, and was helped on Quickstep by Uncle Colby. I thought for sure he'd throw me right off, but instead he actually calmed down a little bit. I guess he knew that a rider meant he was about to be let off that stupid fence post. I rode him around a bit for everyone before Uncle Marcus and I caught the train, and he seemed to enjoy the attention.

During the trip to Houston and then on to Galveston we talked about various things and I learned a good bit more about the world on the way. He showed me the automobiles there in Houston and explained how they worked with the burning gases and all. I saw a telephone for the first time and we listened in as various people chatted about their lives, and at night I saw the electric lights for the first time. We still didn't have any in Varner Creek and that was something to see the night suddenly pushed back by artificial light from bulbs that sat on street lamps. Uncle Marcus told me how they used to use gas from oyster shells and coal to light up the city, but how the first electric street lamps were turned on May 31, 1884. I realized just how far behind the times Varner Creek really was.

And when we reached Galveston, instead of going straight home, we rode Geronimo and Quickstep down to the sea. A cool breeze was coming in from the south and Uncle Marcus told me about the great storm that hit the island Sept 8, 1900, killing somewhere from six to ten thousand people. They never got an official count since so many got swept away in the storm surge. It was kind of a scary thing to tell a new resident, but he assured me the new city was taking precautions against such things for the future. He told me that's why he'd moved here, along with so many others. They were rebuilding Galveston and it would be the finest city in the state of Texas. They were building a giant wall to keep the sea from washing the people away again, and they were even going to raise the city itself. It all seemed like a fantasy place to me as I sat atop Quickstep looking out, nothing but water as far as the eye could go. I wondered what amazing things hid beneath the waves so far out into the world. Off to my left, right where the land seemed to meet the water on the horizon, the sun was dipping to its rest. The sky was lit up a brilliant parade of yellows, oranges, and purples just like home, but now it was painted over a canvas of silver sea.

"Well, this is home, at least for as long as you like," said Uncle Marcus. And as long as I liked turned out to be a long time indeed. Of course I eventually went back to Varner Creek, but it was many years later when I retired. Roots are like that, sometimes they just lead you back again. But I stayed with Uncle Marcus and Aunt Mary Jo there in Galveston for many years, though. They raised me as one of their own and saw to it that I had a good start in life by the time I was a man. The city did exactly what Uncle Marcus had told me they were going to do on that first day, raised itself and built the wall, a seventeen-foot monstrosity strong enough to hold back the ocean itself.

I met Helen there when I was twenty-eight, got married, had children, and lived. I saw ghosts regular, though, after Sarah. That was something she had passed to me and it never left. The great storm from 1900 left many a wondering soul about. It always scared me during those years I was growing up, and my Aunt Mary Jo was terribly worried I'd been traumatized for life and might never be normal. I gave up on trying to explain to her or anybody else about the things I saw. If they didn't think I was trying to get attention for myself, then they thought something was wrong with me, and neither of those was doing me any good, so I let it be. I never understood just what caused it, either. I thought Sarah had been able to find me because she'd gone looking for me, and I found her the same way, so I never understood why it was that I all of a sudden was seeing other spirits. I guess like Sarah had explained, once some of the layers of that onion had been peeled away, every now and then the opaque lens between the alive and dead became momentarily transparent. Maybe sometimes the souls on the other side were reaching over towards ours and because of my being in that place for a bit with Sarah I was able to see them, or maybe I was accidentally finding my own way back to where they dwell, seeing what happened in another time. I couldn't control it, and while I often felt emotions I knew weren't my own being thrown out like projectiles from the dead, I never had that connection like I did with Sarah, as though we were talking in our own special way.

Chapter 14

Now I was on the other side of things with the souls I had seen in life. I was one of the dead. I wondered what it was that finished me? A stroke, an aneurysm, or maybe something else broke down. At eighty-seven, I guess it could have been anything. Miss Rita would be surprised in the morning when she came to check on me, I thought.

Sarah was standing next to me by the creek where we'd found her body. "Where are we?" I asked her. "Are we really back in Varner Creek?"

"No, we're gone from the place where living people are," she says. "We are where we want to be. It's where we go, I guess."

"Is this heaven?"

She shrugs her shoulders lightheartedly, "Maybe. I think it's different for everyone when they're here."

"Everyone?" I ask. I started thinking of everyone I lost in life. My Helen, where was she? Uncle Marcus, Aunt Mary Jo, Aunt Emma, Mama, Pap, even George had gone before me. Were they all here, too? If we were in heaven, wasn't there a hell? Weren't they different places?

"Well, the ones that find their way," she says.

"Did Mama come here with you, too?" We never did hear anything about what happened to her. We just assumed the creek had carried her to an unknown grave.

She looks down at the creek, and an unnaturally beautiful fish green as an emerald jumps from the water and splashes back down. "Yes and no," she tells me.

I paused thinking on this before asking, "What does that mean?"

"Mama's hidin'," she tells me. "But she's done it so long she's lost herself. Daddy's lost, too, but for different reasons than Mama."

"I don't understand," I tell her. I sensed layers in her words, things beyond me for the moment.

"They're still in the black place, the one you passed through." She smiles at me, "I knew you would, but not everyone does. I didn't at first. I knew I was supposed to, but I was scared and stayed waiting for you to come get me."

I thought about that black ocean I'd been in before the light appeared. It was quiet and peaceful, but I'd imagine if it'd gone on like that, I would have started to get lonely.

"A lot of people are in the dark place," Sarah tells me. "It's where I was when you found me, and part of you has been there since."

I thought about what exactly that meant. I remembered seeing Sarah in that eerie green light with darkness all around. "The dark place . . ." I begin to ask. "Is that why I saw ghosts after I found you, because I went to the dark place?"

Sarah nods. "They're the ones in the dark place. That's where Mama's been hiding."

"Why is Mama hiding?" I ask Sarah. "Doesn't she want to leave the empty place?"

"She's scared of what will happen if she leaves. Mama's got a secret," she told me. "And she doesn't want anybody to know." She looked into my eyes with her own blue pools.

"What secret?"

Sarah's easy smile dwindles a bit and I can feel her happiness dampen as some troubling memory enters her mind. "It's not Mama's fault," she tells me, and I sense the pity in her. "I'll show you if you want, but it's a sad place. I don't go there anymore, but I'll show you if you want."

I nod, asking for something I don't understand. As we hold hands the creek disappears. It doesn't feel like us moving to another place, though, but rather the scenery around us changing just like before. Somehow Sarah is doing this.

And then we're both there, seventy-five years ago for me, and it might as well have been yesterday for Sarah, as she was the same age then as she is now, but just looks different in her new form. We're in the bedroom where Mama was dressing her for her birthday party, both of them are there as the Sarah next to me and I look on, but they are frozen in time. It's like we had traveled back in time.

"Are we really here?" I ask Sarah.

"No," she tells me, "We're in a memory, a bad memory. It feels real, though. That's why I don't come here anymore." Inside I feel myself being filled like an empty glass by thoughts and emotions coming from Sarah. The room around us becomes animated and voices ring out from the past. . .

Chapter 15

"Are you ready for your big day?" Mama asked.

"Yes! Yes!" said Sarah, excitedly.

Mama had sewn a number of easy slip-on dresses for Sarah to wear every day. They were feed-sack dresses so she could run and play without tearing them to shreds, and easy enough to slip on and off that Sarah could manage them by herself. Today's dress was a yellow one that Sarah had been favoring lately. She was bouncing around the room in excitement. Mine and Sarah's souls were in one corner watching things, and when her former self bounded towards us she danced right through us.

"Sarah, come on over here and let Mama dress you," smiled Mama.

Sarah came over and said, "My princess d-dress," demandingly.

"Well, we'd get you in it just as soon as you sit still. Now up go the arms." And Sarah complied by lifting her arms into the air. Mama grabbed the dress and drew it off Sarah in one quick motion. Then she grabbed the pink dress and started to place it over Sarah's still uplifted arms, but she paused when she noticed Sarah's waist. She had gotten a pooch on her that Mama didn't remember seeing. "Good Lord, girl, maybe I shouldn't have made such a big cake for today," she joked.

"Cake!" yelled Sarah, happily, knowing that was the sweet treat she got to eat when someone had a birthday.

Mama put the dress down for a moment and stared at Sarah's little bulge. She had brought in her sewing kit just in case she needed to make a quick alteration, and she reached inside and grabbed the measuring tape. Just a few weeks ago she had used it to measure Sarah for the dress, and her midsection had been a uniform twenty-six from waist to bosom. Mama wrapped the tape around Sarah's little bulge and read the measurement, thirty. Four inches in just over three weeks, that couldn't be right, she thought. "Sarah, honey, you been sneaking snacks when Mama ain't looking?" she asked.

Sarah just yelled "Cake!" again.

And Mama sat back on her haunches looking at the bubble in front of her. Then another thought crept into her, a more sinister one. But no, that couldn't be right, she calmed herself. There hadn't been an opportunity, she thought. Sarah never was left alone with the boys at church. Even when she wasn't there around her, Sol was. But still, the thought nagged at her. Four inches in three weeks was awfully hard to explain away on sweets, especially since she hadn't noticed Sarah eating abnormally. She needed to know for sure. "Sarah, honey, you mind if

Mama has a look at yah?"

The idea seemed like a fun game to Sarah, so she smiled and turned around for Mama like she was modeling a dress that she didn't have on.

"No, sweetie," began Mama, "here, come lie down on your bed." And Sarah complied, lying down on the bed with nothing but her underwear on. "Now I'm going to take these off of yah and have a quick look, okay?" And she stripped Sarah down.

Sarah just giggled. She thought being naked was a funny thing. A game that big people sometimes played, she'd been told.

Mama inspected what she was looking for and stood back in horror when she found Sarah wasn't untouched. I could see Mama's reaction from our place in the corner and it suddenly dawned on me what it meant. "Sarah!" My Mama said in a hushed yell, "You been doing it?" Sarah just started giggling again, but Mama got real serious with her. "Sarah! Listen to me now."

"What, Mama?" she asked, truthfully having no idea what Mama meant.

Mama walked around the room a bit, her hands shaking and her mind swimming. She started chewing on her nails frantically like she did when she was stressed or nervous. Then she knelt again beside Sarah, who was sitting up now in the bed, still nude. Mama looked at her and her mentally retarded features. Who could possibly do such a thing, she thought? What bastard had been at her sweet little girl. "Sarah, sweetie, you been laying with any boys?"

Sarah looked confused. She didn't know what Mama was asking her.

"Listen to me, honey," said Mama, and she got down close by Sarah and held her hands. "Have you lain down with any boys?" she asked again slowly.

"What b-boys?" asked Sarah.

"Any boys," Mama said, "Have you been laying down with any boys?"

Sarah was still a bit confused, but then she smiled as she realized what Mama meant and said, "Sol!"

"Sol?" my Mama asked in horror.

"I lay down with S-Sol."

My Mama was nearly having a fit as she tried not to think of the unthinkable. Sol was just a little boy, it couldn't be him. "Do you lie next to him naked, Sarah?" she asks.

But she'd lost Sarah again. "Naked sweetie," said Mama forcefully, "like now, with no clothes on."

"No, Mama," she responded.

"No?" My mother repeated.

"N-no," Sarah said again.

Thank God, my Mama thought. "Well, have you been laying with any boy naked?"

Sarah didn't like this conversation. It seemed like Mama was asking her hard questions on purpose, trying to confuse her. Did Mama mean just boys, or men, too, the big boys? "Daddy?" she asked Mama.

My mother's heart froze, "You been laying with daddy naked?" she asked.

"Big P-People game," Sarah started to explain.

Mama's fear was like a thick soup in the room. "What's the big people game, baby?"

Sarah suddenly remembered she was never supposed to talk about the big people game. It was a secret and he'd said Mama would be really upset and cry if she knew that they played it without her. "You can't never tell nobody," her daddy had told her. "It's a secret game only big people are supposed to play, but since your Mama don't play, you can have her place. But you can't tell, because whoever you tell will get real sick and maybe even die," he had said. "That's why big people don't never talk about it."

Sarah was scared, now. She had forgotten what her daddy had told her and now Mama might get sick and die if she told her, so she didn't answer Mama's questions and pressed her lips together tightly to show she didn't want to tell.

But Mama was in a frenzy now. She grabbed Sarah by the arm roughly and said sternly, "Sarah Mayfield, you tell me right now what he's been doing with you."

Tears filled Sarah's eyes. She didn't understand why Mama was acting the way she was, and she didn't want to tell the secret that could make Mama be sick and die. And then Mama began to cry, and that scared Sarah even worse. Daddy had said that if Mama found out they played the game without her she'd cry. And now she was crying just like he said. So Sarah thought if she told Mama any more, the other things he said would happen, too. "You'll d-d-die," she tried telling Mama. Sarah knew that dying meant someone went away and never came back again.

Mama was feeling sick. Every word took her closer to something so terrible that the very thought of it threatened to rend her in two, but she had to know. "Listen to me, honey," she said softly, "Mama won't die.

But it's very important that you tell me what you and your daddy have been doing."

Sarah looked at her skeptically.

"Baby, does your mommy lie to you?" Asked Mama.

"No, M-Mama," said Sarah.

Mama wiped a tear that was running at a sprinter's pace down her cheek, "Then believe me, it's okay to tell Mama."

Sarah had always been a complacent girl. She tried to do whatever her parents told her, like a good girl was supposed to act, daddy had said. She told her daddy she didn't like playing the big people game because sometimes it hurt, but he said sometimes she had to do things she didn't always like. That was part of being a big person. Sarah was thinking about the game now and started to tell Mama, "We hug and D-Daddy . . ." but she trailed off.

"What?" said Mama. "What does Daddy do?"

"He g-gets on me," said Sarah.

Mama dropped her head in despair and loss. "Oh, My God!" she whispered in horror. "No, no!" Her voice began to escalate and it frightened Sarah so much she started crying again. "Oh, baby!" said my mother quickly, "Sh-h-h, sh-h-h-, don't cry, baby, don't cry." And she reached out to hold Sarah.

"Mama g-g-goin' away?" asked Sarah, meaning was Mama going to die now that Sarah had done what her daddy had told her never to do.

Mama was rocking her back and forth. "No, baby, it's all right. Everything is all right. Mama's not going away and Mama's not mad." She held Sarah close, wincing with pain.

The tears kept coming for Mama. First a trickle and then a stream. She willed them to stop, forcing them to retreat, but they were getting the better of her. Instead she concentrated on rocking her baby in her arms, her pregnant girl child who was carrying her own sibling in the womb.

As Mama sat there rocking Sarah and trying to think about what to do next, all the people arrived for the birthday party. I could feel Mama's horror, and her shame. She couldn't go out there and look at Pap, or me, or her sister, or Miss Thomas. She couldn't imagine what would happen when people knew about Sarah's condition, and who'd got her that way. It was too much to bear. She knew she'd have to tell someone, Emma, or Miss Thomas, someone . . . but not today. She didn't have the strength to face this now. So she pushed it back into a corner like I'd learn to do so many years later. Her heart had just broke, though, and her mind was quickly following. . . .

Chapter 16

The scene changed and it was us sleeping in our bedroom. Sarah's spirit was still standing next to my own and she said, "This is the bad place." I could feel her not wanting to be here. There was something very sad about this memory to her. We stood side by side, looking down at the memory of our living selves sleeping peacefully. Sarah was still in her dress and I was like a log under my covers. Then I heard something outside the door and it quietly cracked open. When the door opened the fear inside of me coming from Sarah made me expect to see Pap standing there, but instead Mama crept quietly inside the room. She knelt down by Sarah and whispered, "Sarah? Sarah, baby? I need you to get up, now, girl." Mama looked exhausted. Her face looked aged ten years and her eyes were puffy, and the feeling I got from her was of an eerie emptiness, like she'd be drained of emotions and was a hollow vessel.

At first Sarah just tossed a bit, but Mama was persistent and nudging her. Finally Sarah opened her eyes and said, "Mama?"

"S-s-sh-h-h," hushed Mama. "Don't wake Bubba." The boy in the bed didn't budge. "Get your shoes on . . . quietly," Mama told her, "we're going to take us a walk."

"W-w-walk?" whispered Sarah.

Mama gave her a stern look, "Just do as Mama tells yah."

Sarah got up and started putting on her slippers. She followed Mama out into the main room and then outside. We did, too, without taking a step. It was like watching a movie that changed scenes, except that we were inside of it with the characters. Mama took the former Sarah by the hand and was looking up at the moon. "You know, Sarah, when I was a little girl I was very bad," Mama told her. "I didn't listen to my own mother and I laid down with a boy, your daddy, when I wasn't much older than you are now, and I got pregnant with you. It was evil because we weren't married." She looked over at Sarah who was quietly trying to understand why Mama was acting so strange. "Do you know what Mama means by pregnant, baby?"

Sarah shook her head no.

"You, see, Sarah, when a man lays down with a woman like your daddy laid down with you, they make a baby." She bent down and put her hand on Sarah's belly, "Just like you have a baby in you, now."

Sarah looked down at Mama's hand and said, "b-baby?" Sarah had seen babies before in town and lots of baby cows and pigs, and in this way understood what Mama was telling her.

"Yes," said Mama, "but it's an evil baby because your daddy put it there. Daddies are never supposed to put babies in their own children, because it's a horrible sin." She looked back up at the night sky filled with stars that looked down upon everyone, good or evil, with the indifference of her father, "Daddy's always been a sinner, but this one is real bad, baby. He's made it so we'll all probably go to hell when we die."

Sarah was getting scared at what Mama was telling her. She'd heard all about hell at church, and it was the worst place anybody could ever go. A person would be set on fire forever, but never die. They'd just burn and burn. "Hell?" She asked frightened.

Mama's eyes were kind of glazed over. She remembered reading the passage in her mother's Bible so long ago, about how children who were evil were supposed to be punished and killed. You must clear away what is bad from your midst, she remembered. Sarah wasn't evil, she knew, but she had been tainted by it. The devil was in their midst, and Abram had been his instrument. He'd come soul collecting and would take them all down to the fiery pits, soon. Mama knew what she had to do to save Sarah's soul. She remembered her dream about fornicating in the Lord's house, when her own mother had risen up to clear away the evil. *'Harlot! Jezebel!'* Mama thought. Her mother had seen it in her, knew the evil seeds Mama had sown in sin. Now they'd ripened on the vine, and the devil had come to harvest. She knew what she had to do.

She let go of Sarah's hand for a moment and walked over to her flower garden. She had decorated the trim with some large rocks she had asked Abram to bring home from the fields and knelt down to pick out a heavy one, but not so heavy that she couldn't manage it well enough. Sarah just watched her innocently, but Mama told her, "Don't worry, baby, Mama ain't gonna let you go to hell." Sarah seemed to feel better about that. Mama never lied to her.

Mama walked over to the well where she dropped her stone and began pulling up the bucket. "Come over here with me, Sarah Jane," she told her. She drew up the bucket of water and placed it on the ledge. "Do you know that when y'all was little, I took you and your brother down to the creek where the preacher baptized you. Do you remember that?" We had been six and five, respectively. Sarah nodded. She knew what being baptized meant and remembered something about a man all dressed up in a robe standing in the creek and dunking some of the kids under the water. "That's the only way we can get our soul clean," Mama told her. "I want you to pray with me, now, okay, baby?"

She helped Sarah put her hands together and then put her own hands the same way. "Dear God," she began. Sarah looked at her confused. Mama sure was acting funny, Sarah thought. "Say it with me, Sarah," Mama told her, "Dear God . . ."

"D-dear God," said Sarah.

"Forgive me of my sins. . ." and she waited for Sarah.

"F-f-forgive m-me of my sins."

"Let me walk in your light," said Mama. Sarah echoed. "Make clean again my tainted soul." Sarah had trouble saying tainted, but she tried her best since this seemed important to Mama. "Make me whole again so that I may live in Your kingdom." Sarah followed along. "In Christ's name, Amen."

". . . Amen," finished Sarah.

Mama had tears in her eyes but a strange smile on her face. I felt an odd mixture of happiness, relief, and misery coming from her. "Now, sweetie, I want you to put your face all the way in the water, just like that day down at the creek, okay?"

Sarah thought it was awfully cold outside to be putting her head in a bucket of water, but she did as she was told. She bent over and put her head under the water, letting it come up over her ears silencing the world for a moment. As she did so, Mama bent down and picked up the rock. She was crying as she watched Sarah, and I could see her shaking from little sobs that were escaping her like hiccups. Mama walked right up behind Sarah, and when her little head came back up from the water, Mama's arms went up behind her with the rock held in both hands. Sarah opened her mouth to get a good breath and when she did Mama came crashing down on her head. Sarah never saw Mama behind her, and didn't see it coming. Mama had come down at a bit of an angle at the back of Sarah's skull, and her face hit hard on the metal handle of the bucket while her mouth was still open for a breath. Her left front tooth caught the force and cracked down to the root, the separated half flipping out to land on the ground where I'd find it nearly a month later that day at the well with Uncle Colby. Sarah's unconscious body slumped forward, head back down in the bucket. Mama had to quickly drop the rock and catch her to keep Sarah from completely falling over. She gently put her hands on the back of Sarah's head and held her under the water. I thought for sure she was already dead, but after a few seconds her fingers seemed to flinch a bit, and then her hand moved. Mama kept holding Sarah's face down in the bucket as she came to. Under the water Sarah had regained consciousness to a horrid panic. I felt it hit me like a lightning strike, her emotions shooting outward like an exploding grenade. She was very scared and hurting quite a lot. Her head was pulsing with a throbbing pain and her mouth where her tooth had caught was also torturing her, but it was nothing compared to her fear. She tried to scream for Mama but there wasn't any voice, only the little bit of breath left in her escaped, and then she couldn't resist the overwhelming urge to breathe. The water flooded her lungs and she tried to cough it out, but there was no air left to do it with. The panic and pain in her seemed to break like a wave, and then she swayed into darkness. Mama held her for what seemed like minutes, rubbing her back as though Sarah wasn't dead, but merely a sick child leaning over a bucket to throw up who Mama was trying to comfort. Finally, Mama leaned Sarah out of the water and laid her down on the ground.

There was no life in the little body. Her lips were turning a little blue and already she seemed a deathly pale complexion. Mama pushed the hair out of Sarah's face and kissed her on the forehead. "It was to save your soul," she told her dead daughter. "I'll go to hell, now, but not you, baby . . . not you, Mama's special angel." She kissed her again.

Sarah's spirit was still standing next to mine, holding my hand. "Mama didn't mean it," she told me again.

I couldn't speak. I was so horrified by what I'd just seen. All those years I thought Pap had murdered Mama and Sarah both, but now it was replaced by this awful truth.

Mama stayed there on the ground with Sarah in her arms for a while, listening to the sounds of Varner Creek at night. The crickets were chirping and somewhere an owl was hooting in a distant tree. The chickens were restless at the sounds of the predator and started making a loud ruckus. "I remember going into the darkness," said Sarah by my side. "But I could still see Mama. I didn't want to go into the dark by myself, so I tried to stay with her, to stay with my body. I could still see her a little, but it was like we are now, outside looking in. Mama couldn't hear me when I called out for her. She didn't know I was still there in my way."

Eventually Mama got up again. She looked at Sarah's dead body and the guilt assaulted her. But still she was happy, too, in a way. She had found the strength to free Sarah. But now what was she going to do? Her feelings were like a shadow, consuming everything in its darkness. She saw everything as a failure. Her life with Abram, the children they'd had together, the home they'd built together. It was all one huge evil rug the devil had weaved, and now it had to be undone. She'd clear it away, clear it all away. She had to save her children from the fires of hell.

She went back into the house and into her bedroom, walking as though already a ghost. She looked behind the dresser for the shotgun, the double barreled one Pap used to kill game birds, rabbits, and squirrels. She looked at Pap in the bed and raised the gun, but then I felt the change in her. Her mind was falling to pieces but I could feel what it was that stopped her. It was me. She knew if she shot Pap in the bed, I'd hear the gunshot and wake up. Then she'd have to shoot me when I could see it coming, and she didn't want that. She'd wanted Sarah to go peacefully, but she'd come to under the water and probably suffered. Mama didn't mean that for her, and didn't want to make a similar mistake. She'd have to shoot me first, in my sleep so I wouldn't be scared. I couldn't hear Mama's thoughts, but I felt them so strongly, it was as though I could. She was convinced the devil had infected us all, and like an outbreak of disease, the only way to kill it was to burn everything. She felt like she could still save Sarah and me if she acted now. Her and Pap would have to go with the devil, though. Him for what he'd done to Sarah and all the other hateful things he'd done in his life, and her for killing her children, husband, and then herself like she planned. It was worth the sacrifice, though, if it saved her babies.

Mama had just started out of the room towards mine when Pap stirred in the bed. The chickens' ruckus earlier had put him in a light sleep. He opened his eyes and saw her in the doorway with the gun, "Annie?" Mama stopped in her tracks, but didn't turn around. Pap must have thought some animal was outside at the chickens and Mama had fetched the gun to go see about it, because he rose up out of bed and said, "What is it, snake or possum after the chickens?" Mama still didn't turn around or say anything. "Well, you'd better give me the gun. You couldn't hit the broad side of a barn." Pap started getting on his pants like he was going to go see about the chickens, but Mama turned around finally and raised the gun at him. Pap looked at her confused for a moment and then said, "Annie, what the hell are you doin'?" She just stared at him, murderous emotions seeping from her like blood from a wound. Pap was cornered between the bed and the wall and had no place to run. His eyes were wide with fear, "Annie? Jesus Christ, what're you doin'?"

She pulled back the hammer on the shotgun, "I killed her, her and that devil's seed you put in her," she told him. "She's free of you now."

"What?" he said. "Who? What in the Sam hell are you on about? You gone crazy or something?"

"Shut up!" she hissed at him, raising the gun a little more, centering on his chest. "You'll wake him and make it harder for him to go peaceful like."

He was going to ask who again, but he suddenly realized just how serious Mama was. He slowly put his hands up as if offering surrender. "Annie, now I don't know what's gotten into to you, but . . . "

"I know about Sarah," she told him. "I know what you've been doin' with your own daughter, you bastard. You own daughter!" she whispered forcefully. "How could you do it, Abram? How could you take advantage of her like that . . . your own child?" Mad tears came, an angry storm brewing inside of her, but still she barely spoke above a whisper. He'd ruined her plans by waking up. She had wanted to shoot me in my sleep so I'd never see it coming, then finish Pap, but now he'd ruined that, just like he ruined everything. She'd have to kill him first. "She was pregnant." Mama told him. "Did you know that Abram? Did yah know that you had gotten your own child pregnant? Did you know it while you were still laying down with her in sin like you did?"

I felt Pap becoming shocked and terrified. He felt his sins biting at his heels. The hand of judgment was on him and he couldn't find words. He had suffered that nightmare childhood with his uncle, only to become just like the man he'd hated so much, and now it had caught up to him in the eyes of Annie. "Annie, now listen . . ."

"No, Abram," she said with finality. "The devil's waited long enough," and she pulled the shotgun's trigger . . . Click! Pap's eyes shut tight as he waited for the blast, but it didn't come. He opened his eyes again. At first he wasn't sure what'd happened, but then he looked down at the dresser drawer where he kept the shells and realized it was still shut. Mama pulled the second hammer back and fired again, Click! And then she knew it, too. The gun wasn't loaded. She wanted to charge him, to kill him with her own two hands, but she couldn't find the strength. Something in her broke and surrendered. All she wanted was to have it all finally ended, yet somehow she'd been robbed of that. Outside Sarah's body was growing cold under the night sky. Sol was sleeping in his bed, and she had meant to kill him, too. But the gun wasn't loaded. She was going to tear the Devil's web down and clear it all away, but the gun wasn't loaded. It wasn't fair, she thought. The tears were coming now and she lowered the gun. I could feel her surrender, and the hate at this cruel joke fate had dealt her, one more final blow. She laughed an empty and hollow laugh, "Look," she told Pap, "even hell won't have you."

Pap walked around the bed quickly and grabbed the gun. He laid it in the corner and then he looked back at Mama. Sarah's soul and I watched her, a broken human being that could take no more. I half expected Pap to hit her, or maybe even load the gun itself and shoot her with it, but the emotions coming from him were different than anger. They were of guilt and remorse. And for all the evils that Pap had, for the first time ever, I saw him cry. "Annie," he said, but couldn't finish. He wanted to apologize, I could feel it in him, but he knew an apology was worthless now. The demon inside himself always wanted other people to suffer what he'd suffered, and now it'd won out. "I ain't no good," he told Mama. "I know. I ain't never been any good." She didn't say anything. All I sensed from Mama was die, die, die, die. *Just let him die and the devil have him. Let us all die.*

Pap backed away from Mama and sat on the bed, watching her cautiously. He was waiting for her to scream and charge him in a blind rage. She was waiting, too, but couldn't find the spark in her to do it. What did it matter, she thought? All was rotten. If he hadn't gotten up, she would have finished her plan. She would have killed me in my bed, killed Pap, then set it all ablaze and stood in the fires of this hell on earth. But that was past, now. Sarah was free, and she thought to herself she'd have to be content with that. She was ready to kill herself, but that seemed too good for her at the moment. She should have to bear this pain for awhile, she thought. It would be a righteous punishment, the least she could do for Sarah was to grieve for her a while before escaping the pain of this world. "I'm gonna go, now, Abram," she said flatly.

Pap looked at her blankly. I could feel the loathing in him. He hated himself so much, hated his uncle who'd stolen happiness from him, hated his father who died and mother who's sent him to live with his uncle, hated Mama for being better than him, hated Sarah for her innocence, and hated me for the same reason. But it was too late for Pap to try and find the goodness within himself. The irreparable damage had been done and all the repentance in the world couldn't change it now. He'd done too much wrong over the years, and now time was the fire in which he'd burn, because they'd all caught up to him.

"Sarah's outside," Mama said. "Her soul is free and you can't never touch her no more." As if in a trance she started walking towards the door, and then she repeated, as though as much to herself as Pap, "I'm gonna go now." Pap thought he should stop her. She'd cracked and he knew it. Maybe he should drag her kicking and screaming to Emma's and tell them all the horrible things he'd done and what had happened. But even now he was a coward. He didn't want to face the judgment of anyone else for what he'd done. And he was scared of what Annie might do. She had lost her mind, there wasn't any doubt. His sins had destroyed her.

He followed her outside to see what she had been talking about with Sarah. When he saw her, he froze. She looked like a life-size porcelain doll of herself, pale white under the moonlight. He walked over to her and knelt down by her. No breath escaped from her, no beat of the heart, and suddenly Pap realized what Mama had done. I felt the grief spring up inside of him. He'd been a cruel man and done terrible things, but he truly grieved for Sarah at that moment. He cried for her, he cried for Mama, and he cried for himself.

Sarah's spirit was next to me watching as I did, and she told me, "Daddy was broke, and couldn't fix himself."

I just watched everything, taking it all in and trying to make sense of it. All their emotions and the things that had happened to them all their lives seeped into me, and what I was getting from Pap felt like poison. I hated him and felt sorry for him at the same time. He had such evil in him, but now I understood that he probably hadn't been born that way. I understood what Sarah meant; he'd been broken a long time ago. It couldn't excuse what he'd done, but in some way I supposed it helped explain it.

Mama undid the gate to Lillipeg's pen. Pap could only watch her. He was holding Sarah's hand trying to imagine how Mama could kill her. "How could you?" he asked Mama. How could you, I found myself asking Pap.

"I'm gonna go, now," Mama said again in that same odd way like talking to everyone and no one at the same time. She opened up Lilipeg's pen and backed her out. She put Lilipeg's bridle on and harnessed her up. Pap couldn't move. He just stared at Sarah's dead face, trying to wish it unreal. Finally he raised his head as Mama finished setting the wagon.

"Where are you goin?" he asked. She didn't answer him. "Annie?" he asked pitifully.

"I'm gonna go, now," she said for the last time. And with that, still in her nightgown and without any shoes or any of her things, Mama climbed into the wagon and flipped the reins. Lilipeg started with a slow walk, and Mama was gradually swallowed by the night while Pap was left with Sarah.

Still standing within Sarah's memory, we stood there looking down at Pap as he held her dead body. Her own emotions flowed from her to me as though we were spectators to the events of our lives, and yes even her death. All I sensed from her was pity and sadness. She didn't seem to hate Pap at all for the things he'd done.

I looked down at Pap and tried to feel the same way, but couldn't. I still hated him. I had never known about him using Sarah like he'd done, and it made me realize he'd been false all the times I thought he'd been sweet to her. I thought back to the times he'd played his sick games with me, holding me over the well as though ready to drop me, or the time he beat Mama, or the hundreds of times he pushed and smacked me around. The only person he treated with kindness was Sarah, and it'd all been a lie. He'd abused us all, but hers was the worst.

As he knelt down there with Sarah I could sense him wondering what to do. Should he run after Annie? Or maybe go and get Colby? No, he couldn't do that. All the options seemed wrong. Annie was gone and who knows where she was headed. Sarah was dead in his arms, and Sol was sleeping through it all. Hide it, I knew he was thinking. Nobody has to know what happened. If Annie really leaves and doesn't come back, who would know? He could just tell everyone she left him and had and taken Sarah with her. He'd get rid of their things and everyone would think they just left. Nobody would know, not even Sol. And that's when he probably thought of the creek, down by the bend where we went crabbing sometimes.

It took Pap a while to finally get up and start to his task. First, he went inside and gathered up all of Mama and Sarah's things. He must have been quieter than he'd ever been in his life not to wake me. I still couldn't believe I'd slept through Mama coming into our room for Sarah, and then Pap coming in and taking all of Sarah's things.

When Pap emerged from the house again he had all of their things, Mama's brushes, clothes, books from Miss Thomas . . . all of Sarah's clothes and toys, including the gifts I'd given her for her birthday, they were all wrapped up in a big blanket. All except the little castle he'd carved from cedar for her. Pap walked out into the woods and buried the big blanket as best he could, as it would only be a short-term solution until he could burn it all, but the little castle he left by Sarah. After burying the other things he came back and laid out about a four by five section of chicken wire. He dragged Sarah's body on top of it and gave her a long last look. He wanted to wrap her up so he didn't have to see her when he hid her away, but that would make it hard for the creek to do its work. I could feel the regret in him, but I tried not to let myself feel sorry for him. Pap folded her arms on her chest and put the little castle in her hands. Then rolled up the chicken wire with her inside and fastened it with bits of barbed wire.

It was a long walk for Pap down to the creek with Sarah's body wrapped in the heavy wire. Unlike Uncle Colby, who had carried Sarah's body like a bail of hay the day we found her, Pap could only walk a little ways before needing to stop and rest. Sometimes he tried to drag her by one end, but more often than not the wire would get tangled on brush and he had to carry her. All the while her face was uncovered, and his eyes kept falling upon her mask of death. I can't say how long it took Pap, because everything seemed to change and Sarah and I were standing by the creek again, except it was daytime and beautiful. We were back where we'd started, next to place where Pap would hide her body that night.

"It's a sad memory," she tells me again.

I looked into her eyes, thinking about how she must feel knowing now just what it was Pap had done to her, and about how Mama had killed her out of some sense of sacrifice. "Yes," I told her, "it sure is." We stood together as I took in all I'd learned. I thought about Mama, traveling to some unknown destination, falling apart as she went. And Pap, who'd tried to cover up his sins despite his regrets, I remembered seeing him that morning with muddy boots and wet hair. Now I knew where they came from. I guess his regrets would get him in the end, though. He'd end up dead in town a month later. "Pap shot himself," I told Sarah. "I'd always thought he'd killed himself because everyone found out he'd killed you and Mama. Turned out he didn't murder anyone, though I guess he might as well have."

Sarah squeezed my hand and said, "I saw." matter of factly.

"You saw?" I asked. "How could you have seen that?"

"When I got here," she said. "I could see everything, even things that happened a long time ago.

"How?" I ask.

"I don't know. I just think about something, and I see it. I'll show you. Do you remember how Daddy stopped hitting Mama?"

"Yes," I said. "Sometime around 1905, like someone had just turned off a switch. I often wondered about that."

"It was Uncle Marcus," she tells me.

"Uncle Marcus? But he wasn't even there."

"Just think about it. Think real hard why Daddy stopped hitting

Mama, and the answer will come."

I closed my eyes and tried thinking about it, and slowly, I could feel something change.

Chapter 17

When I opened my eyes again I was in a field somewhere and there was a man working near us. I recognized him immediately as Pap. He was out feeding the cattle Mr. Pyle had in one of the fields. He was by himself in that particular area of the pasture when a man came riding up towards him. The horse was a beautiful gray with white spots along its side and running along its mane. The man dismounted and Pap barely paid him any attention at first, but then he stopped what he was doing as the man approached. By the time he recognized who the man was, it was too late. He had been knocked down with a swift punch. And before Pap could get up again he was staring down the barrel of a Colt .45 pistol that was being pressed up against his nose. On the other end of that Colt was Uncle Marcus. He still had that intimidating look he was so recognizable by, but he looked not a day over thirty, "I never liked you," he told Pap. "And if I had it to do over again I wouldn't never've let Annie get mixed up with yah." He put his right knee on Pap's chest and knelt down close, still holding the barrel of the gun against Pap's face. "But what's done is done and you're my sister's husband, now." He pushed his thumb down and cocked the pistol. "But if I ever and I mean ever, hear about you laying one finger on her again . . . I'll blow your head clean off, and smile while I do it. I bought this gun just for you, and if I ever get another letter from Emma saying you've hit Annie, you're a dead man. Nobody knows I'm here 'cept you and Emma, but if I ever have to come back you'll be the last to know, because the last thing you'll hear is what this gun sounds like when I shoot you with it. You understand?"

Uncle Marcus had a way with words, brief but powerful. Pap looked scared shitless. Uncle Marcus had scared Pap back before he had married Mama, but seeing him like he was now with that stare of death on him and that gun in his hand terrified Pap. "Yeah," he told Marcus, but apparently Uncle Marcus didn't feel convinced because he pressed just a little harder, "I understand!" Pap shouted. And only then did Uncle Marcus get off of him. He uncocked his gun, stood up, and walked away without another word. He must have taken the train all the way from Galveston to Houston and then all the way down to Varner Creek just to deliver that message in person to Pap. But even though he'd made the trip, he didn't visit anyone else except Aunt Emma that same day to ask her where he could find Pap. She didn't ask him what he intended to do and didn't have any idea what was said, but she saw the result same as us, even if we didn't know the cause back then. Pap quit hitting Mama after that day.

"That explains who flipped the switch," I said to Sarah. "He never told me he had done that, even after I went to live with him."

"Marcus was with Pap when he died, too," she told me.

"What?" I asked. "I never knew that." That's not what I had been told. Uncle Marcus said Pap was already dead when he found him at Miss Thomas'.

I didn't have to ask her to show me, because once again everything around us changed. I could see Pap leaving Mr. Pyle's farm early the day I found her in the creek. He went home and started in on his last bit of whiskey. At the same time me, Uncle Colby, and everyone else were sitting in front of the sheriff's office with Sarah's body in the wagon, Pap was walking into town to go and buy another bottle. He didn't have a horse or wagon anymore, so he was on foot and coming through a little wooded area that ran up against some cropland on the edge of town. Before he came out onto Main Street he saw us off in the distance sitting in the wagon. Then he saw Uncle Colby going towards it with Dr. Wilkins by him. Pap froze and his heart jumped up through his lungs. He stood with his feet growing roots in the ground as he watched the Doctor look into the wagon and appear to pull back a bed sheet. Shit, he told himself. So that's why Colby had left early. Somehow one of them knew where she might have been. I could feel his disappointed curiosity at how she'd been found. He should have burned the body, he scolded. He had been smart enough to gather up her things that night and hide them until after Sol left for Emma and Colby's, then make a fire and burn them to ashes, and now he wished he'd done the same with Sarah's body, because there she was. He started back the way he came and was going to head back home, but then he thought better of it. The sheriff will know by now, of course, and he had horses. By the time he could walk home that old fat bastard would likely be waiting there with three or four other fellas. So instead he crept back in the wooded area and found a spot where he had a pretty good view of town without anyone seeing him. We watched him creep behind the tree line, protected by the brush. His head was spinning with the whiskey and he tried to concentrate and think straight.

Time skipped ahead under Sarah's control as she painted the picture of that afternoon. At about the time my living self was having dinner back at Aunt Emma's, Pap was still sitting on the edge of the wood thinking about what to do. He replayed events over and over again in his mind and remorse started eating at him. All the things in his life were coming back to haunt him. He decided to just sit and gather his thoughts on what he should do now. And as the light began fading away he saw the train pulling into town. A few people got off and on, and one of them that had exited went to the back car to get a horse. It was a gray horse with white spots along its side and neck that Pap could see from where he was. He had seen that horse before. There wasn't another like it in the whole town. That was Marcus. *Annie!* cried his thoughts. She must have gone to Galveston and told Marcus everything. Now Marcus had come back to kill him. He waited until the horse and its rider entered the town and disappeared between some buildings. Then he decided the light was fading enough that he might risk getting a little closer. So he crept down from his hiding spot and sneaked his way towards town. It took him a few minutes to get into town under the shadow of dusk, but when he did he noticed the gray horse was tied to the hitching post near Miss Thomas' house. Then he saw Marcus come rushing out of the door and head towards the Sheriff's office on foot.

Sarah and I watched him as he crept to the back of Miss Thomas' house and into the back door. He had been in her home on a number of occasions. Whenever they came to town Annie liked to stop in and visit Miss Thomas and of course they'd had dinners here on a number of occasions. Pap knew where the guest room was and he snuck inside. The first thing he thought was that he'd get Marcus before it was the other way around. He must have brought that gun with him, he thought, and he started rummaging around the room. Sure enough, there under some underwear that had been folded and put by the nightstand was the Colt .45 Peacemaker. Pap grabbed it and opened it up. No bullets. They weren't far, though. He spotted them near the traveling pack Marcus had brought with him and proceeded to load the gun. Now, what, he thought. Sarah and I watched it all like a living picture show. Pap sat on the bed and his mind began to wander. His emotions were like butter being churned over and over. He was scared of being caught and having to explain things. Even if Mama hadn't told Uncle Marcus, then everyone would just think he'd killed Sarah. Either way, he was in bad trouble with no way out. He thought about all the things that'd happened to get him to this spot. So he'd shoot Marcus, what good would that do? Even if he did manage to get away and run, the sheriff would have a posse after him, and when they caught him, he'd still die. He'd buried himself, he realized. All those sins had buried him. No good, went his thoughts, I ain't never been no good.

While Pap's mind raced we disappeared. Sarah was moving us to a new place, and it took me a moment to recognize the sheriff's office where Uncle Marcus, the sheriff, and Uncle Colby were all sitting. He'd just been told about them finding Sarah's body. "There's something you ought to know, also, Marcus," said the Sheriff. "Colby here found out same time I did, but I don't think it's anything that bears too much repeatin' outside this here room."

"What?" asked Marcus.

Sheriff Covell sighed deeply, "Doc Wilkins say that little girl was pregnant when she was killed."

"Pregnant?" said Marcus. "How could she be pregnant?" Nobody answered. "Who'd get her pregnant?!" he demanded.

Colby and the sheriff both looked at each other and then the floor. "Dunno," said Colby, "But seem to me most likely . . ." He couldn't finish it. It was bad enough just thinking it.

The sheriff summed it up. "I reckon we might know now why Abram's done what he's done."

Marcus' face went first white, then blood red and his blue eyes seemed to shine with rage. It was too much. He couldn't have. What father could . . . but it made sense. Annie found out and he killed her for it. He killed them both. He looked at the sheriff and told him flat out, "I'm going to kill him."

The sheriff took the words in slowly, "I know. I've been looking for him, but ain't nobody seen hide nor hair since this morning. I tell you truly, though, Marcus, if I find him, it's my job to bring him in without any harm if I can, not that'll it do him good for long, you understand, but it's my job." He lowered his voice a bit, though, so if anyone was listening in from outside they wouldn't hear. "Now normally I'd have to tell you to sit at home and not take matters into your hands," Marcus's eyes were cutting through the sheriff as he heard this last statement, but the sheriff raised his hand a bit as if to say he wasn't done yet, "But I know you ain't gonna do that givin' what all that's happened. And the truth is it might be easier for everyone if you did find him first. I'm not sure we need everyone in town learning all the sordid details, if you catch my meaning. So, I'll tell you what I can do, Marcus. If you do find him first, it'll be self-defense so far as I'm concerned. No matter what really happens, I'll call it self defense, but that's about as much as I can do being a law man and all."

"That's enough," said Marcus.

Uncle Colby looked like he wanted to protest, but the knowledge that Pap had probably been the one to get Sarah pregnant was enough to silence him. It was out of his hands now, and he knew it. Pap was going to die one way or the other.

The sheriff picked up something off his desk and handed it to Marcus, "They found this with the body when they got all that wire off her," he said, passing it to Marcus who held it up a bit like Miss Thomas had done not so long ago.

"What's this?" he asked.

Uncle Colby had been sitting quietly up to this point, but he looked up at what Marcus had in his hands and said, "That's what Abram done give Sarah for her birthday." And so it was the same little castle he'd placed in her hands the night she died.

Uncle Marcus held on to it and said, "I'll make sure to return it to him," and then walked out.

And then Sarah and I were back in Marcus' room. We heard the front door slam. So did Pap. He walked around to the very back of the room, behind the bed and away from the door. When Marcus walked in Pap had the gun on him.

I could feel Pap's anxiety and Uncle Marcus' shock. He hadn't expected Pap to come into town, let alone be in his room holding his own gun. "You," he said. He started forward as though he'd rip Pap apart then and there.

"Don't move, now!" yelled Pap, and he clicked the gun back. Marcus was close enough that he could see the bullets were loaded. He was tempted to keep going anyway, consequences be damned. He wanted this man dead more than anything, but he thought of Mary Jo and the children. It wasn't fair to do that to them, he told himself, so he stopped.

"Real man, aren't yah?" he asked Pap. "Sleeping with your retarded daughter, knocking her up and then killing her." He wanted to lunge at Pap so bad he was shaking. But he didn't do it. He was thinking of his own family, and despite his fury he didn't want to leave them without a husband and father.

Pap's mind, on the other had, was rattled with confusion. His emotions were like a jigsaw puzzle someone had just tipped out of the box. He was the one with the gun but he was terrified. He wasn't feeling that sense of anger I'd of expected from him in this position, and didn't seem to really want to shoot Marcus anymore. Pap was just scared. He knew he had reached the end of his rope and didn't want to have to face up to it.

"I don't know what you're talking about," he tried to tell Uncle

Marcus.

"Oh no?" Uncle Marcus tossed the castle he still had in his hands on the bed, and Pap's eyes stared at it with terrible resignation. It was over. Everybody knew what he'd done. "You murdered my sister, too, didn't yah?" Uncle Marcus asked Pap. "Where is she? What'd you do with her!?"

Pap was still staring at the castle. He didn't know what happened to Mama, but he figured she'd gone off somewhere to die. She'd lost her wits that night, and if she hadn't gone to Galveston, she either died on the way or killed herself. And I knew Pap felt the burden on his shoulders. He felt all of it at that moment. It was his fault, all of it. "Reckon I did kill'em both," he told Marcus. "I just ain't never been no good." He looked at Marcus and remembered Mama's words from that night. "The devil's waited long enough," he told Uncle Marcus, and with that, he put the gun to his own temple and pulled the trigger. I closed my eyes with the sound of the gun, like a crack of lightning during a bad storm, and when I opened them again, Sarah was still holding my hand and we were back at the creek. I looked at her and wondered what she'd thought when she first saw him end his own life.

"And Pap went into the dark place?" I asked.

"Yes," she said, "but it's different for him. He's in his memories, and they're a bad place."

"He can't come here?"

"He has to let go," she says. "Daddy's still angry, and he can't come here until he stops being mad at everyone, even himself. Like Mama, she's in the dark place, too, because she can't forgive and can't forget. "

I saw her again, being swallowed by the night in the wagon. "How did she die?" I ask Sarah. It's the last piece I'm missing, and Sarah has already taught me how to find it. I concentrate on the question and Sarah comes with me.

Chapter 18

One last scene changed. Lilipeg walked along, flicking at the bugs that kept chewing on her. It was a rough ride as Mama had long since left the road. Her mind was blank and the morning sun gave her no cheer. We sat with her, in the wagon, as Lilipeg pulled us along. Mama's emotions were chaotic, like a house being pulled down, board by board, nail by nail. Marcus, a fragmented thought murmured, he'd save me. She wasn't sure where Galveston was, but knew it was south where the land met the ocean. She'd never seen the ocean and wondered if it was really as big as Candace has told her about in her letters. The edge of the world, she thought to herself. That's what Candace had called it. 'When you look out over the horizon and see nothing but the ocean all the way until you can't see anymore, it's like looking out at the edge of the world.' That's where Mama wanted to be. It was easy enough to stay south, just keep the morning sun to her left and when it set on her right, and eventually she'd find it. I thought I could sense her thinking that it was where her salvation lied, but then I realize no, not salvation, just an end. Mama believed it was too late for salvation.

I grieved for her. "She's in such pain," I told Sarah.

"Mama's real sad," she tells me. "She won't forgive herself for what she did to me, and I can't tell her it's okay because she's hiding."

Time progressed ahead and I saw Mama sleeping in the wagon, Lilipeg still attached but having a little bit of grass. There wasn't anyone else around. Mama was staying clear of any place that looked like there might be people. I knew she didn't want people to see her sins. The next day she came to thick woods. South was still ahead through them, so she unstrapped Lilipeg. She hadn't eaten anything but did drink from some of the water they had come to. After unhitching the wagon, she climbed up on Lilipeg bareback. She had never ridden a horse bareback like that, but Lilipeg was gentle and didn't mind. So Mama left the wagon and there on the edge of the trees. It'd be found a few days later by a man out hunting, and he'd take it home with him. Mama didn't care about material things anymore, anyway. Let them be scattered to winds. South, said her thoughts, keep going south.

The next night she tied Lilipeg to a nearby tree and slept on the ground next to her, but she was up again and moving before the light. Her thoughts were like the drums of old when ships were at sea and someone pounded out the rhythm for the slave rowers. South, south, south, boom, boom, boom.

It took Mama three days to reach the ocean and when she did she was a very long way from Galveston. It was many miles East of where she found the sea. It was midday when she crossed over some sandy dunes and saw it stretched out before her. Sarah and I were there, our feet in the sand as the waves caressed them. Mama climbed off Lilipeg and in a daze stumbled towards the water's edge. Lilipeg walked off to find some grass to eat. Mama walked into the ocean up to her knees and marveled at the sight. The sun danced off the water in the distance, glittering in a way she'd never seen water do. The waves were small and calm, breaking white around her legs as the tide went out. As the ocean's water swirled around her she felt the sand beneath her toes give and the current sucking at her ankles. Yes, she thought, it was like Candace had described. It was like looking at the edge of the world. And she walked forward, hoping to walk right off the world itself, and in a way she did.

Mama had never learned how to swim, but she kept walking towards the horizon, towards the end. The ocean swallowed her and she let it sweep her away. She had drowned her daughter, and now she herself would be drowned. The last thing I could feel from her was the thought that this was a righteous punishment. And then there was no more from her.

It was so sad how Mama had chosen to end her life, but I understood what was in her thoughts as she did it. I knew she had forsaken all hope and only wanted to escape the pain in her heart.

"And she's in the dark place, too?" I asked Sarah, already knowing the answer.

"Yes, because she wants to be. She went looking for you, though. I saw her when you died."

"When I died?" I thought about all I'd been shown, and it seemed to make sense how Sarah had known I was passing from the world and able to reach me before I'd even made it to the light. We'd shared something special during those days when she was in the darkness, and I knew our bond had held us together. I didn't know what she meant by seeing Mama, though.

"When you died," said Sarah, "She was there in the in-between place. You saw her, too."

And then I remembered. "The woman?" I ask. "The one with no face?"

"Mama," says Sarah.

"But she had no face," I say.

"Mama's hiding," she tells me again. And then I thought about the shiny black hair the woman had. I knew it had been familiar, but just didn't think to place it. She had hair like I remembered Mama having. And the blur where the face should be, that was Mama' mask of shame, guilt, and her despair. Sarah was right, Mama was hiding from what she did and didn't want me knowing it was her.

"Do you think she will ever come here?" I ask Sarah.

"I don't know. It's her choice. Even Daddy could come if he wanted. I don't think we're ever supposed to stay in the dark place for always."

And I knew what she meant. They could come here if they'd learn to let go, to forgive themselves and let the past be past. But if they can't let go of the memories that are haunting them, then they'll always be in the dark place, ghosts themselves, ghosts of Varner Creek.

Sarah looks at me deeply, through the mirage of the bodily image and straight to the soul that is all I am, and I can see hers, too, there just beneath the surface of the girl I see. It is light, sound, memories, emotions, an entire universe in itself.

"No," I say, "I guess no one is ever meant to stay in the dark forever." Sarah embraces me tightly, kissing my boyish cheek. "I'm glad you're here, now. I was never lonely here, but I've missed you."

"I missed you, too," I say.

She looks to me with a smile and says, "And you've missed other people, too." She gives me one more hug and says, "I know. I have to go now, but we can see each other any time we want."

"What?" I ask. "No, not yet. Where are you going?"

"She let me say hi first because it's been so long, but I know she can't wait anymore. You can find me when you want, but someone else is waiting for you."

And then she is gone. The sand beneath my toes, the ocean in front of me, and the sky above, it all fades again. Nothing remains but the bright light I had first seen. Then I see someone start coming towards me. I sense her happiness and am filled with joy as I begin to suspect who it is. Her hair is the loveliest copper color, her eyes green and her smile heart stopping. "Hello, husband," she says to me.

Thank you for reading.

-Michael Weems